He took the hand she offered and handled her delicately boned fingers with the familiarity of a man who was used to touching women. Raising it to his lips, he kissed each finger in turn until Paige was speechless with awe. Every nerve ending in her body suddenly became alive with the unexpected sensual onslaught, and before she could descend from the blissful moment of surprise, he gently pulled her into him and caught her further unaware with a curt kiss on her lips.

Paige weakly pushed against his chest in vain, finding herself helpless in the well of feeling that suddenly erupted in the pit of her stomach. It was an innocent, informal greeting, but she could feel the slight warmth emanating from his body beneath his jacket as his exotic scent tickled her senses, enveloping her in a whirlpool of frankincense and myrrh.

It was the briefest of kisses, yet she felt as though every inch of her mouth had been devoured. He caught her breath and made it his own, claimed her tongue for one fleeting taste of her ardor, and captured her lips with such fervent need, she felt the gasping pants of her heart being pulled out of her body and abandoned in infinite freedom.

The public intimacy of the moment did not escape her when his eyes, sparkling in their incredible soulful depths, finally ensnared her own. It was a heart-stopping moment. Paige swallowed convulsively, hoping she could dispel the image that provoked her. *I wonder if you're as wild in bed as you look.* From where she had acquired such shameless thoughts about him, she did not know.

He licked his sexy lips. "You needed that."

SMITTEN

Sonia Icilyn

ARABESQUE
BET BOOKS™

BET Publications, LLC
http://www.bet.com
http://www.arabesquebooks.com

ARABESQUE BOOKS are published by

BET Publications, LLC
c/o BET BOOKS
One BET Plaza
1900 W Place NE
Washington, DC 20018-1211

All Kensington Titles, Imprints, and Distributed Lines are available at special quantity discounts for bulk purchases for sales promotions, premiums, fund-raising, and educational or institutional use. Special book excerpts or customized printings can also be created to fit specific needs. For details, write or phone the office of the Kensington special sales manager: Kensington Publishing Corp., 850 Third Avenue, New York, NY 10022, attn: Special Sales Department, Phone: 1-800-221-2647.

First Printing: June 2003
10 9 8 7 6 5 4 3 2 1

Printed in the United States of America

For Parissa and her furry little friend, Buttercup

Prologue

"Girl," Rupert King screamed, ducking for the nearest available cover behind the tiny kitchenette situated close to the cockpit. "Don't do me like this."

Paige Alexander measured the weight of the empty champagne flute in her hand and decided it was heavy enough. With enough force, she flung it across the small interior of the chartered four-seater private jet, watching in satisfaction as it landed with a crash onto the expensive carpeting beneath her feet.

"You lied to me," she seethed, reaching for a second flute. "You led me to believe we were more than just good friends."

"Now baby," Rupert tried to reason, wincing as splinters of more glass crashed against the broken champagne bottle on the floor. "Whatever gave you that idea?"

"You've played me for a fool," Paige gasped, aiming unerringly for the aluminum ice bucket on the small hospitality table. She heaved a sickly breath, trying hard to recollect her thoughts. At thirty thousand feet above sea level, it was not easy to formulate how she should deal with the discovery that she had been dating a player. "All those phone calls, text messaging, faxes to my office . . ." Paige paused long enough to hurl the half filled ice bucket in Rupert's direction. She cursed herself when the damn thing missed and hit the jet's fiberglass wall instead. "What on earth were you thinking of?"

"Baby, believe me," Rupert began lamely, softening his

British accent as he raised both hands in mock surrender. "I had no idea you had any feelings for me."

"What?" Paige's midnight-blue eyes widened as she murderously searched for the next available object.

"Baby, I didn't mean to give you the wrong impression," Rupert continued, not giving much thought to what he was in fact saying. "I've always enjoyed your company. I just think you need some time to—"

"Baby this, baby that," Paige cut in, reaching for his silver attaché case, which she spied on the floor close to the chair where Rupert had been seated. "This is about me not jumping into bed with you, isn't it?"

"Honey—"

"You just had to try and wear me down the moment I told you I'd taken a vow of celibacy." Paige's voice weakened at the discovery of how transparent she must have seemed to him. "How long did you think it would take? Three months? Four?"

"Sugar—"

"You want, you need, you must have," Paige seethed, tossing the attaché case in the air with such force, it landed with a harsh bang against the cockpit door. The concerned voice of the Danish pilot suddenly intruded on the rising heat of their argument.

"Is everything all right back there?" he inquired loudly.

"Yeah, we're fine," Rupert's deep baritone replied. He returned his attention to Paige. "Why is every woman I've known angry with me?"

"Have you ever thought it could be how you're treating them?" Paige was not deterred. "So . . . *baby,*" she summarized sarcastically, "considering you suffered what . . . nearly two months without it, exactly where were you getting it, if not from me?"

"Now Paige," Rupert broached harshly, standing to his five feet seven inches, offended as he threw his come-to-bed eyes at her. "It wasn't like that."

"No?" Hands on her hips, looking every inch the self-respecting woman she was purported to be, Paige asked, "Just how was it?"

Rupert threw her a sheepish grin. "Baby, she was clean."

Her brows rose marginally. "Excuse me?"

"Guys like me do it all the time." Rupert volunteered the information like a true male chauvinist. "It's no big deal using a professional service."

Paige reeled back on her high stiletto heels in shock. "You used a . . .?"

Rupert saw the glaze of tears in her eyes. "Lady love—"

"While you were waiting for me to break, you went to a . . ." She could hardly bear to say it. "Hooker?"

"What can I say?" Defeated, he threw his hands into the air. "I'm a man. I have physical needs that you weren't taking care of."

Dazed and wounded as the blatant confession and accusation were flown at her in the same breath, Paige took refuge in a chair. Her voice broke. "You paid for sex?"

"I used a service," Rupert corrected.

"You were serviced . . . like a car?" Paige choked.

"Honey!" Rupert came closer and deposited himself in the chair he had been seated in earlier, before their altercation began. "Now that I know how you feel about me, this doesn't affect us. She doesn't count."

Paige raised her head and looked at Rupert, appalled. His boyish happy-go-lucky grin, with the shadow of a well-trimmed mustache above his mouth, looked so enchanting, she felt her heart shift at how handsome he still seemed. His grin had been the first thing that had attracted her to a man who looked much younger than his twenty-eight years. As had his chubby olive cheeks, the thick tight curls of his short Afro hair, and the broad tilt of his nose. But it was his slanting brown eyes that had endeared her, though she could see the deceit behind them now. She had to hand it to Rupert. He was a smooth player.

"What do you mean *she* doesn't count?" Paige queried, hardly believing what she was hearing. "Doesn't this woman have a name, or did you think you were doing the bedroom Olympics with something inhuman?"

Rupert had the audacity to reach for her fine-boned fingers. Taking them into his large hand, he laced them through his own. "She didn't mean anything. It was just—"

"Sex!" Paige finished. "Did you use a condom?"

Rupert glanced at her horrified. "Of course I used a condom." Vexed, he added, "I always blanket my rocket before I cock it."

"To cheat on me," she said.

"I didn't cheat," Rupert blurted. "I . . . retaliated."

"What?"

"At least she appreciated what was on offer."

Paige stared, then dipped her head and studied her manicure on the very hand Rupert was holding. She could not stop the tears that threatened. "I believed in you," she told him quietly, her voice quaking in betrayal of how deeply hurt she was. "I was stupid enough to believe we had a good thing going. That was why I waited." She looked him dead in the eyes. "I wanted to be sure."

"We've still got a good thing going," Rupert told her in earnest. "She was just a mistake to tide me over."

"I was worth the wait," Paige said, dejected, though her voice held steel. "I thought this was going to be the happiest weekend of my life, but you don't deserve me."

"What?"

"You don't deserve anything honest and pure," she told him, absorbing in pleasant satisfaction Rupert's sudden amazement. "I was a fool because I gave too much attention to you when you clearly didn't deserve it. I listened to all your difficulty making decisions and I fell for your charms and good looks. You played with my heart and I allowed you to, when all the time you didn't feel the same way about me as I did for you." She spat out the words like venom. "And I doubt very much that you will ever care for anyone except yourself."

"I didn't know you wanted us to be exclusive," Rupert insisted, in full denial of his actions, though Paige's anger caused him to quickly remove his thick brown fingers from her own and protectively clasp them against his crotch. "I was just—"

"Lusting for me," she said. "When all the time you didn't really want me. There, we have it." The tears rolled down Paige's cheeks in hot fury. "What a victory it is to know that whenever I think of your sorry ass, I will always be reminded that I was unconquered territory."

"You can't do me like this," Rupert repeated, resentful. "What about—"

"The chocolates? The flowers? The restaurant bills?" Paige gloated. "Put it down as a tax loss. You didn't profit from the investment."

Rupert forced his large shoulders back into his chair. "I ought to ditch you for—"

"Not closing on your initial outlay," Paige concluded, so enraged that she reached for her Christian Louboutin canvas shoe, pulled it from her foot, and threw it at him. WHOOSH! The shoe came flying through the air, caromed off the Plexiglas window, and hit Rupert on his right brow before it fell with a thud onto the floor. Paige was immediately remorseful. She was out of her chair in an instant, with a sorrowful expression on her face, upset that her reaction had been so resentful as to potentially cause damage. "Oooh," she gasped, reaching to the floor to pick up her shoe, bypassing Rupert entirely. Hugging it apologetically to her chest, she checked that the heel was still intact before replacing it on her foot, adding an impassioned "It's okay."

Rupert stared at her in disbelief. "You care more about your shoe?"

"More than you cared about me," Paige revealed, slowly retaking her seat.

"I did love you," Rupert admitted, rubbing his brow gently.

"Exactly which minute of the day was that?" Paige taunted, deeply wounded at how easily he could lie.

"Okay." Rupert was outraged. "Who told you?"

"You made the mistake of bragging to your best buddy Edmund Barrington, who blabbed to his girlfriend Norma Ramsgate, who gossiped to our mutual friend Claudia Delaney, who confided in my cousin Francine, who told me."

"So you got me," Rupert chided, annoyed. "You can't blame a man for looking for milk when the cow at home ain't milking."

Paige's blood ran cold. "Take me home," she insisted. "Now."

"I can't just order the pilot to turn the plane around," Rupert chided, attempting to force a smile on his face. He knew she was upset, but not this upset. "We've only been in the air twenty minutes. We can still enjoy our weekend in Portugal."

"You're a two-timing, double-dealing, twisted little rat," Paige croaked hotly, in the spirit of a woman scorned. "You think women are like floor tiles. If you lay them properly the first time, they can be walked over forever and a day. Not me. By hook or by crook, I'm going to make you pay for this."

"Now, baby," Rupert said, frightened by the depth of revenge he could see in Paige's eyes. "You don't mean that. I'm the best catch you're ever gonna get at your age."

"What?" Paige spat out, flinching at the reminder that she was closing in on thirty. "I've still got it going on. I can get another guy just like that." She clicked her fingers, brandishing the simple gesture in Rupert's face as though it were a deadly assault weapon.

"Prove it." Rupert laughed out loud, trying to see the funny side of what was going on. "I'll take you back to England, but you'll be begging for me within the space of a week."

"I'll have *you* replaced within the space of a week," Paige said through clinched teeth, narrowing her eyes like a hungry fox overeager to taste blood. "Come hell or high water, you just watch me."

She had crossed the threshold of the private jet with a heart full of hope and dreams, and the promise of a future, though she now loathed herself for wishing it. For in less than an hour, Paige Alexander stepped off a disillusioned woman.

It had been one of the most crushing days of her life.

It was hardly three days later when she began to feel the pressure.

One

"I'm not good at talking to women. " The bold words appeared in Times New Roman on the LCD flat plasma screen. "I'm much better talking *at* them."

Paige Alexander, sitting behind her desk at precisely 9.30 A.M. in the wood-paneled property development office at the realty agency where she worked, peered closely at the laptop screen in wide-eyed bemusement. The blinds at her windows were closed, shutting off the early morning sunlight that had forced its way through the rainy showers typical of a day in early February. Her office door was locked, with the key placed securely by her telephone where she could see it. She had taken the phone off the hook, and switched the network to her answering service for fear of being disturbed.

This was a daredevil approach for a person who considered herself much too open, too sensitive and fragile. Today, Paige Alexander felt rather secretive, as though the insecurities of the last three days in her life had left her helpless and weak. Yet beneath the frailty, there was a level of excitement, too. A buzz that suggested that by experiencing the whole panoply of the World Wide Web, she would find solutions to choose from. Paige had decided to go online.

The telephone circuitry she had attached to her portable computer was making a cacophony of sounds as though it, too, was conspiring with her in its own code to converse with a complete stranger. All the warnings she had received from her cousin over the weekend had worked their way to the back of her brain, where they festered momentarily, while she typed a response. The adrenaline pumped while the pain in her head caused a nuisance, and she frowned, reminding herself she had taken two tablets to abate the ache. Still, the discomfort was not enough to sway her from embarking on what was, to her, a brave new encounter.

"I'll buy half that line," Paige typed into the vacant window space facing her, a smile tugging at her lips as she deftly pressed ENTER before deciding to move on.

The site was aptly named *www.totallyblackdating.com,* and boasted a directory of three hundred thousand strong. She had been allocated a membership number after supplying credit card details that enabled her to log in with platinum status. Then, after giving her user name, she was asked to assign herself a moniker that identified her to other users without displaying her real name. The site listed profiles, personal advertisements, e-mail addresses, mobile numbers, and jpeg photos of the many suitable candidates looking for love. As a woman with a busy life schedule, the idea of using a matchmaking service—even one such as this with its video-dating, chat-up rooms, e-greeting service, and daily sex positions from the "Nubian Sutra"—was a fresh indulgence, one that left Paige completely in awe.

"You can tell a lot about a woman by the way she dances," another stranger tapped in. "If you can dance, you're a good lover. I'm a badass dancer."

"I can get jiggy with it, too," Paige replied with a rich, fruity chuckle under her moniker guise as the Egyptian goddess Isis. Again, she moved on.

"Sometimes we don't even meet for a drink," wrote another. "I just sleep with 'em."

"So that's why they say cybersex is overrated." Paige giggled, and kicked off her Damier leather shoes. With the speed and agility of a startled bird, she moved from her chair and seated herself among the lilac-colored cushions on the purple dralon sofa in her office, folding her long legs into an agreeable arrangement before placing her laptop on her knees. She moved on.

The conversations grew more lewd. There were the desperate lyrical ones: "I is a brother man and me want the same t'ing as any other man. Sex, sex, and more sex."

"Then all you need in life is a bed," Paige told him.

The bawdy ones: "Sometimes they fall in love with me. I always end it with an e-mail."

"You can't burn an e-mail," Paige returned, in awe that she was on the world's number-one Web dating site for minorities. "I don't want to get my fingers burned either."

And the thrill-seekers: "I'll try anything once with total discretion."

"As long as it's not with me," she wrote, recognizing the codeword *discretion,* which invariably meant the person offering the thrills was attached. "I don't date married men." The Web host, aptly named Cupid, should stipulate rules against this entrapment, she mused.

Not all were so transparent. Many were lonely and centered their conversations around divorce, starting over, single parenthood, and the challenges facing a man forced to discover his female side. This was something new. *They've got feelings after all,* a tiny voice whispered at the back of her throat, as memories of Rupert King surfaced to torment her. For the first time in her life, Paige found herself questioning her choices in men.

Rupert had not been the only one to hurt her. He was simply an addition to the others who had come before. Suddenly, as she began to read more of the profiles, she came to realize that she had been attracting the ultra-trendy Mr. Ghetto-fabulous, who liked his lady to be well-groomed, made-up using brand-name products, and impeccably dressed. That meant high heels, plenty of gold jewelry, short skirts, hair worn in a weave, wrap set, or wig, and possessing a penchant for being seen in the best clubs in town.

Warming to the complex psychology theme, she realized this was not who she was. Admittedly, she was a well-maintained woman. Her ear-length brown, relaxed, salon-cut hair was her own, along with her cosmetically altered teeth, though a slightly wonky front tooth lent her a particularly endearing appeal. She had come to work that morning dressed in a lime-green cashmere polo-necked jumper, Spanish hipster blue jeans, and high-heeled shoes, but it did not follow that her mask of self-sufficiency meant that inwardly she was secure and in charge.

Paige paused for breath. Suddenly, she found herself typing, "I want a man to accept me for who I am, not what they think I should be or who I think I should be." She did not care whether it made sense or not. She simply pressed ENTER.

The chat line fell silent. It was as though a dark thundercloud had appeared and hovered above her head, enveloping her and everyone who was online at that precise moment. Paige had caused a stir. What had she said to cause a slew of people to become dumbstruck? Silence. Then abruptly, she got a reply.

"Who do you imagine yourself to be?"

"Someone who wants to *feel* half of another person," Paige replied in return.

Without warning, her computer instantly began to make further communication sounds with its modem. Paige's midnight-blue eyes grew in wonder. She did not know what was going on. All she knew was that she had been taken out of the mainframe window of the chat-room she was in, and suddenly taken into a much smaller window frame with a heading above it which read: "Private Room."

Her moniker Isis was still there, along with the moniker of someone else who identified himself as Omega. He evidently had more to say, and wanted to make it of a more personal nature. "Do you think you're someone who uses her feelings?" he asked.

The question took Paige by surprise. Glancing at her screen, she could not see the "X" indicator on the top right-hand corner of the new window frame to kiss it good-bye. This was not a question she wanted to answer, particularly as she was a little unnerved at chatting one-to-one with a total stranger. But an inner instinct took over, deep and strong, and prompted her to confide with some honesty. "Yes," she typed in.

"Men use their heads."

"Don't men have feelings, too?" she asked.

"The only reason a man feels he needs a woman is to get sex over and over without having to pay for it, and the only reason a woman feels she needs a man is for a home, kids, and financial security. If the sex is good, even better."

His answer was crude, but Paige was not thrown. "And if it isn't?"

"Am I dealing with your sexual frustration right now?"

"No," Paige lied.

"Liar."

"Okay. It's been a while."

"His problem or yours?"

"I was hoping I'd be worth the wait," Paige wrote candidly.

"Ouch. Into traditional values. A rare commodity."

Paige gave her computer screen a wide-eyed look of curiosity and carefully told the truth. "That does not mean I think marriage and monogamy go hand in hand."

"But you'd feel more secure if you had some paperwork to prove his commitment?" Omega tapped back.

"I'm not sure that marriage cements and validates a relationship," Paige went on, "and if it does, that does not mean I should share everything, including a mortgage."

"A real estate agent. Hmmm."

"How did you know?"

"I'm a sensitive guy and I sense that you've lost your role in life as a woman. You have trouble relating positively to men."

Paige pulled back into the haven of her sofa. "What?"

"You're counter-phobic," Omega worded out. "You have mixed opinions about sex and marriage. Up front, you probably give off mixed signals, too."

"Is this the sensitive bit you were telling me about?"

Paige's question demanded, her emotions becoming all-over uncomfortable and defensive.

"You deserve to be told the truth."

"From someone who doesn't even know who I am?" Paige tapped back.

"*You* don't even know who you are." The hard fact was returned.

"I'd like to leave this room now," Paige typed protectively, looking about her screen for an exit indicator. This man was homing in on something. He had succeeded in getting into her psyche and was defining her in a manner she had been unable to do herself. How could a stranger manage such a thing? And in less than five minutes. She had to get out. Now. It was time to move on.

If only Omega would let her. "Go on. Run." The words hit hard like a solid rock. "Run away from who you really are. I suspect you've been doing that all your life."

The tears rose quickly and stung at the back of her eyelids. "You know nothing about my life."

"I see you as a person who is the center of the party, bowling everyone over with your seductive smile, and your assertive décolletage," Omega began with a selection of choice words, all taking Paige by surprise. "But it's a mask. Inside, you're unsure of your intelligence, your beauty, and perhaps even your bra size."

"How dare you make perceptions about me like that?" Paige hit back.

"I can dare anything," Omega's words reminded. "I'm on the Net."

"I think you're rude and if I were a man, you'd feel the sting of my fist."

"Irrational and aggressive, too," Omega worded out. "Is this premenstrual tension?"

It was all too much. "What do I have to press to get out of here?"

"Still running?" Omega typed back. "Let me make it easy for you. Scroll down."

Paige took the advice quickly. She wanted nothing more than to get away from this man, but since this was her first time dating online, she had not yet learned how to use the service, and was still finding all the window options and flash indicators bewildering. But she did as instructed and found the relevant exit indicator.

"I'm outa here," she tapped in, feeling she was giving Omega more courtesy than he deserved.

"Run." He had no qualms about keeping her chatting. "But one more thing," he added without care. "Stop identifying with a man. You're a woman. The only way you can knock a man out is with a kiss."

"Fat chance you'll get one from me," Paige relegated in bold typeface.

"I thought as much," Omega replied, taking the bait. "I bet you don't dare yourself to do anything."

"Meaning?" Paige felt pressured to know before leaving the private room.

"C'mon, Isis." His reply goaded. "You're afraid to say what you really want, which is to have someone else do the risk-taking for you."

"I'm not afraid of taking my own risks." Paige could not type the words fast enough.

"In that case, I dare you to meet me."

"I don't do blind dates," Paige tapped back.

"Sounds like you don't *do* much when faced with a man."

Paige felt the sting of his remark. She had told him too much. Irritated past reason, she pressed the EXIT indicator, and paused for the brief five seconds it took to return her to the site's home page. With the new window back in view, Paige drew a breath in relief. Her heart was thudding so fast and there was such a deep amount of sated anger at the pit of her stomach, she was forced to take another breath to vent out her frustration.

She had read in a newspaper that on average four out of ten people now dated online, but if their experiences were anything like what she had just encountered, Paige failed to see the attraction. Failed to see why anyone would want to converse with a complete stranger just to be insulted and made a fool of. He was probably a dangerous Lothario. An ill-bred one at that. She imagined he did this all the time, perhaps every day of the week. Logged online to deliberately reduce women to tears by expertly dissecting them to pieces.

What a nutcase, she mused, inwardly calming herself, deciding whether she should have another go. She had told Rupert King she would have another man within the space of a week, and asserting herself on the Internet was certainly an option. The thought of trying again enthralled her. Surely, not all the men on *www.totallyblackdating.com* could possibly be as conceited as Omega? After all, she had chatted with a few good ones who were trying to come to terms with their own collapsed relationships. It couldn't be all bad. With this thought in mind, Paige reshuffled her position, and was reaching for her keyboard to have another go when her laptop alerted her with a prompt bell-like sound, indicating that she, under her guise as Isis, had been retaken into a private room.

What's going on? Paige thought in alarm. It occurred to her, as she saw Omega's name reappear in the top window, that though she might have left the room, it did not stop him from causing her to reenter it.

"Haven't you got a videocam?" he asked.

Paige fumed. This was too much. Had this man not got the message that she no longer wished to talk to him? She decided it would be far best to stick to one simple answer. Then maybe he would allow her to move on.

"No."

"Jpeg scan online?"

"No."

"Microphone?"

"No."

"You're a novice at this, aren't you?"

"No."

"Know any other language?"

"No."

"Guess what? I like *yes* women."

This should get rid of him, Paige decided. "I intend to keep my legs crossed and my options open."

"Liar," he wrote for a second time. "You're a woman and all women have needs."

"And you would know?" Paige typed, rising to the bait.

"I don't want to argue. I can sense that you're feeling quite overwhelmed about something and need someone to talk to," Omega replied. "I'm all yours. What's the problem?"

Paige pondered for a moment, feeling shaken by this man's guile and sheer blatant audacity. Again, he was accurate at deciphering her mood, and she wondered at the small percentage of harm it would cause by telling him the truth. It was hardly negligible to worry about. It was not as though they were likely to meet. That he could cause her further harm should she tell him what was really on her mind. *Let's see what this stranger has to say,* an inner voice even challenged.

"I'll be thirty years old this Saturday," she found herself typing. "I'm having a big party and have already invited one person from every area and walk of my life so far to be there."

"Wow. A milestone," Omega wrote.

"It would be if I had someone to be there with," Paige divulged, wondering why in God's name she was feeling compelled to tell him anything at all. She decided it was the anonymity of it. Almost like making a confession to a priest. It was the sense of getting it off one's chest. Off-loading and being done with it all.

"You need a lover," Omega homed in. "Chocolate or vanilla?"

"Black cherry and strawberry actually. I don't respond to rhetorical questions," Paige wrote in reply.

"Are you ugly?"

"Cheeky," Paige typed back, deciding she would not tell him about Rupert King. "The year's just kicked in. I haven't had time to look around."

"Tell me you're a desert princess from the Sahara and I'll be right over."

"You're in Africa?" Paige tapped back, surprised at the surge of disappointment that coarsed through her veins. It had not occurred to her thus far that the dating site was open to the entire world.

"Where are you from?"

"I was born in Wales."

"That hump at the side of England?"

"It's home."

"Damn. If you were a celebrity, who would you say you look like?"

"Whitney Houston. You?"

"Ja Rule."

"Who's he?"

"A rapper. You have heard of hip hop?"

"Not in Africa." Paige then aimed the pun. "I don't play rap as a rule."

A funny face with a smile appeared on her screen. Paige quickly realized it was a computer icon used by Internet chat rooms to convey emotion. Uncannily, she found it soothing. It signified that this man was listening. She did not expect him to have all the answers. She did not expect him to find solutions either. He was listening. And in that moment, Paige was to know that this was all she required from him.

"I'm an American," Omega wrote. "And you need a life. I think you might be in luck. We could still get it together."

"What do you mean?" Paige asked him.

"I mean I can be at your party."

"I don't know," Paige tapped into her laptop, her heart suddenly skipping at the mere possibility that he could be exactly who she required. Surely it could not be this easy? "It's a long way just for a party."

"I'll be passing through," Omega explained, his typeface oddly seeming suddenly suggestive. "In London by Friday, on a plane by Sunday. You can meet me at the airport. I promise to be at your side when you blow out your candles, and I'll even buy you a present. How's that?"

"Let me think about it," Paige typed in, feeling pressured

to agree right away without giving the matter some thought. After all, this man did not know what she looked like, and she certainly had no idea about him. "You could be a mad ax murderer."

An icon of a sad face appeared on her screen with an appropriate suggestion. "I'll e-mail you and attach a jpeg." Omega seemed deadly serious. "I got your e-mail address from your profile. It doesn't say much. This your first time?"

"Yes," Paige told him, recalling simply typing in her moniker, her age, and a few details, leaving a point of contact in her profile.

He retyped her profile to ascertain accuracy. "Slim, five-five, 110 pounds, short brown hair, age twenty-nine, friendly, laughs easily, can only pull one face, and bootylicious!" Another icon face with a smile appeared.

"That last bit was just a joke," Paige laughed, adding a few exclamation marks so he could see that she truly meant to jest when detailing her love for Destiny's Child.

"I like those three brown sugar pieces, too," Omega replied.

"You don't sound like a mad Lothario as I suspected." Paige typed her confession with an easy conscience, curious now to know what this man looked like after all. She found herself secretly praying that he would be someone with nice eyes and a nice smile, and began to look around her screen for the profile indicator that would allow her to read what he had to say about himself. "You're okay."

"Of course I'm okay," Omega confirmed. "I'm a man with certain philosophies in life."

"Which are?"

"A successful man should make more money than his wife can spend."

"And a successful woman is one who can find such a man." Paige giggled to herself as her response appeared on the screen.

As though almost hearing her chuckle, Omega wrote, "No joke. A man knows that every woman worries about the future until she gets a husband. But a man never worries about the future until he gets a wife. In today's age, he has to compromise, and that means working on his career to keep her happy."

Paige was intrigued. "Why then, when a woman marries a man expecting he will change, he doesn't? I've seen it with my cousin. Her husband doesn't compromise anything."

"Because when a man marries a woman, he expects that she won't change, but she does," Omega wrote back. "A woman wants everything from one man."

"And a man wants one thing from every woman," Paige typed in return.

"Are you feeling sexually frustrated again?" Omega sent his reply with another icon.

"It'll pass."

"Not all guys are out for that. I'm really a nice guy," Omega wrote back.

"Don't push it," Paige tapped in a reply, chuckling. "Nice guys appreciate simple things like the color of roses."

"If you want to know my favorite color, just ask," Omega tapped back before his answer filled her screen. "It's has to be the blue-violet streak across a sunrise. When you see such a color, it's so beautiful, it's like finding the gateway to heaven. You really should see it sometime."

Paige was instantly moved. Who was this guy in Africa who liked to poetically describe to her his innermost thoughts? Encouraged, she ventured further with the first teaser to enter her head while her gaze fell on his profile indicator. "Storms, cool or scary?"

"Scary," came Omega's response. "I like to hear God dropping his apples down the stairs, though I have a niece who insists they're pineapples and watermelons."

Paige laughed out loud as she pressed the profile indicator. She had gleaned more information from this one man's mind than she had out of Rupert King or her boss in all the months she had known them both. To her chagrin, she began to imagine Omega smiling, even though she could not picture a face in her head or imagine what he might look like.

"If you were to write your autobiography . . ." she asked.

"I'd be arrested," he joked.

Paige giggled as a profile window appeared at the side of her screen that told her that he was "thirty-two years old, five eleven, 42" chest, 34" waist, 33" leg, slim-medium build, affectionate, sensitive, liked good food/wine, music, theater, sport, reading, conversation, and was seeking a sincere long-term friend and lover." *Ambiguous,* she thought of the last bit while closing his profile window. She had made no mention of what she was looking for by way of a mate, or what her likes and dislikes were. Perhaps this was why he was grilling her so adeptly.

"What is most important in life to you?" Omega's question suddenly appeared on the screen in front of her. Paige was thoroughly intrigued.

She thought for a moment, amazed that her heart felt unusually warmed by Omega's inquiry. "Love of oneself, of God, of life, of those close to me, the quest for knowledge, peace, wisdom, financial security, raising a family, and the love from those nearest to my heart."

"Go, girl," came his prompt encouragement, with the display of another icon of the face that smiled, this time with a tongue plunged out and licked to one side.

Paige laughed out loud again. Her eyes widened and then she asked, "What's your favorite number?" She was flirting and it felt good.

"Four, for the kudos of it."

"Do you eat broccoli?"

"Stems, leaves, fluffy bits. The lot."

"What book are you reading now?"

"I'm reading about the ancient Egyptians. We know that their language belonged to the group known as Afro-Asiatic or Hamito-Semitic, which simply means that they shared some common traits with the languages of parts of Africa.

That's why your name attracted me, Isis. It's Greek for the goddess Aset, a great ruler in Egypt. I like it. I like you."

Paige's heart skipped a beat. She was warming to the new feelings Omega was evoking in her. "Is that why you're in Africa right now?"

"Egypt," Omega amended. "I'm chilling out and learning about a pre-dynastic period which shows a mixture of racial types which stem from Negroid."

"You should write a book on the subject," Paige suggested.

"Not a bad idea," Omega replied. "Especially if we find anything, like the tomb of Atum for instance. It's part of an excavation site I'm looking over at the moment."

Paige's heart was thudding. Omega seemed so unreal. It went beyond his being just a name on her computer screen, someone in whom she was confiding more than she imagined she ought to. They were two people who had not yet met. Who had not even seen each other. Were they to meet, it could all change. It could be that he did not like the look of her, even if she were to send him a jpeg beforehand, as he had promised he would send to her. Maybe she would not like the look of him. And suppose she did, what then? In Paige's mind, it was all about savoring the moment. Living in the guise of the moniker she had given herself.

"Say one nice thing about the person you're chatting to," she typed in, smiling like the true goddess she was. She pressed ENTER.

"An imaginative, like-minded spirit," were the words that came back on her LCD flat screen.

Paige was reading this when she heard the knock at her door. "I have to go," she tapped in quickly.

"Don't go."

Her emotions jarred at the sudden interruption, Paige typed, "I'm at my office desk in London. It's the boss."

"A real estate tyrant who likes cracking the whip?"

"And more." It was the honest truth.

"Poor girl." An icon of a sad face arose. "Look out for my

e-mail," Omega wrote back, a reminder of his promise to send her a jpeg.

"Okay. Bye."

Paige's heart fell as she hurried and placed her laptop among the lilac colored cushions on the sofa. The knock at her door became more persistent. When she grabbed the key from beside the telephone and released the lock, it was to find Blanton Blake, her boss, standing at the other side.

"What are you doing locking your office at"—he looked at his watch—"11:02 in the morning?"

"I was . . . ," Paige began. "Is that the time?"

"I didn't realize that my invitation for you to think about becoming a partner at this firm would give you liberties to be sleeping on the job," he announced, his entire frame appearing imposing as he remained standing at the doorway.

"I wasn't doing any such thing," Paige insisted. "If you must know, I had a headache. I thought it'd be nice to feel a little cocooned."

Blanton looked around the room, finding the blinds closed and the telephone off the hook. "What are you planning, a murder?"

Paige laughed nervously, realizing she had gone to extremes, especially as her brain reminded her that she had already accused one man on the other side of the world of being a mad ax murderer. "No."

Blanton's gaze wandered, following the long, plainly visible cable wiring that led from her desk, over her shoes on the floor, and across to the cushioned sofa where her laptop was located. It was still connected to the World Wide Web, and he could evidently see the window's caption, *www.totallyblackdating.com,* headlined along with its colorful home page. A measure of alarm instantly grew across his face and his gaze transferred to Paige.

"What are you doing?"

Paige trembled, notably aware that she had been caught logged online to the world's most renowned Nubian introduction agency. Blanton Blake was much too handsome to be her boss, certainly not someone she would find it easy to disclose her extracurricular activities to. He was tall and imposing, with an incredible intelligence behind his dark eyes that oftentimes projected a smoldering glaze in an understated sort of way.

As he stood at the entrance to her office, his amazing pecs were crouched inside the soft cotton of his white Christian Dior shirt, where his strong column of a toasty brown throat was coated with a well ironed Fendi tie. His toned thighs were hugged inside expensive tailored Dunhill gray pants, the waistline trimmed like a man who worked out three times a week. And the boyish, intriguing dimples that were often in his mischievous smile were barely evident in the grim set of his face.

It struck Paige anew, as she caught the reflection of his diamond cuff links, just how very different Blanton could be when she was faced with his pragmatic side, that he could be so shortsighted of his own sex appeal to women. Even though she was tangibly aware of it, she had to also remind herself that at thirty-six, Blanton was engaged to be married to the coveted winner of the Miss Zimbabwe beauty pageant. Dismissing this dubious thought from her mind, she answered him astutely.

"If I tell, promise you'll understand." she implored, knowing that Blanton could be a regular stick-in-the-mud. Mr. Sensible on all counts.

"That depends." He raised a brow.

Paige detected the judgmental brow movement and heaved a sickly breath. "I'm going to date someone I've met on the Internet."

Two

"I might have known this would be about a man," Blanton Blake accused, venturing into Paige's office and closing the door behind him. Towering within a foot of her, he shoved his hands deep into his trouser pockets, anticipating a full explanation.

"What's that supposed to mean?" Paige bit back harshly.

"This!" Blanton pointed at the laptop. "Your affair with Rupert King ended three days ago and—"

"He hurt me, remember?" Paige finished. "This is me moving on."

"That's what happens when beautiful, young girls like you go playing with the devil," Blanton derided without an ounce of sympathy. "Men like Rupert King don't grow on trees. They grow on charm and lots of it. He ditched you—"

"I *ditched* him just before my thirtieth birthday party," Paige corrected, adding the most dire piece of information. The stinging pain of it still felt like a knife wound in her chest. "My ego is wondering what people are going to think."

"About you being the birthday girl all alone at your own party?" Blanton questioned in annoyance. "Or him cheating on you with a woman probably ten years your junior?"

Paige stared at him, feeling terribly sore. "I don't want to squabble with you," she pleaded, "but what you said just now was hurtful."

"You made a mistake." Blanton sighed, his African accent

softening slightly. "All people will be saying is what a dog-gone shame it is."

"You just don't get it, do you?" Paige announced, tears now threatening at the back of her eyes, her wonderful chat with Omega now suddenly ruined. "I can't be seen at my own party without a man at my side. I'm going to need someone, like yesterday."

"So that's why you nearly went off the rails trying to find an escort agency in the *Black Links* directory when you came back to work yesterday," Blanton suddenly surmised. "That's not the answer."

Paige leaned back on her heels, recalling the scenario at the back of her mind. She had not considered locking her office door, so it was made easy for Blanton to find her drooling over her desk with her finger on the relevant directory listing. And when he had inquired, she was not too shy to tell him—in light of the news he had delivered that morning on his forthcoming engagement to Miss Zimbabwe—what she was doing.

"Make your dreams come true," she had announced, seconds after he leaned over her shoulder in open curiosity. "*Ebony Escorts*. A fine selection of beautiful men and women, all nationalities for all occasions, twenty-four-hour service."

"You're not serious," Blanton had gasped.

"Visa and MasterCard accepted," she voiced.

"You're going to rent a lover?" he shrieked, struggling to assemble the words as calmly as he could.

"Discreet and prompt service," Paige finished. "I wonder if they take American Express."

"It's still a possible answer," Paige now insisted, dismissing the scenario as she shrugged the embarrassment of him catching her in the act from her mind.

"Look." Blanton pulled his hands from his trouser pockets and planted them firmly on Paige's shoulders. She felt the frisson of his touch run along her veins, and the scent of his Rocabar cologne invigorate her senses as he held her gaze while attempting to explain. "I didn't want to tell you this, but I think you're suffering from what is commonly known as post-split syndrome."

Paige's brows rose. "What?"

"It's the breakup blues," Blanton continued, assessing her carefully. "When a relationship ends, most women's natural tendency is to impulsively indulge in a short-term fling to put distance between them and the last relationship."

"You mean to get over a guy I need to get under one instead?" Paige derided.

"That's not what I'm trying to say." Blanton sighed, releasing his hold. Paige felt the tangible loss of him as he ventured into the room and took a position in front of her desk, leaning his back against it, folding his arms across his chest. "You need to feel attractive and in control again," he went on. "That was why you tried to get an escort."

"Which I may still consider," Paige chided, annoyed that Blanton had shifted from boss and potential business partner to part-time psychiatrist.

He exhaled an exasperated sigh. "Look," he said, clearly agitated. "What you're doing is trying to break your emotional ties with Rupert by hiring a lover. It will not boost your ego and it will not develop into a relationship. It will end in chaos, confusion, and disaster, and you will be left feeling much worse."

The silence that followed Blanton's awful prediction seemed to cascade around them both as Paige walked over to her desk and began to put on her Damier leather shoes. "You think I won't be able to handle an escort, don't you?" she accused hotly.

"I'm saying that when you're at your most lost and vulnerable, plunging into a lurid man-for-rent kind of affair might seem tempting, but in the long run you'll not feel better about yourself."

"So you think I'm going to layer trauma upon more trauma, like a sort of lasagna?" Paige seethed, feeling the rise of her temper. "That if I can't handle a hired escort, how then could I possibly handle a date from the Internet. How dare you?"

"How dare *you?"* Blanton raged in return, pushing himself from the desk and rising to his majestic five-ten frame. "You can't try to build a barrier between yourself and what went on with Rupert by using someone else."

"He'll be getting paid," Paige yelled.

"And will you be getting laid?" Blanton threw back.

"That does it," Paige said, walking over to the sofa, yanking her laptop from among the cushions, and returning to her desk. Turning to face Blanton head-on, she felt her heart lurch in gloomy despair that he was sadly unavailable to her. "This general rash of principle, is it consideration for me, or do I detect that you may actually resent me attempting to sort myself out?"

Blanton's deep charcoal-colored eyes narrowed. "What do you mean?"

"Well, I didn't expect you to agree with my plan to find a mate to be with at my birthday party, but I had expected you to understand," Paige told him smoothly, placing her laptop by the phone.

"I do understand."

"No, you don't," Paige said, taking refuge in her office chair, feeling quite sorry for herself. In doing so, she stared at her laptop. The home page for *www.totallyblackdating.com* glared back at her as an alternative option, a reminder that there was someone out there named Omega who did understand. "I'm better off with a transitional object right now—someone safe whom I know I can rely on for a short period."

"Paige—"

"I'm not rushing into a passionate fling with an exciting stranger as you seem to think I'm about to do," she insisted, "who may push all my buttons and leave me feeling more lost. I'm simply choosing to be more discerning about myself by either hiring a mate who will do as he's told, or picking someone off the Web who will do as I suggest."

"Which is immoral," Blanton scoffed in disgust. "You English women never cease to amaze me."

"You see," Paige told him, quietly noting that Blanton's Afro hair had been freshly trimmed and cropped around his face "You don't understand."

Blanton turned to face her, bending over to brace both hands on her desk. "Paige, I do understand," he said, his voice softening suddenly. "I understand that you need to have the courage to learn about yourself through being on your own. I understand that if you have low energy and you're not feeling good about who you are, you'll attract similar types. This escort you want to hire, or perhaps this man you say you want to date from the Net, could be your worst nightmare reincarnate."

"And what do *you* suggest that I do?" Paige harangued, leaning back into her chair, feeling loath to tell Blanton her true intentions in trying to locate a man.

Blanton pulled himself away from the desk, pondering to himself as though the question had come quite unexpectedly. "Maybe . . . a recommendation from a friend."

"Know any eligible bachelors?"

Blanton shook his head in the negative.

"I thought not," Paige breathed, disappointed. "It's hard for a woman to find a mate these days. I can't expect you to know because you're engaged to be married. Maybe I don't need a man on a leash, which is your way of looking at this. Maybe I should try the classified ads—people looking for love—maybe that would suit you." She immediately reached for the *Nubian Chronicle* by her desk, and opened it to the relevant classified advertisements section. "Would doing it this way boost your opinion of me?"

"Paige—"

"No," Paige insisted. "Let me read one for you. *Retired Nigerian banker, 47 years old, enjoys traveling. WLTM young woman for fun.*"

"That translates to: tax exile, balding, into offshore money-laundering, looking for an easy lay," Blanton explained.

"Really." Paige raised eyebrows acknowledging the element of truth. "Then what about this one. *Born-again Christian, middle-aged, seeks honest woman for a nice meal, good wine, and magic."*

"Cult follower, beer belly, seeking naive woman who is easily led for a one-night stand."

"You do like to throw in the X factor," Paige gushed. "Okay, does this guy sound good to you? *Locksmith merchant, 29, looking for a Caribbean princess who can find the key to my caged heart."*

Blanton actually chuckled. "Incarcerated, apprentice con, looking for a meal ticket when he reaches parole."

"Family-minded male, 42, hard worker—"

"Married with kids, having a mid-life crisis, can only see you on weekends," Blanton corrected.

"Pharmaceutical assistant, new to London city, looking for an accomplished daughter of Zion with—"

"Rastafarian drug pusher, expanding his operations, looking for a place to stash and make new contacts."

"*Optician—"*

"Shortsighted."

"Lonely musician—"

"Hard-luck case."

"Nobody quite good enough for me in your eyes," Paige announced, bereaved. "Maybe I should place an ad of my own—*Frogs, toads, and tadpoles need not apply."*

"This is silly," Blanton bristled, finding it easier to begin pacing the room instead. "Here we are, living in a nation of cheats, liars, and serial adulterers, and you want to be more reckless."

"Why are you being like this?" Paige fired back, secretly hoping that it was because he wanted her. Because he cared. Misanthropy told her differently. "I'm not your problem. We're only going to be business partners, remember—the moment I sign on the dotted line?"

"I happen to consider you to be more than that," Blanton declared, a notch of concern resonating in his tone. "You're a very accomplished woman. I valued that in you when you started working for me a year ago."

Paige remembered the day well—the occasion of their first meeting. His collar button open, his tie askew, her first impression of Blanton Blake was clearly that he was a young African man in a hurry—looking like he had barreled out of one meeting and was perilously late for another. She had sensed that the only way to clinch the vacancy she had seen advertised in the *Nubian Chronicle* was to exert her own importance.

"I don't think I need to define myself in relation to the other candidates seeking this job," she had begun. "However, I feel I can bring new policy, new hope, and new ethics to the way property is sold by this agency, and would feel obliged to do all that I can."

"Which is?" He had smiled at her, allowing her to see for the first time his boyish dimples while he continued to sign the various documents in front of him on his desk.

"You are not where you should be, not where you can be, and certainly not where you want to be in the marketplace," she said with unabashed courage. "I can't say you will not survive without me on board, but I can say it damned well won't be the same as if I were."

"I believe I'm taking a good measure of your womanly commitment even as we speak," he had intoned in his mild African accent, suddenly losing interest in his documents.

"It's not about gender," she corrected him. "It's about an agenda."

His smile widened. "Coffee . . . Miss . . . ?"

"Alexander. Paige Alexander."

"How do you take it?"

"Dark and sweet, like my men."

Before the day was out, she had been hired.

"Your amazing progress as a property surveyor and valuer were the reasons why I recently gave you the opportunity to become an equal partner." Blanton's voice was still resonating when Paige suddenly shook herself and was thrust back into her current malaise. "I can't tell you what to do—"

"Damn straight, you can't," she taunted, saddened by the enormity of her feelings, even more saddened that he had spoiled what little peace of mind she had found that morning by opening herself up to a complete stranger named Omega.

"But . . ." Blanton continued, abruptly stopping in his tracks to face her from the other side of the room. "Casual sex liaisons, even of the most perverse nature, are tragically an accurate guide to the level of promiscuity which now passes for acceptable behavior in this country," he warned her firmly. "I don't want you to get caught up in this chopping and bed-hopping just because you don't want to be lonely."

Paige was offended. "I won't," she promised, a solemn oath. "Why do you think I had to shut Rupert down? I needed to protect myself."

"You guys didn't—"

"No. I thought—"

"He was serious." A flicker of emotion passed across Blanton's face as he spoke. "Ditch this idea of finding some roving, nomadic sensation-seeker to give you a brief moment of thrills," he conceded. "Your birthday party will be just fine without him."

"But," Paige began, denying that she was looking for an applicant to be at her disposal in a climate of self-serving brutishness, "I'm only going to reach thirty once. I don't want to look back and remember it as a washout."

"Meaning?"

"I need—"

"A man," Blanton finished, his eyes fixing her with a look that brought a flush of heat to Paige's cheeks.

Feeling entirely vulnerable to the point that she was almost embarrassed, she said, "Don't sound too enthusiastic, will you? I am reminded that you're not available."

Blanton responded with a distracted "Hmmm," though the deepening tint of color in his charcoal-colored eyes suggested something very different behind his facade.

Disappointment stirred in Paige when she asked, "Have you both set a date yet?"

"Latanya's inviting her parents up this weekend from Zimbabwe for preliminary discussions," Blanton disclosed with a shrug of his shoulders. "I'm just going to go with the flow. In fact, I may bring them along to your party, if that's all right?"

Paige's heart sank as she nodded her acceptance. "At least your life is sorted," she said forlornly, leaning back into her chair, her gaze roving to rest on her laptop just as it began to make a discord of noises. She immediately bounced forward, simultaneous to her laptop sounding out the welcoming voice, "You have mail." "I *need* to do something about my life, too" she told Blanton, accessing her mailbox by a simple prompt on her keyboard.

"What is it?" Blanton asked alarmed, realizing from the look on Paige's face that something had happened. He quickly walked over to face her from across her desk.

"Omega"—she flashed Blanton a brief glance—"my Internet friend, has just sent me an e-mail."

With further prompting on the keyboard, she opened up a jpeg attachment file, which unfolded in full color to reveal the cutest man she had seen since setting eyes on Blanton Blake a year ago. Rhys Langston, as the title beneath the jpeg file suggested, was Omega's real name. He was very good-looking, in a stray, square-jawed, obvious kind of way, unlike Blanton, who was more buttoned up and seemingly oblivious to the impact his own alluring sexuality had on women.

Rhys Langston's texturized short black hair was slick and smoothed away from his face to reveal a rich golden-brown complexion. It complemented a pair of soulful, smoldering mocha-brown eyes, large pink lips that were invitingly kissable, a set of perfectly sculptured teeth, and a smile that was so sweet, Paige could do nothing but stare. Everything about this man seemed to evoke images of sinful lust, of renewed hope, of sultry tropical heat. . . .

Paige gasped. "This is *him.*"

Blanton leaned over and stared, then straightened his position and returned his hands to his trouser pockets. "You do know that this risky behavior might have strings attached," he gritted out.

Paige's eyes narrowed. "Like what?"

"Recompense," Blanton said, abandoning all pretense. "This man you want to date off the Internet isn't going to travel all the way from wherever he's coming from to attend your party on a whim without seeking something back in return."

Paige swallowed. Then she gave a short laugh. "Look at this guy. He's *gorgeous."*

"Like a lamb ready for slaughter," Blanton scoffed.

"You're trying to scare me into not doing this, aren't you?" Paige accused, annoyed.

Blanton's face darkened as he saw the surface level of fearful excitement behind Paige's midnight-blue eyes. "I hope I'm making you see sense."

Paige might have been nervous, but she wasn't cowed. "What I see is you"—*not ever noticing me*—"being late for your lunch date," she reminded him, shrugging away the deep yearnings of her heart. "I'm meeting Francine and you're meeting your fiancée, remember?"

Blanton reluctantly glanced at his watch, worry lines etched on his forehead. "Of course."

"Don't worry about me," Paige yelled with pretended bravado as she watched him take large strides toward the door. "Trust me on this. Everything will be just fine."

Blanton braced himself at the threshold, throwing Paige one last discouraging glance. "That's what the spider said to the fly," he told her, waving a dismissing hand as he made his departure, "before he gobbled him up."

"You're lovestruck," Francine announced as she plowed her manicured fingers into the cheesy packet of potato chips. Paige briefly glanced at her cousin before she toyed with her bowl of chicken soup at the canteen table in the small law firm on Kensington High Street where Francine worked.

A casual passerby would notice that the two women were very different, both in looks and character. Francine was one year older, doll-like and petite, with a dainty face and an auburn curly perm that seemed to accentuate the bright sparkling shade of hazel in her eyes. Paige, on the other hand, was tall in comparison, with a very feminine-shaped figure, skin a much darker shade of honey, with a straight nose and eyes widely spaced under arched, slanting brows. Paige was also more energetic, high-profile, and would easily have run the lives of everyone around her if Francine's down-to-earth instincts had not offered resistance.

"His name is Rhys Langston," she told her cousin, who was seated across from her, immaculately dressed in a pin-striped navy suit. "And he's gorgeous."

"That's precisely what you said about Mr. Blanton Blake when you met him a year ago," Francine reminded her, placing her empty chip packet on the table to reach for a packet of Marlboros from her red Gucci handbag. "Have you now cast him to the wayside?"

"Let's say he did that when he announced his engagement to Latanya Folasade," Paige said, leaning dejected into her chair. "He doesn't have any feelings for me. And if he ever did, he lost them the moment he was invited to become one of the judges of the Miss Zimbabwe beauty pageant and fell in lust with the crowned titleholder."

"Which was why you dated Rupert King," Francine recalled. "You got jealous and didn't give Blanton Blake a chance."

"He noticed *her,* not me," Paige reminded Francine, now wondering why it mattered so much to Blanton Blake whether she found a mate or not. "What was he waiting for? Hell to freeze over before asking me out on a date?"

"So, you both started seeing other people," Francine added. "What's the big deal?"

Regret welled up in Paige's eyes. "I'm thirty on Saturday. I can't wait forever. Now he's engaged, so it's a lost cause."

Concerned, Francine gazed at her cousin. "What's going on with you?"

"Nothing," Paige lied, suddenly tearful.

Francine lit up a cigarette. She inhaled the stench of nicotine before chastising her younger cousin further. "Why are you doing this?"

Paige stared at her soup, one word looming in her mind's eye to glare at her. *Thirty!* Thirty seemed impossible. Thirty and still having the girls round on Friday night to talk men and watch videos, still going to the gym religiously three times a week to work away the cellulite and hope to hell she would not have to go four times a week next year to trim her waistline.

Thirty and tired of spending Christmas week visiting her folks in Nottingham alone, tired of the utter predictability of her life. Most of all, she was tired of the nonsensical, confusing stuff that went on in the vacant spaces of her mind. Thoughts that kept her disgruntled, her self-confessions shocking her rigid throughout the day, most of them dreams of finding love. Now, suddenly, she was about to make changes, and everyone seemed unhappy.

"I'm doing this because I don't know how to fall in love without losing myself. I don't know how to kiss in a way that communicates perfectly what I would like and wouldn't like to happen next. What I would or wouldn't do for love, and how to ask for what I want in a way that makes it most likely I'll get it. Don't you think those are major flaws for a woman on the brink of reaching thirty? I couldn't even land Blanton Blake and I adore him."

"You can't force a man to like you, lust for you, or love you," Francine clarified, sympathetic to her cousin.

"I couldn't tame Rupert King either," Paige went on, her lunch forgotten, the now-overdue sad pathetic tears falling into her bowl of soup.

"C'mon," Francine encouraged, unsympathetic, but

nonetheless rubbing a gentle hand against her cousin's own. "You didn't really like Rupert, now did you? You only dated him to try and forget your crush on Blanton Blake. All rebound stuff."

Of course, Francine was right. Paige thought back to her romance with Rupert. It was not made in heaven, but on the pages of the world's glossiest magazines. Rupert King, a famous British soccer star who was reputed to be taking her to a private holiday villa in Portugal to set the scene for a proposal of marriage. At least, that was what the newspapers were saying, and she stupidly believed the publicity hype—after only two months of dating.

He was described as an engaging young striker who, through hard work and a great deal of vanity, had thrust himself into the London "A" list to much success and notoriety, especially after having played during the World Cup in South Korea and Japan last year. She was said to be the picture of brains and perfection, with a body toned in the best gymnasium in town and a seductive smile that was an easy attraction to the world's most ego-minded bachelors.

They had met at a charity function, where she had learned that his romances had never progressed much beyond the gossip columns. It was little wonder that their two-month affair would be precisely that, airbrushed across the shiny pages of journals and newspapers alike, all charting their whirlwind affair to an unrealistic expectation of marriage.

Paige pushed her bowl aside and stared while Francine absently flicked ashes of spent cigarette into her soup. "I just feel so . . . much void," Paige said quietly, wiping the back of her right hand across her wet cheeks. "Being lied to by Rupert, ignored by Blanton. . . . We argued today."

"What about?"

"Me looking for love on the Internet," Paige confessed sadly. "He made me feel . . . pitiful and . . . desperate."

"And are you?" Francine asked, puffing smoke and fanning it from her face with her hand to prevent it from dulling her pale honey complexion.

"I just don't want to be alone at my party," Paige declared at last.

"So that's what this is really all about. You won't be alone," Francine reassured her, squeezing her cousin's left hand. "Using the Internet isn't the way. We discussed all this when you returned last weekend from your failed trip to Portugal."

"Rhys Langston wants me to return an e-mail agreeing to a date," Paige went on, ignoring Francine's remark. Drying her eyes, ever the optimist that she could actually work things to her advantage, she added, "I want to do it. I want him at my party. That'll show Rupert King I can do better than him."

"You've invited Rupert to your party?" Francine was aghast. "Why?"

"It was before we broke up," Paige explained ruefully. "But bet your bottom dollar he'll be there."

"And you want what? Revenge?"

"No. Leverage."

"Is this some kind of vendetta?" Francine asked, alarm causing her to poise her cigarette in midair, allowing smoke to seep into her pores.

"It is," Paige confirmed sternly.

"Let it go," Francine implored.

"I can't," Paige refused. "You should've heard the things he said to me."

"He's not worth it," her cousin said. "Just handle the rejection gracefully."

"I want him to *see* he's not worth it the moment I walk into my party with a new man at my side," Paige said. "That's when I'll feel better."

"Paige, your life is doing just fine," Francine tried to reason in vain. "Don't do this."

"I want to see his face," Paige insisted, "and watch him squirm."

"No doubt you'd like to see him crawl, too," Francine derided sarcastically.

"Like a snail."

"You're asking for trouble," Francine warned, smoke

pumping out of her mouth with a huge dosage of cold sentiment. "Okay, Rupert King didn't deserve you and I don't know what to say about Blanton Blake, except that he was a little slow on the uptake. Just remember what Aunt Elva used to say: There's good, there's better, and there's the best. Maybe you just haven't met the best yet, that's all."

"And I'm not likely to at this rate," Paige declared, eyeing Francine through tear-stained eyes.

"Paige, you've done some wonderful things with your life," Francine began, flicking more cigarette ash directly into her cousin's bowl of soup. "We live in a lovely Victorian home with Aunt Elva in Chelsea while we work during the week, and you're thinking about buying a small retreat of your own in the country. You're earning enough money to set something aside to fund your old age and you have a résumé to die for." Francine arched her lips into a grin. "You also have eight matching plates, wine glasses with stems, and an iron with twenty-four heat settings."

Paige exerted a healthy chuckle.

"All you need right now is to learn how to live alone, even if you don't like it," Francine said with a smile.

Paige sighed heavily. "That leaves me with little control over my destiny. I *need* to know what's going to happen next."

Francine looked confused. "Like what?"

"Marriage," Paige confirmed. "Is it about blind devotion like you and Mervyn? I mean . . ." She paused. "Does Mervyn bring excitement, love, and adventure home when you're back together in Birmingham?"

"Paige!" Francine was shocked. "Mervyn is my best friend. We share everything."

"But don't you think you married him to escape responsibility, as all women do?" Paige scoffed, ever alert to the cynical perceptions she had acquired about the ultimate relationship. "That's what marriage is, a fortress behind which a woman can hide all her illusions and self-deception."

"You really are losing it," Francine said, her hazel eyes wild as she held her cigarette precariously. "If I didn't know you better, I'd be considering right now committing you to a mental asylum. Mervyn's a man who has always made me feel special. He shares my ideas, opinions, and dreams. That's what marriage is, togetherness."

"I was wondering if it's dependency," Paige corrected, deliberately adding provocation to the subject. "Enslavement, pure and simple. To me, a man is an optional extra."

"I'm ending this conversation," Francine blazed, stubbing out the last remnants of her cigarette directly into Paige's soup bowl. Glaring at her in disbelief, she added, "I'm going back to my office."

"What's the matter?" Paige goaded, determined to satisfy her suspicions as Francine rose out of her chair. "Afraid to admit that you've surrendered everything to Mervyn? Your high energy, ambitions, and dreams."

"I *love* my husband," Francine screamed, causing her work colleagues and onlookers in the canteen to raise their heads from their own lunch plates, curious as to the cause of her outburst.

"That's a high price to pay," Paige concluded, her tone neutral. "Hiding behind your marriage to bury your anxiety about what you really want in your life."

Francine's eyes widened as she retook her seat. "When did this become about me?" she flung out, seething and understandably offended. "Let's get to bedrock here. This is all about you and your refusal to accept that you want to be loved, just like the rest of us. Only, you don't want to surrender anything, not even your precious celibacy."

"I'm waiting to meet someone special," Paige said objectionably, secretly aware that stalling Rupert surely meant he was not the right man for her.

"Yeah, by going onto the Internet," Francine spat out. "You don't want to risk love for dependency, but you're prepared to risk your life for independence."

"I want a youth that I'm content to move beyond," Paige railed in frustrated defense, knowing she had done very little to accomplish this. "A past juicy enough that I can look forward to retelling it in my old age."

"If you had said you want an old love you can imagine going back to and one who reminds you how far you had come, I would've said that you've lived," Francine confided with honesty, her voice nonetheless heavy and stern. "But if this is all you have to tell me, that you want revenge and excitement, then go on this reckless date with Rhys Langston. Go and see if you find your protector, your prince, the one who will rescue you from yourself. Just leave your obituary by the canteen door on your way out. As the resident family lawyer, I'll be sure to send a copy to Aunt Elva, not to mention your parents."

Paige was shaken. "I'm sorry," she apologized, shamefaced at her behavior.

"Not as sorry as I am to see you like this," Francine returned, still unfazed.

Paige bowed her head, then glared at her cousin. "There's something about this man that makes me feel I'm going to learn about who I am," she admitted finally. "I need answers."

"Paige," Francine cautioned, her tone firm and grim. "Take your bat and ball home. You don't know the rules of this game you want to play."

"Rules?"

"There must be some sort of social code for dating and mating on the Internet," Francine blurted quite cynically. "Whatever it is, you don't want to play."

"But—"

"You had your chance with Blanton Blake and blew it," Francine continued, "by dating Rupert."

Paige's eyes widened suddenly. "What?"

"It was obvious to everyone except you that he liked you," Francine declared sarcastically. "You were just impatient."

"Are you saying that Blanton Blake really likes me?" Paige harangued, feeling she had suddenly lost the thread of conversation somewhere.

"He made eyes at Latanya Folasade and so you started dating Rupert King, which forced his hand to date Latanya," Francine confirmed. "And Rupert saw you as just the latest in a long line of beauties to be a charm-plumped cushion of comfort since the breakdown of this . . . alleged heart-and-soul relationship he had going on before he met you. That's your love life over the past year in a nutshell."

"Francine . . ." Paige wanted to laugh. "This changes everything."

"What do you mean?"

"Don't you see? Instead of using Rhys Langston to show Rupert that I can get by without him, I could instead force Blanton's hand by making him jealous," Paige related in a flurry of renewed excitement.

"Now you're being childish," Francine harangued, unamused.

"You said that he likes me, so what's the problem?" Paige croaked. "A girl's got to try something."

"Why don't you just try and find a suitable partner in the church?" her cousin overrode. "Someone homely and genuine."

"What?" Paige was aghast, her brain still trying to piece together what Francine had just told her. "I'm not one of those church girls who's waiting to be approached by a light-skinned pastor, singer, or musician who has Indian hair so that my babies will turn out cute."

"I didn't mean it like that," Francine bristled, growing impatient. "I'm just thinking that you need someone reliable."

"With a name like Godfrey," Paige choked.

"So what if every church has a Godfrey," Francine proclaimed, seeing the pained expression on Paige's face. "There's nothing wrong with that. He's in his thirties, been in the church all his life, wears a small Afro, sensible, non-designer clothing, and has a doting mother in the background pulling the strings."

"I don't want a Godfrey," Paige protested, annoyed.

"You know something?" Francine remarked solemnly. "You remind me of a client I once had who went to the

Caribbean to find herself a handsome visa husband. He was a compromise. She really wanted an African-American with a fancy name like Stanhope or Devante."

"What's your point?" Paige scoffed, detecting the deathly tone in her cousin's voice.

"She thought she could change him," Francine went on, "once she got him back to England. She actually believed that if he went to evening classes, no one would ever know that he used to sell crabs to tourists on the seafront."

"What happened?" Paige asked, gripped.

"She came home early one day and found him in a compromising position with someone else," Francine concluded. "It was a case of her wanting to tell the pastor that her man had come without a ten-year guarantee and that his marriage warranty had run out, and could she give him back or exchange him for another model. But that entitled him to one third of her estate."

"It would cost *her* money?" Paige was shocked.

"Not to mention the emotional scarring," Francine related. "She took my advice and went back to the Caribbean. The Home Office would not allow him to stay without her, so when he found himself right back where she had found him, he settled for a divorce on her terms."

"She called his bluff," Paige acknowledged, nodding.

"The point I am trying to make," Francine concluded, "is that when she eventually returned to England, she found a good man in the church and was happily married a year later."

"Like you and Mervyn," Paige finished.

"I learned from this woman's story," Francine explained. "I went to church and found Mervyn. He's hassle-free."

"But don't you think men in the church are . . . ugly?" Paige opined thoughtlessly before seeing the shocked expression marring Francine's face.

Her cousin rose abruptly from her chair. "I'm offended by what you've told me today," she snarled, appalled. "Don't go projecting your hardships on anyone, especially me. I know you too well to fall for it. If your life is sour, it's not anyone's fault but your own. I'm happily married because I choose to be and intend to stay that way." She shook her head, exerting a deep sigh. " Just sort out your life, Paige. You can't keep punishing everyone for what your parents went through. And if I were you, I'd offer Blanton Blake an apology."

"What?"

"He and I at least see one thing you don't," Francine jabbed angrily, reaching for her Gucci bag. "Who can vouch that Rhys Langston even exists?"

Paige was silenced. This was true. She may have reformulated her game plan, but suppose Omega had not revealed his real name. Until she tangibly met him in the flesh, or met someone who knew who he was, she could not be sure. As a stranger, he could be just about anyone. "You're right," she conceded, quite rueful. "I'll give him a rain check. What was I thinking?"

"That's more like it," Francine agreed. "I'll see you at Aunt Elva's later." With that answer, she was gone, leaving Paige with her bleak and dismal thoughts. She was still engrossed in her malaise when she left the canteen and hit the sidewalk, immediately turning blindly into someone.

"Paige!" the newcomer announced. "Paige Alexander?"

"Lizzy," Paige enthused, dropping out of her trancelike state. "How are you?"

"Fine, now that I've got my act together," Lizzy replied with a smile. "What about you?"

Lizzy Chadwick was an old acquaintance who had organized Paige's twenty-first birthday party years before. They had lost touch when Lizzy, deciding she was good with food, had opted for setting up her own catering service. Paige had heard that she was now the owner of the flourishing London party planners *Chadwick & Co.,* and could boast an impressive list of clients.

Paige hardly recognized her now. Lizzy was older and slightly wrinkled around her large doe-shaped brown eyes. Similarly, her relaxed black hair was much shorter, but salon-styled and trimmed to perfection. She wore no makeup, except lashings of lip-gloss, and was dressed in a dark navy suit with a slash-necked white silk blouse and high stiletto-heeled shoes, all of which projected the image of a woman who meant business. Not quite the shy girl Paige remembered.

"I now work for *Blanton's*, the London and country real estate agency on Sloane Street," Paige revealed to her old friend. "You're now looking at someone who deals in residential sales, lettings, and commercial property, and is considering a partnership."

"That's great." Lizzy smiled, clutching at her handbag. "I'm still into catering. In fact, just off to see a new client."

"Good luck," Paige offered kindly.

They were silenced as a passerby intruded between them, glancing briefly at both women, perhaps in bemusement as to who was the prettier. Paige had to admit, Lizzy was very much like her in build and size, and though only marginally older by months, could still knock the lip gloss off women ten years younger.

"How's your love life?" Lizzy could not resist asking, narrowing her well-plucked eyebrows in curiosity. "I've been reading about you and Rupert King."

Paige winced at the reminder. "Over with," she said simply. "And you?"

"Still unlucky."

Paige felt the sentiment as only a lonely woman could. "Look," she ventured thoughtfully. "I'm having a thirtieth birthday bash this Saturday. I know it's short notice and I don't know what your plans are, but—"

"Who's going to be there?" Lizzy probed, noncommittal.

"My family, friends, some of whom you've met already."

"And Rupert?"

Paige's brows furrowed. "He's invited, not that I will be sparing him any mind if he shows up, of course. I made the mistake of asking him before we broke up." She failed to see the flicker of entrancement that passed across Lizzy Chadwick's eyes.

"I tell you what," Lizzy said. "Why don't I help you add the finishing touches to your party. That way you can fill me in on the love gossip that went on about you two and I can give you an update on mine. No charge."

"That sounds great," Paige said, excited.

"And I have a friend who can do your hair," Lizzy added as an incentive.

Paige's smile broadened. "Thank you. You're on. I'm at the same address in Chelsea. The party starts at nine."

"Shall we say I'll see you at ten in the morning that day?"

"Fine," Paige agreed.

The two women briefly embraced their farewells and parted. Paige was taken into the malaise of her life once more. She moseyed back to her office in a preoccupied state, getting caught in a brief rain shower as she wondered just exactly when was it she had lost some semblance of herself. Once upon a time, she had been a lively, energetic, active woman full of opinions and ideas, and though she could still admit to herself that a part of her retained those qualities, the larger part was in an abyss of despair.

Could she trace her feelings to when it had all begun? In her case, it was simple. It was the day she had started working for Blanton Blake. On accepting his job offer, she had asked herself what sane woman would forgo the pleasure of discreetly ogling him. But his reluctance to respond to her flirtations had been a devastating blow to her psyche. When she had found it fascinating to tell him all about how she had traced her family origins to the small black dockside communities of Cardiff in Wales, where her grandfather had been born, he did not seem so enchanted with her.

Not once did he even inquire about her mobile phone number, which—and this was something he knew throughout all the months working with her—she rarely gave to anyone. From the start, there had been an element of friendliness that never once strayed beyond the conduct of their profession. She would time and again tell herself that she understood his privacy and forgave him. There was, after all, a fundamental rule to working closely with one's boss.

The fact remained, she was attracted to Blanton Blake. Everything about him made her crave for his kiss, his touch, his affection . . . his love. And when he had suggested he might take a business partner and gave her first refusal, in spite of knowing he had already begun dating Miss Zimbabwe, she had begun to fantasize about his warm body beside her in the night, making love until dawn. Until . . . yesterday, when he announced his engagement.

In a wild panic, she had nearly made a barbaric decision to consult *Ebony Escorts*. When Blanton had caught her, she had come to realize that, like many a black immigrant, he was cruelly secretive, fiercely ambitious, and would not stop until he had fulfilled his dreams, and that included the perfect woman at his side. Sadly, she had slowly come to terms with the fact that his future wife would not be her. Such was the consequence of unrequited love. Now what Francine had told her changed everything. There was still hope.

At her desk, her mind refocused. *I bet you don't dare yourself anything* lingered. When Paige switched on her laptop, she decided she would apologize to Blanton Blake, accept his invitation to become a partner at his realty agency, and send an e-mail to Rhys Langston.

Three

"That's peculiar," Francine said.

She was standing in the doorway of Paige's bedroom, reading a copy of a morning newspaper. Though both women still wore their nightdresses, Paige's pert face was half buried in her pillow. She seemed perfectly at rest. Perfectly still. Only one eye was open, throwing a hazy midnight-blue gaze across the room.

"What is it?" Paige murmured, resenting the early intrusion, begrudging the crumbling image in her mind of someone new, a man with mocha-brown eyes, kissable pink lips, and a sweet smile.

"Hackers Strike Fear into Net Businesses," Francine went on, reading out loud the one-sentence headline. "To think, we were just talking about this whole online cyberdating thing only yesterday."

"Francine, it's Wednesday morning," Paige complained, thinking only of getting more sleep, though she could not guarantee this would dismiss the wonderful image of Rhys Langston in her head. "Can't we talk later, after work?"

"I'm driving back home after work," Francine reminded. "To see my husband, in case you've forgotten I have one. Besides, I thought you were taking the day off."

Paige's open eye veered sideways, peering through her tousled brown hair, which was spread out around her face like an aura, to find exactly where Francine was located. She darted this way and that around her bedroom, flicking sideways to catch a glimmer of the morning sunlight forcing its way through the thin lacy curtains at the window, then across the room to her dressing table and the French Provincial armoire. Finally, her glance fastened on the motionless woman standing in the open doorway.

"What time is it?" she asked Francine.

"Seven-thirty."

"That early?" Paige was dazed. "Where's Aunt Elva?"

"In bed."

"Anything about Rupert King in that newspaper?" she questioned with a huge yawn.

Since their split, she had been checking the press, aware that Rupert's publicity profile was like that of a pop star. Were there any news, however small, it would have been deliberately planted by his personal bagpiper to benefit him enormously with advertising and sponsorship contracts. But so far, she had seen nothing.

"If you mean have your private canoodlings been catapulted to the front pages as newsworthy to mere mortals like me, then the answer is no," Francine derided. "Aren't you going to get up and listen to this?"

"I thought you were going to help me with the last-minute arrangements for my party," Paige slurred while struggling to open her other eye. "There's a thousand things to do, and you'd never guess who I bumped into who's offered to help me. Lizzy Chadwick. You remember her?" Paige prompted. "She was the party planner Aunt Elva hired when I had my twenty-first birthday party. Anyway, she's offered to help, so I've invited her."

"It says here that agents of the Federal Bureau of Investigation are frantically trying to catch the mysterious hackers who brought down half of America's top Web sites last night," Francine announced, distracted. "They bombarded a number of service sites, and were successful in obtaining access to user names and credit card details. Sites that are particularly vulnerable are those that had been trading for less than one year and were not adequately insured to cover theft of assets, liability to other companies, and the illicit release of confidential data."

"What's all this got to do with me?" Paige croaked, raising her head from her pillow.

She blinked once, then again. Something new to cope with? Some new problem? Another crisis? She inhaled deeply, as if she were struggling for oxygen. There were the caterers to pay, the cake to recheck, the sherry glasses had not yet been delivered, the waitresses were still awaiting confirmation. She could not decide. Did she need two or three? She had already dealt with the DJ, the food selection list, the champagne and wine varieties. But there were the napkins to buy, more paper plates and plastic cutlery, refuse bags for the garbage, non-alcoholic beverages for the younger relatives. . . . More problems?

"What was the name of that Web dating service you used yesterday?" Francine asked.

Paige frowned. Francine was always this way. Always the factual one. Always asking questions. It was her lawyer's brain. Never switching off. "Totally Black Dating dot com." Paige added, "Problem?"

"There could be," Francine proclaimed. She ventured into Paige's bedroom and sat down on the edge of the bed. "It was one of the sites that got hit last night. Look." She handed over the morning newspaper.

"What?" Paige immediately sat up in bed and scanned the headline.

She read how over one hundred cyberdating sites had been attacked and were inaccessible for about four hours, though *www.totallyblackdating.com* was one of the few that had come back online for about two hours before going down completely around midnight. At the time of going to press, over half of America's top Web sites were still not restored. Users of Web site services were strongly advised to check with their credit card companies to see if extortionate amounts of funds had been removed from their accounts.

Agents at the FBI and in the U.S. government were taking the matter very seriously.

"You should phone your bank," Francine advised.

Paige wanted to chuckle. Things somehow did not seem real anymore. Her guise as Isis. Chatting with Omega. She could not put her finger on when it all began to feel hazy and dreamlike. *This is neurotic,* she even told herself. "Surely, this can't be affecting me?" she said at last.

"I don't know." Francine was honest. "What details did you supply?"

"My full name, address, telephone number, credit card number, expiration date, date of birth . . ."

"I'd say that was more than enough," Francine mocked in a superior tone.

Paige saw the look, the one that said *I told you so,* and wanted to scream. "Feeling vindicated, are you?"

"Don't be silly." Francine flinched. "Just call your bank, now."

"And say what?"

"You're testing my consternation." Francine warned. "Tell them the truth."

"That I had a lapse of indiscretion." Paige laughed hysterically. "I'm sure they will disapprove of my code of ethics very severely."

Francine rose from the edge of the bed. "I'm going to Birmingham," she remarked coldly. "If I know you as I do, your credit card, like everything else you own, is probably insured anyway. How amazing it is that you can install security to protect all your possessions, but let your values fly out of the window. No wonder you're forgetting you have a bank balance to preserve. There's the matter of your reputation to address, isn't there?" Francine left, allowing the bedroom door to slam behind her.

Paige was out of her bed before her drowsy mind could fully come back to its senses. She was immediately in front of her dressing table, removing her laptop from its holdall and attaching the cable to the nearest socket on the wall. She switched it on and connected her phone line. The LCD screen flashed and began to load up its operating program. The few minutes' wait was more than Paige could endure. She found herself pacing the carpeted floor of her bedroom, wondering whether she would be able to log online.

What she did not tell Francine was that she had sent an e-mail to Rhys Langston. *How could any woman in her sane mind resist?* she told herself convincingly. Furthermore, she had included a jpeg attachment of herself, and had agreed that he should attend her birthday party. In doing so, she had even written out his invitation on one of the few remaining fancy white gold-trimmed cards she had ordered and mailed to her guests. Of course, her plans could all change if he did not like her picture. And in view of the news she had just read, Paige was now wondering whether she had done the right thing.

Why she felt panicked, she did not know. Perhaps it was the recklessness of what she had done that worried her. Or maybe it was the concern that he might never respond to her e-mail. Maybe it would be a good thing if he did not; then she could put the entire experience behind her. But that would mean she still had to find someone before her party on Saturday night.

The laptop now loaded, Paige logged online. To her chagrin, a voice instantly announced, "You have mail." She seated herself at her dressing table and accessed the first in a line of three in her mailbox. It was from Rhys Langston. She read it out loud.

" 'Hello, Paige. I thought I was dreaming when I saw you. It was like staring at a real live goddess among the desert sands, and I am humbled to be accepting your invitation to be with you at your party. Thank you for leaving your name and mobile number. Sometime soon, I shall call you.' "

"Sometime soon?" Paige squealed, aware that in the pit of her stomach was a low level pool of pure excitement. Moving on to her next e-mail, she saw that Blanton Blake was in protest mood. Paige saw the words in front of her and groaned.

"I need to talk to you about the property at Holland Park. Unfortunately, you're not in work today, so I should like you to meet me in my office first thing tomorrow."

It was a confrontation she did not want to have. To find herself explaining to her handsome boss why she had not yet booked a third showing of the property that was proving popular with two buyers. *I'll think about that later,* she resolved, moving on to her third e-mail. Paige was surprised to find it to be another one from Rhys Langston.

"Hello, my desert princess. Change of plan," he wrote. "I'm flying into London today. Someone made an attempt to hack into my bank account last night. CNN online is reporting some scary stuff. My nearest international offshore bank is London. I'll call you from Heathrow Airport."

"What?" Paige said out loud.

She jumped out of her seat. It suddenly dawned on her that before the day was through, she could be meeting her princely stranger at the airport and taking him home! Paige was now indeed alarmed. She rushed over to the door, almost falling over her nightdress in the process. She had to tell Francine and Aunt Elva. But when she braced her hand on the doorknob, she was paralyzed with fear. Francine could not be told. Francine would skin her alive. Aunt Elva might even faint. She could not face either one of them at the breakfast table either. The strain of it would show on her face.

Paige inhaled a deep sickly breath. "I can do this," she told herself calmly, taking another breath, reminding herself of her oath to clinch her boss and teach Rupert King a lesson. "He'll have some ID and . . ." She looked at her laptop. An idea hit her. The search engines!

Paige rushed back to her computer and immediately went into Yahoo. She typed in Rhys Langston's name. It was a long shot, but in her present circumstance, it was the only way to find out whether this man did in fact exist. Pressing SEARCH, Paige waited. Her eyes widened in startled amazement when, almost instantly, information presented itself on her screen.

"Rhys W. Langston . . . of Omega Private Equity Funds Ltd. . . . makes donation for research into African diasporic studies, African cultures, African archaeology; African American archaeology, and . . ."

Under EVENTS, she read: ". . . family history. Dr. Warrington of London, a workshop in 'Jewish-Jamaican Genealogy, A Spiritual Journey,' sponsored by Rhys W. Langston."

And again, she saw: 'Finding Lost People: Rhys Langston funds photographic presentation at Liverpool Slavery Museum."

Paige was enthralled. She read all seven Web page matches, visiting some of the Web sites themselves to find startling revelations about her wonderful Internet friend. There was no mistaking that Rhys Langston existed, and was a man who had an active interest in the research on global black culture. Paige eventually switched off her computer and stared at the patterned wallpaper in her bedroom. Sometime today, she would be getting a call from this man. This icon. Suddenly the stupidity of her not having a partner at her birthday party, and the schemes she had invented to bring two men to their knees with their tails wagging, seemed microscopic in comparison to his work.

Certain he would surely find her a nuisance, Paige went over to her handbag and located her mobile phone. She stared at it for all of three seconds, then decidedly switched it off. Taking a breath, she told herself it was for the best. She had already made a fool of herself by telling him as much as she had. Now knowing how worldly this man was, Paige felt positively weak with idiocy.

Such a man would not want to play her games. Such a man would have better things to do with his time than indulge her fantasies in trying to make Blanton Blake jealous, and least of all being used against Rupert King at her party. No. She would get dressed, skip breakfast, and go about her chores. She would put the whole matter behind her. If she kept herself busy, she could forget just how brainlessly she had behaved.

That was the plan. It lasted three hours. Paige was not accustomed to having her mobile phone switched off, especially midweek. Between picking up a range of napkins at Selfridge's and fancy serving plates at Harrod's, the fretful thought that Rhys Langston was waiting for her at Heathrow Airport niggled at her conscience in such proportion, she found herself seated in a taxi switching the damn thing back on.

Only the date, time, and network glared at her. Thankfully, there were no messages. Rhys Langston had not yet called. Perhaps he was not coming after all. It was a thought that gave Paige a moment's relief. She leaned comfortably into the imitation leather of the taxi seat and watched the noisy traffic amble by. Contemplating the remainder of her day, the majority of her chores done, she decided she would return to Aunt Elva's in time for dinner, maybe watch some TV, then get ready for bed. That resolution firmly implanted in her mind, she glanced at her watch. It read 5:33 P.M.

At 5:39 P.M., her phone rang. Paige was immediately jolted in her seat. Her heart began to pound with such intensity, the feel of it resonated in her head. Adrenaline ran along her nerve endings until her hands shook. Nervously reaching for her mobile, she released the flip and accepted the call.

"Paige Alexander, please," a man's voice said. It had a pleasing Southern American quality to it, as though the single thing on his mind was to locate her and her alone.

"Yes," she answered.

"Hi there. It's Rhys Langston. How are you?"

"Fine, thank you. You?"

"Just arrived at Heathrow. Slept most of the way here. Are you busy?"

"No."

"Care to pick me up?"

"Okay."

"I'm at terminal four, British Airways arrivals. See you in—?"

"Just under an hour."

"Cool."

"Bye."

It was short and sweet, just like their online chat. Returning the flip, Paige remained motionless, feeling as though she were working her way out of a trance. All thoughts of her earlier decision had vanished. She was hardly aware she had tipped the taxi driver to reroute toward Heathrow Airport until she saw him working his way along the spiral roadway that led toward the various terminals. She heard a number of airplanes zooming overhead and for a wild moment, had the urge to cut and run. But that would be denying herself a youth she would one day be content to move beyond, and Paige did not want to do that.

"This is gonna cost a pretty penny," the taxi driver alerted, bringing her attention to the rate charge on the clock. "I can wait, but they'll probably move me along. Airport rules. I can circle the building."

"Okay, I'll be right back," Paige told him, departing his cab and running into the arrivals building. Nothing less than divine intervention could stop her now.

Her high-heeled burgundy-colored boots were not designed for running along polished floors attempting to find someone she had not yet met, but Paige had not contemplated finding herself in such a predicament. British Airways arrivals at Heathrow Airport was vast. Her gaze roamed among the endless number of seats, among the endless number of people who were seated, or walking with trolleys, standing at phone booths, at the duty-free store, on the conveyor belt. . . .

She was dressed in a dusky-pink hand-knitted sweater and blue-denim skirt, with a dark-pink beret crowning her head, and no one would have taken her for a woman who had gone too far. The pitch of her shoulders was confident; the expectant way in which she looked around the arrivals lounge was brisk. Only the mouth betrayed tension. The lower lip was trembling with nervousness and a dozen other conflicting emotions.

Why am I doing this? Paige mused, darting an eager gaze from left to right. Then she had an even more disturbing thought. *If not this, then what?* Paige told herself she had the savoir faire to deal with it. She had started this charade and she would finish it. Beneath her breath, she even uttered her credo—*ad finem,* to the end—then allowed her gaze to wander across the lounge once more.

Two minutes passed. Four. *Where is he?* Paige brooded, her tolerance wearing thin. She was reminded she had a taxi waiting with bags of purchases littering in the backseat. She really should get back before the cab driver chose to abscond with her purchases. It seemed divine intervention was beginning to play its hand after all. Throwing a final anxious glance around the terminal, Paige was suddenly hit with the notion that Rhys Langston had gone. Another minute passed and she turned on her heels, walking directly into a hardened chest.

"Excuse me. I'm sorry." She looked up and was immediately struck dumb. He was right in front of her, though for one insane moment, he was like a shadowy oasis and Paige was forced to blink. But Rhys Langston was real enough.

Paige stared at him and blinked again. If she had thought his jpeg file had done him justice, she was even more pleasantly surprised by what faced her in the flesh. If, likewise, she had been seriously seeking to fulfill her own personal fantasy adventure with a desert prince who would whisk her away on a fiery black stallion, Rhys Langston would fit the role most admirably.

He was wearing washed-out denim jeans that hugged his muscled thighs and a pale blue shirt opened at the neck, revealing a glimpse of dark curly hair on his chest. A thick beige-colored camel-skin jacket protected him against the elements, while heavy-set pale-brown boots covered his feet. He towered above her, and his smile was captivating and his magnetic presence seemed to hold her hostage.

She noticed that the dark soulful eyes were in fact deep,

bewitching, and mesmerizing. His gaze garnered her attention like a hypnotist with mutual recognition, instantly forcing Paige to swallow the breath caught in the back of her throat. Reassessing her original impression, she realized he did not simply ooze sinful lust or provide her with renewed hope. Rhys Langston was like a dream come true, and that was all any girl could ask for.

He smiled. "Miss Alexander?"

"Mr. Langston," Paige gasped, breathless on hearing the mild Southern accent up close. "How long have you been standing there?"

"A few minutes, watching you," he answered.

"You might have alerted me sooner," Paige breathed, quite flustered. "I have been—"

"Waiting for me," he said.

Paige felt the hot flush of blood rush into her cheeks. She was aware he noticed it, too. If her suspicions were correct, she also knew he could visibly see the palpitations of her heart. Hoping to disguise her reaction well, she decided to offer her hand to affect a friendly handshake. It seemed the most polite thing to do. And it would have been had she chosen a more conventional man. But Rhys Langston was far from formal.

He took the hand she offered and handled her delicately boned fingers with the familiarity of a man who was used to touching women. Raising it to his lips, he kissed each finger in turn until Paige was speechless with awe. Every nerve ending in her body suddenly became alive with the unexpected sensual onslaught, and before she could descend from the blissful moment of surprise, he gently pulled her into him and caught her further unaware with a curt kiss on her lips.

Paige weakly pushed against his chest in vain, finding herself helpless in the well of feeling that suddenly erupted in the pit of her stomach. It was an innocent, informal greeting, but she could feel the slight warmth emanating from his body beneath his jacket as his exotic scent tickled her senses, enveloping her in a whirlpool of frankincense and myrrh.

It was the briefest of kisses, yet she felt as though every inch of her mouth had been devoured. He caught her breath and made it his own, claimed her tongue for one fleeting taste of her ardor, and captured her lips with such fervent need, she felt the gasping pants of her heart being pulled out of her body and abandoned in infinite freedom.

The public intimacy of the moment did not escape her when his eyes, sparkling in their incredible soulful depths, finally ensnared her own. It was a heart-stopping moment. Paige swallowed convulsively, hoping she could dispel the image that provoked her. *I wonder if you're as wild in bed as you look.* From where she had acquired such shameless thoughts about him, she did not know.

He licked his sexy lips. "You needed that."

Paige lifted one brow. "Did I?" Her voice came out in a feeble sound.

"Yes," he whispered against her lips, never once taking his eyes off her.

His voice was low and mellow, soothing Paige into a hazy daze. She was too overcome to confirm his decision, and yet very tangibly aware that she had become suddenly quite liberated. There was a different taste of victory now that she had met Omega, one that was wonderfully sweet on her tongue.

"I have a taxi outside." To her surprise, her tone was hoarse and needy.

He took his wallet from his jacket pocket and handed it over to her. "Let's not keep it waiting."

It was a promise that worked on Paige like an aphrodisiac as Rhys Langston reached for his black leather bag by his feet on the floor. Paige was rendered mute when he took hold of it with one hand, laced his long fingers through her own with the other, and decisively led the way ahead. Like she was indeed his desert princess, Paige silently tagged along, all thoughts of Rupert King and Blanton Blake momentarily abandoned into oblivion.

Four

"I insist you taste the carrot juice," Elva demanded, pouring a large glass of the orange milky cocktail and handing it over to Rhys Langston. "It's my own recipe from Jamaica, you kno'. If the bite lick you, it'll be the Guinness and the drop of rum. No mind that. A trillion calories, but me can see you is a strong man." She nodded and added with gusto, "Me sure your stomach can take it."

Turning quickly to Paige, she went on. "Make sure you eat up all your dumplings and the jerk chicken, to'. Me no want you momma to t'ink me no feed you up good." Retaking her seat at the head of the table and sighing with the relief of a woman who was more than satisfied with her day's handiwork, she added, "How you grow. Me can hardly believe you a bring man come to my yard for me to clap me eye on him. You not going to ask me what me t'ink?"

Paige was speechless. She had not thought what her Aunt Elva would think of her beau, if she could possibly refer to Rhys Langston with that term. Evidently, it was how her aunt was interpreting the situation. Not wanting to give away her secret on how they had met, Paige hardly knew how to react. Aunt Elva was an inquisitive old bird, though she was within her rights, given that this was the first occasion on which Paige had invited a male guest to her home.

"I was wondering—"

"You have manners," Elva said, directly returning her attention to Rhys Langston in approval, while pushing her wire-rimmed spectacles closer to her eyes to scrutinize him further. "Which part of Jamaica you family from?"

Rhys swallowed a large gulp of the potent carrot juice and smiled his wonderful, captivating smile. The old lady seemed fearless enough, he told himself, judging Elva discreetly from across the table. He gauged her age, estimating fifty-eight . . . sixty, and found her velvety dark eyes, white curly hair, unwrinkled sandalwood-colored complexion, and spectacled, steely expression rather more trite than imposing.

"I'm an American," he declared warmly. "My parents were both born in Leland."

"Where?" Elva was bemused.

"Mississippi," Rhys said. "In the United States."

"You not from the Caribbean?" Elva was alarmed. "But you is a church man?"

Paige gulped. "Auntie!"

"I believe in God," Rhys answered, throwing Paige a kindly wink.

"Which church you from?"

Paige grew uncomfortable. "Auntie!"

"Me just trying to establish what kind of man is sitting at my table," Elva proclaimed on seeing the embarrassment in her niece's face. She turned to face her young male guest, admiring his handsome features and the way in which he seemed to enjoy her food.

Aunt Elva had to admit she was a little more than surprised when Paige had walked in and introduced him right off. She had not known her niece to be so impulsive. Since she had not heard any mention of Rhys Langston before, he had come as quite a shock. It was not so much his impeccable manners or the soft lull of his voice as he spoke, but more the fact that he seemed such a suitable match for her niece. And that was an admission Elva Cartwright did not make easily. It was clear to her, on seeing Rhys Langston, that any young sensible woman would give her eyeteeth to be in her niece's position.

He had placed his bag on the floor in the hallway and politely taken off his jacket and boots before entering Elva's carpeted conservatory. Paige had informed her that she had just picked him up at the airport and he would be joining them for dinner. If she had received prior warning, Elva would have dressed differently instead of greeting such a striking young man clothed in the simple frilly patterned frock she often wore when cleaning, with her head wrapped over with a pale yellow silk scarf to hide the growing emergence of gray.

She had made a mad dash to the bathroom, had considered wearing her church wig, but instead restyled her thinning hair, sweeping it up into a little topknot on her crown. Every woman, whatever the age, deserved a little vanity, and so she had applied a little red lipstick for effect. Though she never had any children of her own, Elva had often nursed the daughters of her two sisters, and had grown to know the slight nuances and foibles of all five nieces. As she arrived downstairs marginally more presentable, it was evident to her that Paige was more than fond of this man. Likewise, he seemed inebriated with her.

Rhys Langston had kept his eyes on her niece while Elva poured Earl Grey tea and offered him biscuits before dinner. He courteously linked Paige's hand over his arm as they walked to the dining room to eat, like a true gentleman. There was a brief moment when he whispered something quite scabrous in Paige's ear, and Elva had watched her niece laugh with the kind of gaiety a young woman exerted on meeting her fancy. And now he was seated at her table, his dark brooding eyes watching Paige as she tried to curtail the probes from an old lady.

"So how you two meet?"

"I told you," Paige gushed, fearing that their secret might be discovered. "Rhys is an old friend who arrived a little early to help me with the arrangements for my birthday party."

"But where you meet him?" Elva was not deterred.

"In a bookshop," Paige lied. "I . . . I was interested in a book on black history and—"

"I recommended she read one written by a friend of mine,"

Rhys interrupted, placing his glass of carrot juice on the ivory-colored tablecloth. "*The Lost Tribes* is his latest title in print," he continued, noting the measure of complete surprise across Paige's face. "It traces the history of the Sephardic Jews when they were booted out of Spain during the Spanish Inquisition and resettled in Jamaica, making it their new homeland."

"It's a history on Jamaica?" Elva gasped approvingly, allowing a smile to form on her face. "We have Jews back-a-yard?"

"From as early as 1663," Rhys clarified, transferring his gaze to Paige. "I'll be sure to arrange a copy to be sent to you before I leave."

Paige's mouth fell open. She had read very few books, mostly the occasional Jane Austen. When she was a child, her sister Penelope did the reading for them both. Whatever would her family think knowing she was dating someone who could boast he had a historical writer as a friend?

"I don't know what to say," Elva breathed.

"Say yes," Rhys challenged, throwing her a smile.

"Mr. Langston is researching Egyptian history," Paige piped in. "I think he should write a book on his findings."

"I've funded an excavation site," he clarified.

"So you not staying in England?" Elva ignored them both, not missing the implication that he had arrived from overseas.

Paige was immediately saddened. "He's passing through," she confirmed with a woebegone ebb to her voice, the reminder of her original intention to use him as a guise against Rupert King and a provocation for Blanton Blake suddenly beginning to plague her mind.

"Me kno' there was trouble," Elva drawled with annoyance. "In my day, t'ings no work like this. A man no leave his woman behind to travel pastures new."

"It's not like that," Paige said meekly, darting her eyes from Rhys's comely face to her aunt's reproachful one. "We haven't—"

"Talk marriage," Elva chortled in staunch disapproval

while vigorously shaking her head. "Me have three before me widow, and them all meet their maker and leave me with happy moments to cherish. So little of that these days."

Three husbands, each one wealthier than his predecessor, Paige thought, recalling her childhood. Uncle George, who figured early in the chain and owned a small farm in Jamaica, fell from a tree and died instantly. Aunt Elva sold the land and emigrated to England. His successor, Uncle Clevy, of whom Paige had vague memories, was murdered during the Notting Hill riots of 1958, leaving a tidy sum in an insurance policy. Uncle Herman, the last in the sequence, had been chief executive of the local West Indian Community Association and pastor of the church. He died in his sleep and left a generous estate. The house Elva now resided in was a reflection of her wealth, and she happened to be the richest person in their family. Not bad for a woman who still believed in marriage and did not consider herself too old to take the plunge a fourth time.

"It's too early for us to be talking about wedded bliss," Paige objected, placing her knife and fork on her empty plate, not wishing to contemplate taking a husband, let alone burying one. "We're not even dating."

Aunt Elva was not daunted. "Do you believe in marriage, Mr. Langston?" she probed.

Paige noted how his smile lit up his face. "It's the best way to live your life and a place for giving your emotions in a relationship. Becoming the property of someone else is a wonderful thing," he told her.

Paige also noted her aunt's full acceptance of his answer before the same query was aimed in her direction. "What about you?"

Paige gulped. "I don't believe the hunter should lie down with the prey," she relented, disarmingly forthright.

"You will find that my niece has a certain toughness honed to the sharpness of a lizard—like the kind we have back home in Jamaica," Elva said, furrowing her brows. "She gets it from my sister Gwerfyl, her momma."

"Auntie!" Paige protested a third time.

"Me tell her that aggressiveness, drive, and a certain will to succeed are not qualities men want in wives."

"That's because men have a problem dealing with achievement and femininity," Paige wavered, alert to the sudden change in Rhys Langston's face. Gone was his wonderful, captivating smile and the smoldering misty-eyed gaze he had continually presented to her on his arrival in London. In its place was a surface level of serious intent, expectant of answers.

"Am I to understand that you don't want to merge with another human being?"

The polite directness of his question caught Paige unguarded. "Men rule, women endure, and hang the consequences," she told him, feeling quite miffed.

"You like trading your sharp wits for brawn, too," Rhys remarked, not missing the irony. He, too, placed his knife and fork on his empty plate and chose to down the rest of his carrot juice. Placing the empty glass on the table, he threw Elva a courteous gaze. "My compliments, Mrs. Cartwright, but I'm afraid I have to leave."

He rose and Paige joined him. "My niece should bring you again," Elva offered, extending the invitation without detecting a whiff of Rhys's sudden mood change. "If you t'ink your stomach can hold out, you come and try a little rum punch, you hear?"

"Perhaps," was Rhys's simple answer.

At the dining room door, Paige was aware of his hurry to depart. "What are you doing?" she whispered.

"Leaving." he declared.

Out in the hallway, his rushing to put on his camel-skin jacket and his boots posed an immediate dilemma. This was the man who had agreed to be with her at her party and now, suddenly, he wanted to be out of her life. Paige knew she had no other male person to rely on. No dashing allies or knights queuing up for the rescue. If she were to let him go, all would be lost, and she could not risk losing such an attractive man.

"Have I offended you?" she sighed, watching as he bent to the floor and began to tie his boot laces.

A reluctant Rhys paused for a brief second. He looked up and examined Paige's face, allowing his gaze to travel across her features slowly before he spoke. "Why am I here?"

Paige froze. "To see your bank."

"With you," he clarified.

Paige was aware that his enthusiasm for her had decreased. Perhaps, she thought, he had decided to himself she would go the extra mile to attempt to become more than Internet friends now that he was actually at close quarters, now that she had actually kissed him. Maybe, he even mistook her avid interest as a clear basis to build on. And, she had to admit, he was a very tempting prospect. It was the fact that he was leaving that forced her to contemplate how far she wanted to take this.

The mention of her alternative plans to use him was significant, but making the confession to a man with such worldly intelligence as Rhys Langston would be a grotesque admission of defeat to Paige, one that she chose to evade. She reminded herself that it was Rhys who volunteered to travel to see her before she had offered her invitation, that his plans had changed because of Web terrorists, and that although they both might well be attracted to one another, he was going to move on when her party was over. While the element of manipulation still existed on how they came to be together, she had to keep her head.

"We agreed you would join me at my party," Paige said finally, exerting a professional tone to her voice. "As my friend. If you don't—"

"Why are you afraid?" Rhys suddenly thundered, rising steadfast to his feet.

"Me, afraid?" Paige feigned a certain degree of surprise as his tall frame dwarfed her completely. "Of what?"

"Trusting yourself."

"I'm not afraid," she lied.

"Then tell me why you don't like letting go and having fun?"

"I . . . I like to be in control," Paige panicked.

"I was right about you," Rhys declared finally. "On the outside, polished, self-assured, with a tough chocolate coating. On the inside, soft-centered, vulnerable, too fearful of losing identity to even enjoy yourself."

"You don't know what you're talking about," Paige accused hotly.

"No?" Rhys was not forestalled by the surface level of tears he suddenly detected in Paige's eyes. "I suspect all your earlier boyfriends were irresponsible, flamboyant, and passive, which allowed you to be quite domineering and efficient, throwing everyone, even yourself, off track."

"I . . . I . . ." Paige was flabbergasted.

"Most likely they had reputations which preceded them, enjoyed the chase because you played hard to get, and were never where they were supposed to be," Rhys continued.

Paige's mind immediately conjured up an image of Rupert King.

"Or they were the sharp designer-suit sort of guys, good-looking, but pretending they didn't know it, and kept you guessing on whether they liked you or not because they couldn't handle the fact that you have a sharp mind that likes to do as it pleases," he went on.

A vision of Blanton Blake superseded.

"And because you never know where you are in the big scheme of things, you use all your energies to construct a life and style that allow you to try again with your defenses redoubled and played out on a nice guy like me."

His conclusion took Paige right back to their initial discussion on the Internet. In the same vein, he was analyzing her inner emotions, and was not far removed from the truth, either. Paige naturally felt her conscience prickle her. Rhys Langston had assured her then how down-to-earth he was. In her mind, he deserved to be told the real reason as to why she had surfed the Web for a mate in the first place. After all, he was showing her true kindness. But the words failed to spring to her lips.

"I'm sorry," she told him.

"What was it, a vow of celibacy?"

Paige blinked as the sudden inquisition threw her. "Something like that," she mumbled by way of an answer.

"So . . . it's not strictly traditional values?"

"I don't like being rushed into anything," Paige admitted finally. "In my last experience, it was a good thing. Every time I think of his sorry ass, I'll always know I was the one who slipped through the net."

"Ah, so it was tactics gone wrong," Rhys summarized, assessing the situation as best he could. "You must've had some sense about him not being good enough for you to play strategies."

"I had a sense of being worth the wait, as I told you," Paige relented, not liking Rhys's tone. "I . . . I think if the situation is right with someone, it just happens, and I would of course like to get to know the person first. And I'm feeling pretty confused why someone as wonderful as you doesn't have someone of your own." That much was true.

"I work hard, but never seem to find the time to play hard," Rhys admitted, zipping up his jacket. "As a result, my social life has suffered. Meeting you like this is quite bizarre. Believe me, I don't normally conduct my love life this way. On reflection, I'm wondering if I've behaved a little—"

"Reckless," Paige finished. "Me, too."

Rhys nodded knowingly. "Yesterday was my fifth visit to Totally Black Dating dot com," he confessed. "You're the first time I actually met someone."

"And there I was thinking I was the only novice." Paige chuckled.

Rhys joined her with a chuckle of his own. "Now, with Web hackers running rampant . . . that'll teach me to move beyond my more orthodox approaches to meeting a girl."

"That we will never know." Paige smiled.

"Not unless you decide to join me for dinner tomorrow

night," Rhys suddenly offered. "My treat for saying thank you for meeting me at the airport and inviting me to your party." He spoke in a low voice, suddenly seeming very shy and coy.

Paige was touched by his bashfulness. "You don't need to do this—"

"Please," he said. "I'd like to get to know you better."

Aware that she would no doubt soon be introducing him to her friends, her relatives, colleagues, and acquaintances, Paige immediately realized the prudence in accepting Rhys's invitation. She pictured the scene of her party in graphic detail, the showing of shame and hurt on Rupert King's face, how she would gloat knowing she had proven he could be upstaged so soon with another handsome man. And Rhys Langston was more than man enough that she also imagined Blanton Blake looking quite threatened. Knowing a little more about him was paramount. Familiarity was how she could gain the upper hand.

"Thank you, I'd like that," she accepted with a smile.

"Good." He reached to the floor and picked up his black leather bag. "I'll call you tomorrow. We'll eat at my hotel."

"Oh," Paige gasped, overlooking the important aspect of him needing to find a place to stay for the night. "I . . . I hadn't thought—"

"I arrived early," he countered quickly, sensing her moment of embarrassment. "I need to see my bank tomorrow and I'm sure you have things to do during the day. I wouldn't expect to encroach on your hospitality further."

"At least take your invitation," Paige enthused, quickly reaching to a small table in the hallway, where she picked up the white and gold embossed card she had written up the day before. Handing it over to Rhys Langston as he reached for the door, she added, "Now it's official."

Rhys read the card silently. *An extravagant 30th birthday do for my very closest family and friends on Saturday, February 10, at Aunt Elva's, 14a Royal Avenue, Chelsea.* He placed it in his jacket pocket and looked at Paige. His hand on the doorknob, Rhys was overwhelmed. His mouth desired to taste those luscious pink lips of hers again, but he forced down the lustful urge. He had some rethinking to do and did not want to complicate the issue.

"I'll see you tomorrow," he reaffirmed before heading into the night.

Within three seconds and without a backward glance, he was gone.

He had hoped to find the epitome of a desert princess, and he had. Never in his wildest dreams had Rhys thought he would ever kiss one, but that had become possible, too. Now he felt panicked at the consequences.

What it came down to was sympathy. From Paige, he was getting tension, her sense of helplessness, her anger, and sooner, if not later, he would be sure to see her pain. All very much the same emotions he had left behind in Leland, Mississippi. What he had run away from. He did not want to look back. Not ever. His life was his own now.

And that meant he had to be careful with Paige Alexander. Some feelings were best kept hidden, and she looked like the kind of girl who could tempt him to dig things up he had buried a long time ago. He decided it was her eyes that were his biggest problem. Rhys loved the way her midnight-blue gaze made direct contact with his dark soulful one, causing his body to tingle at the electricity that sparked between them.

He was sure she felt it, too, but there was an absent nature to her response that left him wondering what motives lay behind her wanting him with her. Rhys was a man who found friendship an easy bridge to forge, mend, and maintain. He was sure, even before having seen Paige's picture, that the addition of someone in England to the stable of friends he had made around the world would be as simple as boarding the plane he had taken to meet her.

Now in his hotel room at Claridge's, pulling back the fresh sheets on his bed, Rhys pictured her, more beautiful than he could have imagined, and knew Paige had weakened his every resolution to move on. Things did not seem simple anymore. This was a woman he understood.

Deep down, Rhys wanted to run again. It was something he had been doing all his life, too. But as he turned out the lights and stared into the darkness of his empty room, something told him he could learn a lot from Paige Alexander. If he helped her to come to terms with herself, she could teach him to heal. To find peace. Maybe love. And that was a hope he felt he had no right to ask from anyone.

Five

"Mr. Rhys Langston," Franklin Coates-Davis at Adabi Mercantile bellowed loudly, offering his greeting at the door of his offices at Canary Wharf. "Please, take a seat. Coffee?"

"My usual," Rhys amended, making his way toward a chair.

"It's good bourbon," Franklin announced with a thick Arabian accent, reaching to the small glass cabinet beside his vast black marble desk, where he extracted two glasses and a bottle of Kentucky's finest. Doing the honors, he passed a half-filled glass over to Rhys Langston before replacing his large bulk of a body in the imported polished leather Italian chair he loved so well.

Franklin Coates-Davis was plain ugly. A randy, middle-aged, Middle Eastern man, with an oily olive-toned complexion, receding hairline, and dark eyes that glistened like the oil pumped in Saudi Arabia. Though his bank sported a foreign name, he had legally Anglicized his own by deed poll to attract European clients wanting to make risk investments that he presided over with tactful care and vigilant attention.

He had built a reputation that spanned boardrooms, royal courts, political cabinets, and Congress in equal proportions, and was never known for giving a hot tip twice to the same client without money changing hands. With a Monte Cristo cigar hanging from his lip making his puffed-out cheeks seem much in need of deflating, he appeared the perfect accessory to his elaborately and expensively decorated office, as did the eight-hundred-euro shoes on his feet.

Rhys took a sip of the strong liquor before leaning his back into the soft leather chair he was seated in and allowing a brief smile to spread across his face. "So everything's safe?" he asked, throwing Franklin a concerned glare.

"You could have saved yourself the visit," Franklin assured him, puffing smoke. "Your millions of euros are in good hands. That idiot assistant of mine needs to be flogged. I'd give him one hundred lashes myself for bringing you out here for nothing."

"I read the online news," Rhys persisted, downing more bourbon. "Electronic banking leaves no paper trail. I was worried."

"C'mon, Rhys," Franklin berated him, his invisible antenna raised. "We're as secure as Fort Knox at Adabi Mercantile. We've got the best computer security in the world. No one can move a penny without us knowing about it. We could've settled all this with a phone call. So what gives? What really brings you into the metropolis?"

Rhys chuckled. "Always the sly old fox," he told his banker. "You never miss a thing."

Franklin barked out his own chuckle. "A woman's got you spooked, right?" When Rhys remained silent, he laughed even louder. "I thought I'd never see the day. So who is she?"

"She's someone who doesn't know who I am," Rhys confided with a mild burp. "I met her on the Internet and she's zero publicity."

"The what?" Franklin was so amused, he reached for the bourbon bottle and refilled his glass. "I thought only lunatics and nutcases were stupid enough to try and find love on the Web."

"Watch it," Rhys warned. "She lives right here in London, at her aunt's house. She's a real estate agent."

"And did you tell her that you're a private equity investor with vested interests in companies all over the city?"

"No."

"You have investments in over three countries?"

"No."

"She has no idea you're a millionaire?"

"No." Rhys was adamant.

"What the hell did you tell her?"

"That I'm researching Egyptian history. She suggested I write a book on the subject."

"You told her about your part-time hobby?" Franklin intoned with another huge chuckle. "How long do you plan to play this one out?"

"I promised to be at her birthday party on Saturday, then I'm leaving," Rhys chimed in, hating himself for his deceit. "I'm going back to take a look at that dig I funded in Egypt."

"And she has no idea about you at all?"

"Nope."

"Look," Franklin began, knowing this was none of his business but, as someone who was often used to advising people, he could not help himself. "I've been investing your money for ten years. I still remember the day you walked into my old office with eighty thousand dollars, a bruise on one lip, wearing the only suit you owned, and with tears in your eyes. Like a lion, you roared and told me you wanted to make money. You were a desperate bastard full of fire back then, and now you're a rich one. We've made deals, bent rules, and pulled strings together, and for a piss-poor kid from Leland, Mississippi, you've come a long way. We both have. You don't want to go messing that up over a skirt."

"You're right," Rhys agreed. "I should drop her."

"Like a hot brick." Franklin nodded, puffing away at his smoke. "No woman is worth losing your head over. Do you still play squash?"

Rhys nodded.

"Love is a game. Two players each looking to score," Franklin revealed in the same shrewd manner he used when conducting business. "The investment only pays off when you watch your back. If she's a small bet, you're a bigger man now. You don't need to be playing with loose change. Keep your eye on the prize for when the big one comes rolling in." He downed his bourbon. "Fancy a game later?"

Rhys gazed at his wise mentor, swallowing his last drop of bourbon. "Why not."

Paige accepted Blanton's greeting complacently, aware of the judgmental glare he threw in her direction as she closed his office door and made her way toward a chair situated close to his desk.

No one could accuse him of missing the racks of tweeds and saxonies, flannels and serges, stripes and checks that composed the male wardrobe and rigidly codified it for every occasion. Today, in the style he had made his own, he was classically dressed in a Huntsman dark suit—the little black dress of the male wardrobe—with a cornflower-blue poplin shirt, Charvet tie, and polished Berluti shoes. As usual, Blanton was projecting the highest expression of civilization that was required when selling property.

"What's so urgent?" Paige asked, thinking how Rhys Langston was so unlike her boss. His mission in life seemed to be to achieve a level of streetwise invisibility, though his wild looks could present a new lease on life for any ambitious sexagenarian designer.

"Tonight's the night," Blanton said, unable to restrain himself.

Paige widened her midnight-blue eyes at him in wonder as she took her seat opposite his desk. "Excuse me?"

"I heard he's here."

Paige was aghast. She had not told anyone. "The courier pigeons must be on steroids. How did you know?"

"Your Aunt Elva just called. You were on the other line. She left a message," Blanton explained. His face was closed and impassive, as it always was when he was angry.

"What's the message?" Paige queried, keeping her voice calm and appeasing.

"Your aunt said to let you know that she will be going to the church meeting after all and that there's a bottle of sherry in the kitchen parlor for you and your young man," Blanton repeated, plucking a gold pen from among the papers on his desk. "If you want to invite him back later, after dinner of course."

Paige felt the heated rush of blood singe her face. But she smiled slightly, reminding herself she should be silently applauding the effect Rhys Langston's presence was evoking.

"I hope it's good sherry," she told Blanton with polite serenity. "Aunt Elva's choice is often poor."

"So he *is* here," Blanton croaked, slamming the pen he held between his fingers onto his hardened-wood desk. "Your Internet lover?"

"You ought to know that when I set out to do a thing, I inevitably do it," Paige said defensively. "He's here for my party."

Blanton's eyes fired a blaze of stark jealousy at her. "And what else?"

"I expect he wants to give me a birthday present," Paige answered, diverting from his lewd suggestion and quietly delighting in the clear vision of lust and envy she had hoped for so long to see on Blanton's face. Now that it had presented itself, she was sure her plan was working to order. "Any further messages?"

Blanton was agog. "Is that it? Is that all you have to say?"

"Ah yes," Paige recalled. "I received your e-mail. I'll be arranging a third showing of the Holland Park property this coming week."

"Paige!"

"And I'll have Francine take a look at the partnership papers when you've had them drawn up," she concluded.

"Didn't you read the newspapers?" Blanton raged, thrusting a copy of the one he had in front of him toward her. "There was a raid on half the service Web sites that take credit card members the very evening you logged on. Aren't you concerned this may affect you?"

"It hasn't," Paige confirmed, having checked with her bankers.

"Then does it not concern you that your Internet lover may not be all that he pretends to be?" Blanton continued, planting the seeds of suspicion.

"His name is Rhys Langston," Paige reminded him, now somewhat amazed at the opposition she was facing. She had expected to make Blanton jealous, but not to such degree that his suggestions should make her edgy. "He has been pretty straightforward about who he is and his purpose for being here," she added, which was more than she could say for herself, "and he has booked into a hotel and extended an invitation that I join him for dinner there. He'll be contacting me later. He's been quite formal."

That was not quite the truth, Paige realized, on recalling that Rhys had also kissed her senseless. The spontaneity of it brought back memories anew of how wondrous it had felt to be smooched in such a manner. Even though it had been the briefest of moments, it had shaken her, incited and roused her very being, and stoked away at cinders where there burned a deeper fire within. If she were to make any admissions, it would be to taste again such a kiss, but that hardly seemed realistic when she knew Rhys Langston would be leaving England after her party.

Best to stick to the plan, she resolved. And with that, she added, "I admire his well-mannered behavior." It was a direct provocation and one that worked quite effectively.

In that instant, Blanton saw something. It was in the way Paige wore the black and white striped slash-neck sweater, black cropped trousers, and black leather sling-back shoes that gave her an air of regal importance. The bend of her short brown hair combed perfectly around her immaculately made-up face made him aware of her strength and beauty. How she amiably flashed her white teeth at him, where a slightly wonky tooth, hidden behind the cheeky, sexy curl of her lips, attracted his attention. It was in the way her eyes baited and teased until a fantasy began to play its way into his head.

"How available is your personal mobile number?" he suddenly demanded, aware he only had listed the one she used for work.

"It gets bad reception. You'll get nothing but crackle."

"I like crackle," Blanton crooned.

Paige rose from her seat. "I can see it's still a very long way to the altar," she bedeviled, enjoying the chase. "I'll see my way out."

They spent a vigorous hour, one on one, at the Wimbledon Racquets Club, where Franklin Coates-Davis held a membership, before returning to his penthouse apartment building at Seacon Wharf, overlooking the Thames River. The physical exertion was just what Rhys needed. Franklin was not built for active sport, but he at least tried to keep pace even though his body mass slowed his mobility to below par. Not quite the competitor, but sufficient enough.

"You don't give an inch," Franklin accused when their hour was through.

"Because I like to win," Rhys shot back.

They showered and changed. Rhys desperately tried to put the features of a wonderful desert princess out of his head. He had decided not to text her, not even to cancel their date for dinner. Reclined in one of Franklin's Japanese sofas, this time with a glass of brandy in his left hand, both men relaxed and talked money.

"It's a 'wambam,'" Franklin advised in Internet parlance while exerting a healthy chuckle. "Just up your alley."

"Careful." Rhys repeated his stern warning on seeing Franklin's white teeth dancing in his Arabian face. The joke of meeting Paige Alexander on the Web was wearing thin, and he just wanted to forget it. Forget her. "What's the long-term aim?"

"Flotation."

"Tell me."

"It's a software house, offering services to established "bricks and mortar" companies," Franklin began, opening a hand-carved wooden box to offer Rhys a cigar from a collection he had purchased when he last visited the tobacco barons of the Cibao Valley in the Dominican Republic. "What I like is that it has all the fundamentals of an old-economy business model with high-technology ideas. What they're looking for is development capital."

"Management team?" Rhys asked, refusing the cigar.

"There are gaps, but introducing new members will bolster the company ego."

"I'd like to see a trading history and evidence that demonstrates an old economy profit-and-loss model," Rhys decided, "but I'm more interested in having a stake in that diamond-cutting factory in Belgium you were telling me about before Christmas."

"I'm still assessing integrity," Franklin drawled. He lit up a cigar and contemplated his client. "Do you still plan to stay in the south of France?"

"Monaco and I are doing just fine," Rhys answered absently. His mind was back on the subject of Paige Alexander and his conscience was telling him he at least owed her a call.

"You did the right thing keeping your head low after the shit hit the fan two years ago," Franklin agreed. "I should buy a pad out there myself. I heard property prices are climbing steeply."

Rhys thought of Paige and the profession she was in. "I could check with—"

"Your real live goddess." Franklin laughed. "You still got her on your mind."

Rhys remained silent.

"I tell you what," Franklin began. "Why don't you bring her along to Sotheby's tomorrow, let me take a good look at her. They're showing something you may be interested in, actually. According to the catalog, Egyptian legend has it that whoever owns the piece will find and keep love right through to old age. It was made for Isis."

"How did you know?" Rhys asked in amazement as the memory kicked in.

"Know what?" Franklin's brows rose.

"Her name."

"She was an Egyptian goddess," Franklin prevaricated, his eyes flickering slightly at the inadvertent slip about how he liked to keep tabs on all his clients. "You could do with a little luck in that department. It's supposed to be the last in a collection of six. Bids are opening at fifty thousand. Interested?"

It sounded familiar, but the only thing Rhys was interested in was seeing Paige Alexander again. He really should send her a text message or give her a call. He pictured her waiting to hear from him with details on where and when they were destined to meet. He had thought eight o'clock, but it was already past seven-thirty. The sky had darkened. He contemplated rain. He was leaving precious little time for her to get dressed and prepare herself for a date. He questioned himself. *Should I see her again?*

"Yes," he declared, speaking his thoughts out loud.

"I'll tell you what I think when I see her," Franklin promised, immediately putting out his half-smoked cigar in an ashtray. "After that, it's up to you."

"What?" Rhys had lost the gist of the conversation.

"Tomorrow," Franklin confirmed. "You're bringing your Internet friend along to Sotheby's for my approval."

Rhys laughed. "I've got to go."

"Wait a minute," Franklin drawled as he watched Rhys bolt to his feet. "Where are you going?"

"I have a personal investment to check over," Rhys stated tersely, fast making his way toward the door. "This one requires some forward planning of my own."

* * *

Her mobile sounded a bell-like tone. Paige read the brief message: "I'll meet you at 9:00 P.M. in the foyer at Claridge's."

She immediately exhaled a breath of relief and glanced in her bedroom mirror. Reminding herself she was on the brink of reaching thirty, she searched for any signs of decrepitude. There were none. With that came the reassurance that Rhys Langston had not forgotten her after all. She had just enough time to change into a skirt and blouse—not too formal, not too casual—tousle her hair, and reapply a touch of makeup to her freshly washed face before the taxi arrived.

Paige was looking forward to seeing Rhys Langston again. It was uncanny that she felt no guilt, considering she had spent most of her working day enduring the sneaking, pensive glances from Blanton Blake. It should have excited her that she had now, finally, garnered his attention, but Paige was more amused than interested.

Behind her desk, she had watched under the veil of her long lashes as Blanton found any and every feeble excuse to enter her office and strike up meaningless conversations. She had got him on the run and he was definitely picking up pace. By 5:30 P.M., he had tried on no less than three occasions to pry for details on her date with Rhys Langston.

She, of course, had nothing to tell him. Her disappointment that Rhys had not contacted her all day had been mercifully assuaged by Blanton's enthusiasm. It was not until 7:44 P.M. that she received Rhys's text message. That had given her less than one half hour to change and prepare herself for seeing him again.

Now, as the taxi drew up outside the building on the corner of Brook Street and Davies Street, where she could see national flags from several countries flying on poles outside and a concierge—dressed like something out of the Art Deco age of the 1930s—politely walking toward the car, Paige felt a sudden pang of nerves.

She told herself there had not been time enough to style her hair, select suitable evening wear, apply makeup with her usual dexterous precision. But it was too late to turn back. She had made the decision to familiarize herself with Rhys, and he wanted to know more about her. It was mutual. It lacked the bizarre nature of how they came to meet.

Paige paid the cab driver and entered through the main doors. The front hall was vast, and led through to a foyer with an elaborate eighteen-foot ceiling crowned by a magnificent silver light sculpture made from what appeared to be individually handblown glass pieces. There was a reading room, too, with two Art Deco cult marble fireplaces and rich leather columns, with plush velour banquettes and suede walls.

Paige stood motionless for one brief moment, clutching at her black leather handbag as the deluxe surroundings filtered into her head. If there was one thing she knew about Claridge's, it was that the five-star hotel was ridiculously elaborate and expensive. Of course that made her wonder exactly how Rhys Langston came to be staying there.

As if on cue, she caught him striding toward her. He was clothed out of keeping with the customary code for the plush surroundings in form-fitting blue jeans, a black shirt open to the sternum, revealing plenty of hair on his chest, and a brown, unbuttoned checkered jacket, all of which made her appear much more formal.

"I was wondering whether I should dress to be wooed, to kill, or to please." She chuckled on his approach. "I'm glad I chose neither."

"I'd say you look all three." Rhys smiled, approving of the simple mauve colored georgette skirt, black silk blouse, and the black court shoes she was wearing. Just the right shades for a cool evening in February.

Paige felt the rush of color tinge her cheeks as he bent forward and planted a friendly kiss against her left one. Again the scent of frankincense and myrrh tickled her senses. "Happy you're here?" he asked.

She nodded, speechless, desperately hoping to slow the fast beating of her heart.

"I'm sorry I couldn't contact you sooner," he explained. "I've been with my investment banker all day."

"Is everything all right?" Paige queried, concerned.

"Just fine," Rhys assured her. "How's your aunt?"

"She's fine, too," Paige said, noting the hint of excitement in her voice. "She's gone to a prayer meeting at her local church."

Rhys nodded, then indicated the restaurant where London's only three-starred Michelin chef presided. "I thought we'd try a three-course dinner in the new Gordon Ramsay restaurant," he added, taking hold of her arm and leading the way until they entered the large, distinctive room. It was lit by a dozen or more huge orange lantern-style light fittings that dropped from the ceiling, and curtains seemed to drape from every corner. The tables were covered in white, with all manner of plush and decorative eating utensils, chrome salt and pepper pots, and embossed menus.

Paige stared in awe. "This looks lovely."

"They say the chef is as famous for his temper as his culinary creations," Rhys informed her before giving his name to a waiter, who glared at Rhys's jeans disapprovingly before directing them toward a table for two and removing a card reading RESERVED from it.

Seated, they ordered velouté of fennel with fricassee of clams for starters, roasted monkfish tail wrapped in Parma ham, caramelized root vegetables, and gratin mustard sauce for the main course, and bitter chocolate souffleé with white chocolate sorbet for dessert. Amid brief discussions on politics, religion, world events, and geography, a selection of wines had been served, while Rhys and Paige mentally filed away pertinent details about one another. Afterward, over cocktails, their conversation deepened.

"So you traced three generations of your family in Wales," Rhys said in admiration, adoring the smile he had placed on Paige's face.

"Yes," Paige enthused, enjoying his interest in her family. "My great-grandfather served with his brother aboard the steamship *Algonquin*. On March 12, 1917, a German submarine U-62 sank the ship with gunfire and bombs. My great-grandfather and his brother were on deck at the time when the torpedo hit. The ship was cut in half."

"What happened to them?" Rhys asked, gripped by the story, but equally so by Paige's widely spaced, midnight-blue eyes and the way they lit up and swallowed him in.

"Neither knew if the other had survived the attack," Paige clarified, absorbing the wonderful way Rhys's soulful, smoldering mocha-brown gaze held her captive. "It was several weeks before each knew if the other had survived. It turned out that different ships had rescued them both. My great-grandfather was taken to a dockyard in Wales, and his brother was picked up and taken back to Northern Africa."

"Then what happened?"

"My great-grandfather—his name was Seymour Watts, by the way—he married a white Welsh woman in 1920, which was unheard of in those days," Paige explained, sipping her cocktail. "They had my grandfather Vernon Seymour Watts in 1922, who then married Constance Selby, a Jamaican girl whose father had also been a sea merchant."

"And?" Rhys wanted to know.

"They had three girls during the Second World War, Elva, who you met, Gwerfyl, my mother, and Evelyn, my youngest aunt."

"Fascinating," Rhys drawled, finding the entire story breathtaking.

"You have a Welsh name by the way," Paige disclosed, exerting a soft chuckle as she wondered what the W in his middle name stood for, though she could hardly ask him without revealing having conducted a search on the Web. "It means rash and ardent."

"Really." Rhys was hooked at how easily Paige laughed. It widened the smile on his face. "I was told the nurse who delivered me at birth named me," he admitted after a pause. "Perhaps she was a Welsh-American. We have a lot of that in the States."

"Were you born in Mississippi?" Paige queried, now curious as to Rhys's background, though she did not miss his hesitation before he answered.

"Yes," he declared, throwing her a sensitive smile. "I grew up in a town called Leland. It was okay. Post-civil rights. School was a little tough."

"Are your parents still there?"

"No," he murmured.

"Any relatives?"

"A brother, but he's on the East Coast."

Paige felt her heart sink at his vagueness, and also at the thought that he would soon be leaving England. "I bet you can't wait to get back home."

Rhys noted the sorrow behind her eyes, and felt his own heart heave at the level of deceit he was throwing her way. "Actually, I live in the south of France," he told her, knowing she deserved at least one molecule of truth. "I've been in Monaco for two years now."

"Oh," Paige gasped. *That's not so far,* she quietly told herself. *Just across the Channel and down a bit.* "Why there?"

"Sun, royalty. It's peaceful," Rhys returned with a shrug of his shoulders, the smile falling from his face as he became slightly uncomfortable. He did not like talking about his personal life. It was the one topic he would often run away from. That, and the sore subject of his childhood.

"Does any of your family visit you there?" Paige asked, oblivious to Rhys's inner thoughts.

"One of my nieces, the eldest one, stayed last summer. Tell me," he said, swiftly moving the subject on. "What present would you like me to give you to commemorate your thirtieth birthday?"

Your love, Paige mused wistfully, not daring to hold onto any hopes or dreams of attaining it. It was hardly possible under the circumstances, and she was mindful, too, that her brain was dreaming again of her yearning to be with someone who truly deserved her. "Something I can put beside my bed to remind me of you." She volunteered the information with a healthy chuckle, knowing she needed a new clock radio.

"I'll buy you something special," he promised with a fresh smile that deepened in ever more alluring proportions. "How many people are you expecting?"

"Thirty," Paige sighed, catching her breath. Her heart rate had tripled suddenly, and she knew it had a lot to do with the way Rhys Langston was looking at her presently. "One person from every area and walk of my life."

"Literally?" he asked, recalling her having told him this during their chat on the Internet.

Paige elaborated, picking up the gauntlet of the new topic. "My best friend Claudia Delaney, who I met when I started school at age five," she began, checking her left thumb. "Tina Simmons, a lively acquaintance I met while in the children's hospital having my appendix removed when I was nine. We've kept in touch." She checked her left index finger. "Sara Singh, the Indian pen pal I began writing to when I was in college studying geography, history, and art. She married a sheik and now lives in Bombay, but is flying over tomorrow." She checked her middle finger. "Georgia Bagnoli, my Italian gym instructor. She's been keeping me in shape since I was twenty-six." She checked her ring finger. "Lizzy Chadwick, who organized my twenty-first birthday party. Like you, I caught her at the last moment." She checked her little finger. "Blanton Blake, my boss. I've been working with him for a year and he's now offered to let me buy into a partnership at the agency." She started on the thumb of her right hand.

"Wait a minute." Rhys stopped her on the sixth count, realizing she would probably tally all thirty guests if he allowed her. "Business partnership? How much is he asking for?"

Paige was surprised at his sudden enterprising concern. "Forty thousand," she affirmed without a moment's lapse to decide whether she should be divulging this sort of information. "It's a fair asking price."

"Have you taken advice on whether it is a fair offer?" Rhys queried, trying not to appear judgmental or give away the ruthless skills he had acquired through his own dealings in the world of business.

"Of course," Paige quipped, a little perturbed. "Just because I'm a woman does not mean I don't have a head for making a decision as important as this."

"I would not suggest otherwise." Rhys bridled, aware that she had taken offense to his line of questioning. "But if you need any advice—"

"I don't," Paige insisted.

"I forgot." Rhys swallowed the last drop of his cocktail. "This must be you feeling in charge again."

Paige's mind was taken right back to their initial conversation on the Internet. "I don't need you to tell me something new," she declared, her sharp brows narrowing at how accurate he had been in the past, deciphering the confusing facets of her life. It intimidated her how he managed to tap right to the nerve, and she had no wish to endure his further detections in that area.

"Why are you so defensive over a little male intrusion?" Rhys asked. "I'm not taking anything away from you."

"It's not that," Paige said, afraid to give her own answer in fear of how he might interpret it. "It's just that I depend on my own judgments and make my own decisions."

"The brave new woman," Rhys proclaimed. "Willing to go without the shell. Unguarded, unprotected. Alone."

"If you're trying to imply that I don't need a man—" Paige began.

"Ah, but you do," Rhys interrupted, throwing her a sinful, lustful glance. "And what I want to find out is whether this dilemma would create emotionally and financially entangled scenarios of nightmare proportions in your little mind."

"I'm going to find the ladies' room," Paige murmured, raising herself from the table. Her heart was thudding like a sledgehammer against her rib cage, and had tripled its rate when she caught the enduring look of passion in Rhys

Langston's eyes. It ignited her own cravings and appetite to taste again those large pink lips she had been staring at all night. And that was a yearning she could not let him see when he was quite accurately dissecting her feelings.

In the ladies' room, while shakily reapplying a rich shade of fuschia lipstick to her lips, Paige admitted to herself that she had denied the traditional teachings she had grown up with. It was also clear that Rhys Langston could see it written across her face. She had cast her fate in the feminist camp, become a woman who had learned to earn it all herself and had to keep on earning it. There was something slightly noble about her situation, about the way in which she fended for herself. Paige had grown to know that, long-term, it meant spending a life constructing an impenetrable defense. Depriving herself of love, satisfaction, and happiness in order never to experience the panic, confusion, and anger that came with sharing a life with someone.

But deep down, she wanted that satisfaction of loving someone. If ultimately it meant she gave off mixed signals, then Rhys was right. There was the girl who was running away from herself, and the woman who wanted to find the best sense of herself. If anyone could define it to her, Rhys Langston certainly could. There were just two problems. Paige was unsure if she ever wanted to know the truth. And could she bear hearing it from someone as devastatingly handsome as Rhys Langston?

Emerging from the ladies' room, she paused to take another breath for reflection, deciding to adopt a smile to her face that was sure to camouflage the turmoil of attraction versus denial raging riot inside her. Paige did not want to spoil her date with Rhys Langston. He was a birthday guest at her own party, and she would have to play a united front for her own saving grace. Deciding she would offer him an apology by way of a token to appease him for her irrational behavior, she turned on her heels to begin the short trail back to the table. Halfway there, she was suddenly rendered immobile. A familiar voice behind her spoke.

"Who's the date?"

She turned and was aghast. The man facing her was impeccably dressed in a two-piece navy-blue Paul Gaultier suit with a happy-go-lucky grin spread across his fine, boyish features. Paige recognized everything about him; his broad nose, slanting brown eyes, his olive complexion, which was sporting a fresh shave, and the dark, thick tight curls of his Afro hair, which was groomed for the evening's entertainment.

"Rupert. What are you doing here?" She gushed, alarmed.

"My coach has arranged a team dinner for all the lads in The Clarence on the sixth floor before the finals next week," Rupert explained, allowing his gaze to travel the full length of Paige from her face to her feet, then back to her eyes. "So, who's the date?"

"He's a friend," Paige informed him, conscious of his predatory glare.

"My replacement?"

"You said it."

"He's not a patch on me," Rupert answered, sidling his gaze to analyze Rhys, who was still seated across the room.

"That's a matter of opinion," Paige protested, annoyed. "He's pretty cute."

"Made a move on you yet?" Rupert demanded. The low threat belied his tone, but when Paige remained mute, he laughed out loud. "So, that's the game. You're holding out for me."

"I don't know what you mean," Paige quipped, disliking what she had now knowingly started.

"I can see it in your eyes," Rupert crooned, taking a hold of her wrist. "Baby, they're begging that I make love to you."

"In your dreams," Paige countered sternly.

Without warning, Rupert jerked her into his arms. The embrace came quite unexpectedly and threw Paige completely off guard, though she knew it was not Rupert's way to ever force himself upon a woman. Up against the hardened, ruggedly built frame of his body, she could feel the hot panting of his breath, sense the strong tinge of his aftershave, which made her nose twitch at the potency of it, and detect his clammy hands encircling her body, forcing her to look at him.

"Just say when, sugar." He released her just as quickly.

"You'll be lucky," Paige taunted, brushing down her skirt and blouse as though she were removing any stain of Rupert from her person.

"I intend to be," he determined, fixing her with a long, compelling, and assertive glare. "You're still my girl."

"Is everything all right?" Rhys's voice suddenly intruded.

Paige wanted to escape the moment she saw Rhys Langston standing face-to-face with the very man who had instigated her motives for meeting Rhys on the Internet in the first place. She watched with an awful feeling of foreboding as each sized up and classified the other. It was as though a battle line had been drawn, and she was forced to immediately cut to the chase.

"I'd like to introduce a friend of mine," she told Rhys, without going into specifics. "This is Rupert King. Rupert, this is Rhys Langston." They acknowledged each other with a simple nod.

"Are you going to the party on Saturday?" Rupert did not waste time gleaning information from the opposition.

"Sure. You?" Rhys replied, eager to acquire his own facts.

"I wouldn't miss it for the world," Rupert challenged, with a glint of fire in his eyes. He turned toward Paige. "I'll see you there, baby." Throwing her a secretive wink, he departed.

Rhys was mindful of the gesture as he took hold of Paige's wrist. His eyes ensnared hers, hot, soulful, and smoldering his own furnace of fire. "Ready?"

"For what?" Paige shrieked, her adrenaline pumped up with worry.

"To go home," Rhys whispered, masterfully tugging her an inch closer to him.

Paige bit her bottom lip. "Sure."

"Sure?" Rhys breathed. And just as easily as he had done

before in the full glare of onlookers, he publicly kissed her soft, trembling lips.

In an instant, Paige melted, dissolved, and for a long lingering moment, surrendered herself and gave Rhys back everything her soul possessed. She met the marauding silk of his tongue with all the siren sweetness at her disposal until, quite boneless, she drifted into total oblivion. She wanted this. She wanted Rhys. She forgot quite quickly the gamble she was taking against Rupert's serial womanizing. The more dangerous antics she had brought into the fore in an attempt to make Blanton jealous. That Rhys knew nothing about what she was doing or that he was the object of the game playing.

Beneath the insistent, provoking heat of Rhys's tongue, Paige was aware of one thing only. Without understanding it herself, she knew that in some way she had won. She had found someone who was pretty much going with the flow. Who was not confusing her, but was making his intentions perfectly plain. There was no guessing as to whether he liked her. No feeling that she was about to be upstaged by another younger, less flawed beauty. Rhys was taking her as he found her: a woman who truly wanted to be loved.

She almost swayed and staggered when he finally released her. Her body was protesting with unfulfilled longing, and she knew it was evident in the rushed panting of her breath, which suddenly caught in her throat when Rhys's soulful eyes locked into her own. *Let's get it on,* they said amorously, coaxingly causing her heart to skip a beat.

"I'll call you a taxi," he murmured instead, his tone hoarse and throaty.

"What about the bill?" Paige gasped, desperately hoping she did not appear as disappointed as she felt.

"Still wearing the mask of self-sufficiency," Rhys whispered against her ear. "Don't worry. I've charged it to my room."

"Sorry." Paige bit her bottom lip again, afraid to leave

without knowing whether this man really wanted to see her again.

"Don't be," Rhys muttered, catching those very lips with his own for one last, lingering taste of her.

It was a brief kiss, but told Rhys everything he needed to know about why he wanted this woman in his life. As he watched Paige wave her departure and the taxi sped away from the hotel, he was determined. He wanted Paige Alexander more than he ever wanted anything. And he meant to have her.

Six

As usual, the cutthroat competition between the final two rivals had moved everybody else out of the way. Franklin Coates-Davis had happily given up at seventy thousand pounds, but a mystery phone bidder, passing instructions through a dealer, was ripe for finding love right into old age.

The bidding fevered and the atmosphere was charged with a sense of greed and acquisitiveness. Though Franklin was knocked out of the running and had no inclination to make the fight to the bitter end, he was enthralled nonetheless to watch the frenzy to acquire the rare six-inch-high stone statuette from the nineteenth dynasty. He had decided it was worth no more than eighty. Any shrewd bidder would not have gone beyond this point. But someone obviously wanted it for more than investment reasons.

Never had 110 thousand pounds been paid at auction for such a small piece of Egyptian history. Franklin was disgusted. When the crack of the gavel sounded, he threw one last loathsome stare at the attendant porters displaying the ornament to the room before he left his chair—seeing nothing else of value he wanted to bid on from the catalog—and departed Sotheby's. He was surprised to find Rhys Langston in the outer lobby, mopping his brow in mitigated relief. A thunderous applause rung out behind him as Franklin closed the auctioneer's door.

"Ah, you've brought your goddess for me to take a look at?" Franklin chuckled, his spirits momentarily lifted, his mind approving of the fact that Rhys had chosen to take his advice.

"Actually, I've just acquired a birthday present for her," Rhys answered with a huge grin as he recalled the date he had shared with Paige Alexander the night before and that still plagued his mind as a happy memory.

Franklin read Rhys's expression as easily as if it were the FT index. "Not the . . ." He stared in alarm. "The Egyptian figurine?"

Rhys nodded. In his mind, the statuette would be the perfect birthday gift for Paige. "You were right. Bids opened at fifty thousand."

"You've paid over the odds," Franklin seethed, flashing Rhys a canny look of envy.

"No, I haven't." Rhys lowered his voice. "You said something about whoever owns it will find and keep love through to old age. There's a legend to that figurine. I must make a note to find out what it is."

"I hope she's worth it," Franklin added, narrowing his brows as though he was suddenly recalling something—an old story—from the far recesses of his mind.

"She is," Rhys told him just as one of the auctioneer porters approached.

"Cash, Mr. Langston?"

"Yes." Rhys nodded.

"This way, sir."

"You'll join me for coffee later?" he asked Franklin with a grin of satisfaction, so lovestruck, he failed to detect his banker's immense and shrewd recalculation of the situation.

"No," Franklin declined, not having overcome his brief moment of disbelief. "I have a prior arrangement elsewhere. Enjoy your piece while you can."

As Rhys left, Franklin consulted his watch, then his mobile phone. Without hesitation, he barked out an order. "I want you to do something for me," he hissed quietly. "And I want it kept hush-hush."

* * *

Francine was not happy at hearing the sordid details. While following Paige around Aunt Elva's Victorian home in Chelsea, listening while her cousin related details about Rhys Langston, and equally barking orders to the caterers who had arrived to formalize all the arrangements for her party that evening, Francine slowly became enraged at the news.

"You're juggling three men," she proclaimed in amazement. "All at the same time."

"That's not strictly true," Paige said, glancing at the clipboard in her hand, which held a list of the chores she needed to check and complete before the morning was through. "I'm just making sure that the other side does not have the advantage."

"This is not a contest," Francine protested. "Finding love is not a playing field. You're behaving as though there are game moves and you don't want to miss. You want to hit goal first time."

"I've fouled out in the past," Paige answered, ticking her list as two men placed their delivery of sixty rented sherry glasses in a corner of the room. Nodding her acceptance, she turned to find Francine's pale honey complexion had colored with rage. "This time I want to win."

"Aren't you forgetting that Rupert King plays soccer?" Francine warned. "And he likes a good tackle before he scores. You're going to lose this game entirely. He's just looking for comfort since he lost his first love."

"How do you know about this . . . alleged heart-and-soul relationship anyway?" Paige asked, aware it must have been before Rupert had acquired the unprotective veneer of fame.

"I think I read it somewhere," Francine confirmed. "It was a turbulent one, too, which means he's not going to take you seriously."

"Which is why I'm keeping my legs crossed and my options open." Paige repeated her mantra, the same one she had used online when logged into *www.totallyblackdating.com.* "A girl can't risk putting her heart into just one man these days. If it all goes well, then I'm at least guaranteed an alternative option."

Francine was appalled. "What?"

"Like Aunt Elva used to say." Paige repeated with accuracy, "There's good, there's better, and there's the best. I've simply given myself a choice, that's all."

"I need a cigarette," Francine declared, unable to deal with the magnitude of what she was hearing. "You're taking me way out of my depth of understanding here and I need to find common ground."

Paige stared at the two men on ladders hanging her thirtieth birthday banner above the double glass doors that led out into the garden, and felt tense. She was still waiting for Lizzy Chadwick, her old acquaintance from the London party planners Chadwick & Co., to arrive to take over and bring up to speed the exhausting party itinerary. It was very generous of Lizzy to offer, considering she had not been hired, though Paige knew she would more than welcome the helping hand. Lizzy could provide an alternative comfort to her than her cousin, and would no doubt help take her mind of the game playing she had started.

"As long as I know what I'm doing, that's all that matters," she stated tersely, inwardly unconvinced.

"Do you?" Francine was not persuaded. "I'm a lawyer and *I'm* losing the facts. Do each of these men know what you're doing?"

"No."

"Do they know about each other?"

"Sort of," Paige said feebly, ticking her birthday banner off her list. "Actually, Blanton Blake knows the most."

"Then that puts you in a dangerous position," Francine cautioned sternly.

Paige was thrown. "Why?"

"He has the upper hand," Francine conspired, "and it's likely he could use it to ransom your feelings against the other two."

"You're blowing this way out of proportion." Paige flinched, smiling when she saw that her cake had finally arrived. She pointed to the table where she wanted Mrs.

Northcroft, the master baker, to place it. "Blanton Blake's engaged to be married," she finished.

Francine followed Paige on her way to the table. "Notwithstanding that you would rather it were to you," she remarked scathingly.

Paige stopped in her tracks, clipboard and pen poised in midair. "No. I . . ."

"Which is it?" Francine demanded. "Because if you allow Blanton to think he's got a chance, you could well find him calling your bluff and canceling his nuptials at the very last minute to accommodate you and your offer."

Paige swallowed. "I haven't really encouraged him," she bristled, acknowledging Mrs. Northcroft, who opened the cake box to allow her to take a peep. "More like teasing, making sure he's noticed me."

"Three deliveries of flowers this morning, each suggesting heartfelt sentiments," Francine intoned hotly, "speaks volumes. I'd say Blanton Blake, Rupert King, and Rhys Langston all definitely *know* you exist."

"What are you, a scorekeeper?" Paige jabbed, agitated. "Keeping a tally on what's going on?"

"You're the one who's competing for center stage," Francine scoffed. "I'd say you just got it."

Paige closed her eyes briefly, then reopened them to take a look at her cake. She offered the baker a pensive smile in approval. The cake was huge and white, and wonderfully decorated in marvelous red, yellow, and orange colors, with her name emboldened on an image of a champagne bottle. "This is lovely," she nervously told Mrs. Northcroft, snatching a check that she had pinned to her clipboard and offering it to her in payment. "Thank you."

"Enjoy your party," Mrs. Northcroft told her, a smile attached to her face.

"I intend to." Paige swallowed, nodding as the baker left. Turning back to her cousin, who was hounding her like a predatory bear, she said, "What am I going to do?"

"About Rupert King, who seems to think you want him

back?" Francine swiftly moved on. "And who is taking your little game very seriously?"

"But he can't," Paige shrieked, staring dejected at her cousin.

"But he can and has," Francine returned just as quickly. "He's now of the impression that he'll be making up with you at your party. It must be fun for a girl to keep her options open, if she can take the heat."

Paige swallowed her guilt. "Francine—"

"I wonder what Rhys Langston—who'll actually be acting out the role of your current squeeze—is going to think when he finds out," Francine concluded. "The poor man doesn't know what he's walking into."

Now Paige was mortified. After the dreamy evening she had spent in the company of Rhys Langston at Claridge's, her feet hardly felt as though they had touched the ground since she had awakened two days on the trot. Though it was now nine o'clock in the morning and this was the big day of her party, Rhys Langston had been the core train of thought running around in her mind.

Amid the busy rush of deliveries—three sets of flowers, the champagne flutes, sherry glasses, birthday cards, her birthday banner, the food, DJ sound equipment, and now her cake—Rhys had remained a constant memory throughout. Everything about him had immortalized in her brain so that she hardly noticed Blanton Blake's advances when she had gone into work the morning after her date. Only Rhys's short black hair, rich golden-brown complexion, soulful, smoldering mocha-brown eyes, and those pink lips she found so invitingly kissable prevailed in her mind.

Her dream of him carried into the day while she had shown two prospective buyers seven properties, surveyed another three, and returned to her office to find Blanton making her a cup of tea. This was a chore he often left to their secretary, but he seemed eager to please, and talked nonstop about how he was looking forward to attending her party. Whether that meant he would be bringing his fiancée and her family was another matter, one that did not concern her in the slightest.

On emerging out of bed that morning, taking a shower, and pinning up her hair, then dressing in gray bottoms and a white jersey so she could take on the jobs that faced her before her party officially commenced, Paige had concluded that her dinner date with Rhys had been a resounding success. She had gleaned enough information about him to thrust into conversation with her closest family members, colleagues, friends, and acquaintances. *No one will ever be the wiser,* she had even told herself.

Francine's suppositions had changed all that. Since her arrival from Birmingham with her husband, after listening while Paige excitedly divulged the news about what she had been up to, Paige was surprised to find her cousin had done nothing but dish out numerous warnings. She did not feel compelled to heed them. *Surely, Rhys will never find out.* She tried to convince herself that her plan was foolproof. There were no loopholes. After all, she had grown to adore Rhys Langston quite admirably, in more ways than she cared to admit. What could possibly go wrong?

"Rhys and I have an understanding," she proclaimed on reflecting on her decision. "He is nothing more than a guest at my party,"

"And what do you know about him?" Francine demanded. "What is Omega Private Equity Funds Ltd. anyway?"

"I don't know," Paige admitted, ticking the cake off her list.

"Didn't you ask him about what you read on the Web?"

"No," Paige relented, afraid to ruin the ambience that now existed between them. "He does research work, I think, on cultural heritage. I think he's writing a book."

"You think," Francine derided. "Who is his writer friend?"

"I don't know." Paige flinched at the admission. This was information she should know and did not.

"And can he afford to stay at Claridge's?" Francine went on. "I mean, don't they charge the earth for a room there?"

It suddenly dawned on Paige that she did not know much

about Rhys Langston after all. "I'll fill in the gaps later," she croaked.

"I swear I don't know what is going on with you," Francine said finally. "Is it because your life has been eventless that you've developed an anxiety, or fear that it will continue in the same meaningless way indefinitely?"

"You're as bad as Blanton Blake," Paige spat out, her temper now frayed. "Don't either of you want to see me happy?"

"Of course I do," Francine broached loudly. "I can't speak for the motives of your boss, but what I do know is that I'm worried about you."

"Well, don't be," Paige quipped. "I can take care of myself."

"Really." Francine's taut remark came just as the doorbell peeled loudly.

"That'll be Lizzy Chadwick," Paige alerted, glancing at her watch.

"Her name sounds familiar," Francine breathed.

"Don't you listen to a word I say?" Paige gushed. "You've met. She's helping me with my party."

"Hmmm," Francine sighed, shifting back to their main topic. "Or it could be Aunt Gwerfyl and Uncle Jed."

"Mom and Dad!" Paige gasped in alarm. "Francine." She ran after her cousin as they both hurried toward the front door. "You're not going to tell them, are you?"

"That depends." Francine paused and gazed at Paige.

She stared. "On what?"

"That you end this little charade now."

"I can't." Paige swallowed miserably. "It's gone too far."

"It hasn't gone far enough," Francine warned. "But by tonight, it will have."

Paige could hear the 1990s theme fondue from her bedroom while she dressed, aware that downstairs a horde of guests were making their arrivals. She was nervous and rightly so. Francine's dire prediction was playing havoc in her head, and Paige was sure she would explode into a frenzy if she did not calm herself.

Sipping a flute of champagne, which Lizzy Chadwick had brought in before rushing to change in the other room, she thought of Rhys Langston. Perhaps he was already downstairs. Maybe he had not yet arrived. *What if he doesn't come?* She swallowed and stared at herself in her armoire mirror. A panic-stricken face glared back. *What have I done?* prevailed in her mind. Paige did not know what to expect when she finally ventured downstairs to join her invited guests.

She picked up her eyebrow pencil and checked the tip before, with shaky fingers, she applied it to her eyebrows. Marking out a well-defined mark, she grimaced and played out a number of scenarios in her mind. Rupert would be flirtatious. Blanton would be civil, and Rhys . . . Rhys would be . . . understanding. That was it. Surely he would accept any explanation she chose to give him. After all, he was leaving after her party, so it would not be a problem.

Paige marked out the other brow and sighed heavily. It was not fair that Rhys Langston had planned to leave so soon. Just as she had gotten used to thinking about him, about how he had kissed her, about his sinful, lustful gaze, about those large pink lips she so desired to kiss again. *Why is life so unfair?* she mused, throwing down her eyebrow pencil to reach for the eye-shadow shade she had decided to wear that night.

Applying it with fingers still trembling at her having to face the ordeal downstairs, the friends, acquaintances, *en famille,* and potential lovers, Paige paused to take another large gulp of champagne. As the numbing effect began to sedate, she planned strategy. She would be confident, assertive, a little bit sassy, she decided. She would face the hovering male bees with the cool, calm, aplomb of a queen bee. She was good at that. Camouflaging her inner turmoil. The woman who wore the false mask of self-sufficiency like a pro.

I see you as a person who is the center of the party, bowling everyone over with your seductive smile, and your assertive décolletage. Even Rhys's apt description of her had been accurate. She recalled her reply, too. She was going to make him feel the sting of her fist. Instead, she had felt the heated potency of his kiss. Touching her lips with red lipstick, Paige imagined the feel of that kiss again.

What am I going to do? she brooded, patting the stray ends of her hairstyle into place, approving of the swept-up topknot the hairdresser who had accompanied Lizzy Chadwick had applied, which made her short brown hair appear longer than it actually was. *Movie stars wear these additions all the time,* she had been told. Paige was not sure how she felt about it, but it was done now, and all she needed was to step into her dress. It was a selection from her wardrobe, which was a cavern of designer outfits, and was laid out on her bed, unworn, but the perfect choice for a woman who had reached thirty.

She slipped into the pastel-green off-the-shoulder chiffon and lace gown, fastening a halter-neck tie until she felt the lift of her cleavage. She surveyed herself in her bedroom mirror. The classic cut accentuated her womanly curves and showed off her feminine figure to its best advantage. Easing into a pair of lime-green high-heeled sandals, Paige walked over to her dressing table and picked out her favorite perfume. Removing the top, she invigorated her senses with the fresh scent of Chanel Number Five as a final finishing touch. With one last glance, finally she was ready to venture downstairs and greet her guests.

Standing in the doorway upon her alighting the stairway was Blanton Blake in his usual fashion stratagem, a tightly buttoned three-piece suit, with a subversive air that matched his brand of genteel formality. At his side was a woman with elfin features and rosebud lips. In Dior heels and a long silver-colored dress, she looked every inch the coveted title-holder of the Miss Zimbabwe crown. They had just arrived, and were the first two to notice Paige as she disembarked from the last step.

"Paige!" Blanton broached, a huge smile spread across his face. "Happy birthday."

"Thank you." Paige smiled, turning to meet the inquiring gaze of his fiancée. "I thought Blanton was bringing along your parents," she said, holding out her hand to effect a friendly handshake with Latanya Folasade.

"They are . . . how you say . . . very tired," Latanya replied in a rich Zimbabwe voice that plainly revealed that she spoke very little English.

"I see," Paige purred, turning her gaze toward Blanton, who leered at her lustfully.

"Did you get my flowers?" he asked.

"I got your flowers," Paige answered with a nervous smile before a cluster of new arrivals rushed through the door.

"Paige!" another woman squealed. It was Sara Singh and her husband from Bombay. Dressed in traditional Indian garments and looking absolutely adorable, they breezed in showing little sign of jet lag. "Thirty," her friend crooned. "Now you can join the club."

"Happy birthday," Tina Simmons enthused, in close step behind.

"Ditto," Claudia Delaney inspired, finding space to enter.

They all laughed, hugged, and exchanged friendly kisses of camaraderie before Paige made the formal introductions. Hordes of presents were thrust in her direction, until she was forced to hail one of the waitresses to collect them. Closeted by her friends, Paige escorted them all into the main lounge. She was met by her parents, Gwerfyl and Jed, who immediately rushed over and hugged their daughter.

"Oh, Paige," her mother cried, tears forming in her eyes. "I'm so proud. So very proud. Just look at you." She swirled her daughter around like the goddess she was.

"Mum," Paige rasped, hugging her mother in embarrassment. "Don't."

"You know what your mother is like," her father said sternly. "Always a rain shower." He bent forward and kissed his daughter. "Your sister Penelope is flying over from Denmark with her new husband. She'll be here later."

"That's great." Paige smiled. It had been four months since she had last seen her younger sister, and they no doubt had much to catch up on.

"Happy birthday, cuz," Francine crooned, walking over with her husband and two sisters. Nancy and Marcia had not changed a great deal and Mervyn was . . . simply Mervyn.

"Thank you," Paige sighed, filled with emotion. She was surrounded by her family and the few of her friends who had arrived, yet she felt terribly lonely. Rhys Langston had not yet made an appearance, and Paige needed him at her side.

"Have you seen the cake?" she asked everyone, walking directly toward the eighteen-foot specially erected table, decorated and adorned with enough of the finest tidbits of food and cakes to feed a small army.

Lizzy Chadwick had, at the last moment, added the finishing touches to her table. With the DJ equipment set up, the table, the lights, and the drinks table overflowing with an assortment of vintage wine, champagne, and non-alcoholic beverages against the polished wooden floor of Aunt Elva's Chelsea home, nothing could seem more perfect to begin the celebrations.

More presents were forced in her direction as everyone admired the cake. Paige began to feel flustered and overwhelmed when more of her friends entered and began to slowly add to the numbers, until a small crowd congregated to form discussions among themselves. Again, she sensed her loneliness. No Rhys. No man at her side to share in what should be one of the happiest days of her life.

"Where's your young man?" Elva suddenly enquired, offering Paige a flute of champagne. Elva was dressed for the occasion in her best wig and a new frock, and Paige almost felt the pain of knowing that her aunt was equally looking forward to seeing Rhys Langston again.

"He . . . he should be here by now," she said on a shaky

note. Her disappointment was not easy to hide and this surprised her.

"Who you talking 'bout?" Her mother immediately intruded on overhearing the conversation.

"Your daughter has a handsome new beau," Elva revealed.

"Paige have a man?" Aunt Evelyn suddenly impinged in her loudest voice, invading the tiny space where her niece was standing among her family, a champagne glass precariously held in her hand.

The three sisters encroached together, only short years between them, looked amazingly young to have borne children now in their thirties. With the exception of Aunt Elva, Aunt Evelyn and Gwerfyl were now grandmothers, with only Francine and Paige not yet having had children. It was with disappointment that Paige glared at Aunt Evelyn, knowingly aware her voice had carried throughout the room. Soon everyone would be curious about her elusive stranger.

"What him name?" her father wasted no time asking. He had not lost his brashness, acquired having worked in engineering for eighteen years making motor parts. Now retired, Jed still was like a product from the shop floor, loud, brazen, and gauche, as though he were still enjoying the camaraderie of the workplace.

Paige sighed heavily. "Rhys," she finally blurted. "Rhys Langston."

"But wait!" Her father paused. "I thought you was with Rupert King . . . the footballer."

"We've . . . parted," Paige explained. "This is a new guy."

"What?" her mother gushed. "But wasn't you with another man last week?"

"I was with Rupert last week." Paige flinched nervously, disliking the confusion. "And now I'm with Rhys Langston."

Gwerfyl appeared flustered. "You were going to Portugal the last time we spoke." Her mother was more than concerned. "I don't understand."

"I do," a familiar voice intoned.

Paige turned to find the subject of their conversation

standing within inches of her. Rupert King looked no less than devastatingly attractive. He revealed his boyish happy-go-lucky grin to everyone who had eyes to gaze on in bewilderment. His own come-to-bed brown eyes darted across the room, absorbing everything and everyone who filled the main lounge. He nodded his approval, too, as though he found the elaborate decoration for Paige's party something to be admired.

"Rupert, my boy." Jed instantly held out his hand and clinched it with the infamous young man facing him in quiet tokenism, as though they were old pals. "We were just talking about your good health. How are you?"

"Fine, now that I'm here," Rupert replied, transferring his brooding gaze directly to Paige.

"You have the big playoff at the Millennium stadium in Cardiff next week," Jed went on, not heeding his daughter's discomfort at seeing how friendly he appeared with the man she had introduced him to last year.

Rupert welcomed the solidarity with glee. "Yes, sir," he temporized with an even tone. "I hope to do my best."

"I need another drink," Paige interrupted, Rupert's very presence causing her to feel queasy and sick so that she dared not look back after making her departure.

She spied Blanton Blake across the main lounge with Latanya, and noted his bland expression of annoyance on seeing Rupert's arrival. It was clear he did not expect a rival to be there, and she had not mentioned anything to him. Knowing Blanton was aware she had picked someone from the Internet made Paige feel even more uneasy. Francine was right. He did know too much, but Paige consoled herself with the knowledge that he was engaged to be married and could cause her no undue harm. Clearly it was with amazement, when she approached the drinks table to collect another glass of champagne, that she found he had joined her there.

"Did you know *he* was coming?" Blanton spat out like venom.

Paige deliberately lowered her voice. "He was invited," she hissed, "before we split up."

"And he has the balls to show his face?" Blanton scorned with suppressed fury.

"He can't hurt me anymore," Paige retorted, hoping her tone would appease her boss.

"Why is he here?" Blanton derided. He threw a mocking gaze across the room at Rupert before returning his fiery rage to Paige.

"I don't know," she admitted. It was, in part, the truth.

"We need to talk," he whispered, "about us."

"There's nothing to talk about," Paige returned, taking a fortifying swallow of champagne while trying not to appear nervous, even under the hot glare Francine was throwing in her direction.

"You can't say that," Blanton protested, taking a step closer so that Paige was made aware of his imposing stance. "Not after the way we've been . . . looking at each other. You must feel it, too."

"No, I don't," Paige admonished, now mindful of Francine's acute warnings.

"Don't tease me," Blanton debated, his voice changing suddenly to a harsh note. "You've been making eyes at me all week."

"You're engaged to be married," Paige spluttered beneath her breath, "and Rupert's watching." He was, too. His alert slanting brown eyes were trained directly at them.

"What does he want?" Blanton reproved, narrowing his brows as though the question amounted to an equation that needed calculating. Following Rupert's gaze back to Paige, he saw the light. "*You*. He wants you back," he gasped, wide-eyed in awe.

Paige chuckled, behaving as if the entire notion were ludicrous. "Don't be silly," she railed.

"And you know," Blanton judged, jaw agape, his brain putting the pieces together like a jigsaw puzzle. "You picked this guy off the Internet to pitch against Rupert King."

"Blanton," Paige began, struck by the sense of awareness that marred her boss's face. "This is not what you think." She was unable to continue. A cluster of her friends arrived at that precise moment to shower her with their congratulations.

"Our tough little cookie is all grown up," Claudia Delaney stated tersely, reminding everyone that her best friend had now reached thirty. "I hope you have a birthday wish because it's time to light the candles."

"Everyone's not here." Paige panicked, knowing Rhys Langston had not yet arrived. *Where can he be?* Surely he would not come so far to let her down now.

"Who else should we be expecting?" her best friend inquired, curious and unaware that Rhys Langston had yet to put in an appearance.

"A mystery guest," Elva purred quietly.

Paige threw her aunt a scolding sneaky peek before she looked around the room. Everyone who held a level of significance in her life was there. Her parents, her aunts, her cousins, their children. Georgia Bagnoli, her gym instructor, was just breezing in. Paige's godparents had arrived two minutes earlier. She had yet to offer them her greetings. Her friends, her boss, her acquaintances were all there. Rupert, her ex-lover, was hanging in the wings. Lizzy Chadwick had just arrived downstairs, having changed into something more appropriate. How could Paige announce that only Rhys Langston, her Internet lover, was missing?

"My sister," she suddenly bellowed out loud with relief. "We can't light the cake without Penelope, my brother-in-law, and their children."

"Where are they?" Her mother overheard and voiced her agitation. "This is just like your sister to be late."

"I'll call her on the mobile," her father defended, protective of his younger daughter. "You know how difficult it is for Penny with the children."

Paige simply prayed that, for once in her life, her sister would be as late as possible. The further delay would surely provide more time to expect Rhys Langston. She smiled at her friends while Blanton reluctantly rejoined his fiancée. Paige, in turn, plunged into conversations about the horde of presents that were yet to be opened and what her big plans for the future were likely to be. Ten minutes passed before Rupert, unable to contain himself, moseyed on over.

"Baby, I thought you'd be pleased to see me," he leered in her ear, taking hold of her arm and gently pulling her away from her circle of friends.

"Why would I want to be?" Paige asked, her emotions brimming to release an outpouring of revenge as she detached herself from his grip.

"Because my replacement's not here," Rupert proclaimed, his smile fixed to his lips. "Stood you up, has he?"

Paige's heart felt stricken at hearing him say it. "He'll be here," she defended. "Just wait and see."

"Come hell or high water?" Rupert repeated, taking them back to their altercation on his private jet en route to Portugal. "Did you get my flowers?"

"I got your flowers."

Rupert was not deterred. "Honey, don't be like this."

"Why are you here?" Paige seethed, feeling her temper rise. "To gloat?"

"You know why I'm here," he revealed almost in a whisper. "Baby, I want you back."

"I don't want *you* back," Paige snarled, avenging herself. "I'm doing just fine without you."

"You're nothing without me," Rupert taunted quietly.

"What?"

"You know you find me irresistible," Rupert teased, retaking her arm.

"So, I had low standards once," Paige bit back. "Not anymore."

"We had some good times."

"Don't kid yourself," Paige wheeled discreetly. "Dating you was a rough ride. I'm off the carousel now."

"I'm jealous," Rupert finally admitted sheepishly. "Let's quit this game and kiss me."

"Stop it," Paige ordered, keeping her voice low so as not to attract attention. "My date will be here soon."

Rupert released her arm. "He's cutting it very fine then," he told her triumphantly. "Your sister's just arrived."

Paige grew alarmed as she turned to find the last members of her family entering the main lounge. No Rhys. She was gutted. Having put all her ambitions and expectations into Rupert King and finding them dashed, dreaming of Blanton Blake falling in love with her, to find him proposing marriage to someone else, and then having both men pathetically claiming they wanted her after all, had rendered her speechless. She had believed Rhys Langston would be different. He would never let her down. It was like a promise when he had said he would be there by her side. Now, she was truly alone.

"We can light the candles now," she heard someone screech out loud.

Penelope rushed over and gave her sister a hug. "Paige. Why are you crying?"

"Penny, I'm . . . ," she began through tear-glazed eyes, unable to admit the true reason for her tears. "Thirty!"

"By hook or by crook," Rupert taunted into her ear as she was ushered away into the bosom of caring relatives.

There was no more time to wait. No one wanted to wait. Everything began to happen very quickly. A frenzy of chatter, the waitresses offering filled sherry glasses all round, a small group assembling around the fringe of the table while through teary midnight-blue eyes, Paige glimpsed her father lighting each candle in turn. Paige was dazed. With Rupert's taunt still resonating in her ear, she wondered who she would hug after she blew out those candles, made her wish, and cemented her coming of a new age. It would hardly bear thinking about. But her mantra was the same, as always. *Ad finem*—to the end.

"After the count of three," a burst of chorus yelled, before the singing of the birthday anthem began.

Paige closed her eyes, forced back the tears, made her

wish, and blew. To her, it was a magical moment, as if a burden had lifted and she was receiving a rich blessing from God. Paige was spiritually moved as she heard the room fall silent and felt the rush of gentle air pass by her. Then a flurry of whispers provoked her senses. She was indeed still in the world of the living when she slowly, belatedly, opened her eyes. Paige nearly keeled over in profound shock when she found herself sinking into the soulful smoldering depths that only Rhys Langston could possess

He was there. In front of her, the desert prince she had found who had not forgotten he had promised to be at her side. He was handsomely dressed, receiving avid glares from everyone around them, particularly the two love rivals she had engendered into a game plan that now held no motives. Rhys was dressed in a well-cut Italian designer suit in a modern select shade of dyed blue, wearing a pale-blue shirt opened at the neck to reveal his rich golden-brown hairy chest. No tie.

His textorized short black hair was slick and freshly smoothed away from his face so that his square-jawed features and perfectly sculptured teeth captivated the room's attention. His tall, slim build and imposing manner were noticeable to everyone, particularly the two men she no longer wanted, but all Paige could see was Rhys's large pink lips ready for the taking. He did not keep her waiting. He pulled her close and their lips met. She swooned right into him, and an applause of amazement and wolf whistles shook the room.

Seven

"So this is your mystery guest," Claudia Delaney screamed, tapping Paige so hard on the back she was forced to tear her lips away from Rhys Langston's.

The kiss itself had been devoutly erotic. To Paige, it was as though she had come from one dream and into another. Rhys's mouth had sealed over hers and blended like molten lava, causing a scalding heat to pour into her from him as if by magic. Her breath became deep, ragged, panting. Something inside was still building. The room and its occupants disappeared temporarily. All Paige had been aware of was an incredible urge, an incredible need that she was sure would wantonly surge out of control.

His lips teased, his tongue stroked. There was something intensely carnal about the way Rhys enjoyed kissing her publicly. At the airport, the hotel, and now in front of her guests. But Paige was not complaining. Rhys's teeth were on the verge of nipping her when she had felt the hard tap on her back. When she finally, reluctantly, turned to face her best friend, it was with a certain unexplainable satisfaction that she had escaped into oblivion so quickly and returned with the cause of her rapture still at her side.

"I'm sorry," she gasped, apologetic to her shocked guests. "Everyone, I'd like you to meet Rhys Langston." The greetings were head-on and in a flurry.

"That's my little girl," Jed announced loudly, eyeing Rhys in speculative curiosity. "Paige tell me nothing about you."

"What do you do?" her mother invaded.

"You from London?" someone else inquired.

"How long have you been dating my sister?" Penelope even chirped in.

"Let me at least get him a drink." Paige giggled, glancing at Rhys before she protectively laced her fingers through his.

"He's not dating your sister." Blanton Blake's harsh tone intruded, stepping into the fray. His eyes had narrowed with envy, though only Paige was aware of it. "I'm told he's passing through."

Her heart stopped. "Rhys," she gasped, her own eyes pleading with Blanton that he refrain from ruining her party. "I'd like you to meet Blanton Blake, my boss."

"Paige has told me about you," Rhys acknowledged, throwing Blanton a courteous nod.

"Has she," Blanton returned on an agitated note. "I wouldn't trust everything she tells you. We're property brokers. We make very good liars and manipulators."

"That's our job." Paige nervously chuckled, deciding to accept Blanton's remark as a joke, and determined she would speak to him about it in her office at the earliest given opportunity. "If it's a tin box, we know how to sell it." She laughed and pulled Rhys away from the potentially explosive circle of people who surrounded them loaded with questions.

"Is that the real estate tyrant who likes cracking the whip?" Rhys whispered, accepting the champagne Paige forced into his hand.

"That's the realty tycoon and potential business partner," Paige confirmed, mercifully taking a large gulp from the sherry glass she had been given earlier, throwing a nervous glance across the room over the rim. She saw Francine shaking her head as though expecting dreaded doom at any given moment. Then she saw Rupert glaring at her like a bomb about to detonate.

"And that's the guy who winked at you in Claridge's," Rhys

commented. He had seen Rupert, too, and did not miss the knowing grin Rupert threw at him. "Old boyfriend?"

Paige choked. "Just a friend."

"You have a lot of flowers," Rhys noted.

He was shrewd and perceptive, and Paige knew the thinking and assessment had begun. The sudden thought crossed her mind that she should come clean. Tell Rhys the truth. He deserved to know what was going on and that she had been the true instigator of the awful game play that—if she did not put a stop to and soon—was likely to start raging out of control. Blanton needed to be reminded of his forthcoming nuptials, Rupert needed to be told to leave her alone, and she needed . . . she needed . . . to beg Rhys to stay.

"Nice to see you back in my home again." Elva approached them both with a smile. "How are you finding England?"

"A little chilly," Rhys told her.

"And my niece?"

Rhys's mocha-brown eyes were heavy-lidded with wild, sexual yearning as he looked at Paige, absorbing the lift of her cleavage in the green off-the-shoulder chiffon and lace gown she was wearing. "More beautiful than ever."

Paige's breath caught. Rhys was driving her mad. She could not help but stare at him as he talked with her aunt, and later mingled with her friends and acquaintances. Her gaze held as he struck up a conversation with her parents and godparents and generally made his presence felt among the congregation she had invited to her party. He quite unexpectedly led the toast for her coming of age, watched avidly as her father made his speech, and helped take more presents into her aunt's dining room to place on the large table there for opening later.

And she mingled, too, catching Francine planting a kiss against her husband's cheek, Penelope hugging her youngest child, her mother knocking back more champagne than her usual quota, her father occupied with someone on his mobile phone, and Rupert talking with Claudia Delaney. For a time, they laughed gaily together. The next time Paige looked, they were gone. Her gaze roamed to catch a glimpse of them both discreetly disappearing into Aunt Elva's empty conservatory. Paige was not fooled when Rupert closed the door behind him. Ten minutes later, Claudia was to emerge with a satisfied smile on her face, followed by Rupert with an equally sheepish one on his.

The pattern repeated itself half an hour later, this time, Paige noted, with Tina Simmons being led away out into the garden area. The chilly night air did not seem to deter them. When she reappeared, her hair was ruffled, her clothes were slightly disheveled, and Rupert was tucking a stray end of his shirt back into his trouser waistband. Paige was disgusted.

Rupert had no scruples at all to be conducting himself in this disgraceful, outlandish manner right under her very nose with her friends. And at her party, too. She felt ever more eternally grateful that Rhys was a more disciplined man, certainly the type who would never be tempted to do anything behind her back. There were, of course, no guarantees, especially now that Paige began to ponder the caliber that existed among Claudia and Tina and, no doubt, a further handful of her friends. Who in life could she trust if not them? It seemed only Rhys Langston had remained faithful.

True to his promise, he was hers for the duration. It was her night and he appeared to be a hit with everyone. Immersed, Rhys laughed and chuckled, but Paige knew he was mindful of her every move. Caught in the conflict of her spiraling arousing emotions against her harboring deep suspicions that he knew something, she did not know how to react when she watched Blanton harshly brush past Rhys, vindictively knocking his shoulder, and equally at Rupert's clumsiness when he spilled half a glass of champagne deliberately onto Rhys's shoes.

"It was an accident!" Rupert swaggered over to tell her immediately, like a spoiled child not wanting to be chastised.

"I don't want you causing any trouble," Paige seethed beneath her breath, throwing Rhys a sorrowful sigh.

"When are you going to put that clown out of his misery?" Rupert jived, burping an odor with the distinct stench of booze. "And why is that joker over there giving you the eye?" He indicated Blanton Blake, who now seemed caught in a heated argument with his fiancée.

Paige closed her eyes for one brief moment. When she reopened them, Rhys was in front of her. "What's going on?" he demanded.

"She has sexy lips, doesn't she?" Rupert claimed, leaning forward to bring Paige into his arms and take what he considered to be rightfully his.

Rhys restrained him. "You've had a lot to drink, buddy. Let's see if we can get you a cab."

"Take your bloody hands off me," Rupert chided, breaking himself free. "Ask her who she belongs to."

"He's drunk," Paige gasped, dearly wanting to swear at Rupert.

"She's playing some kind of game to get me back."

"That's not true," Paige protested, seeing the shocked expression form on Rhys's face.

"You're supposed to be my replacement," Rupert announced. "I don't know where she got you from so fast, a little prude like her, but she got you from somewhere."

"Rupert!" Francine rushed to the rescue, deliberately prizing herself between Rupert and Rhys. "Look who's here," she added quickly, thrusting Lizzy Chadwick forward until they were both facing each other.

"Hello Rupert." Lizzy smiled. "Long time no see."

Rupert's mouth dropped. "Elizabeth!" He hardly recognized her. His brown eyes widened in such bewilderment, Paige was awed as to what was going on.

"Do you know each other?" she asked, her brows narrowing as Francine affirmed a simple nod, figuring out that this must have been his failed love and soul relationship of time past.

"From school," Rupert gasped.

His sudden switch in concentration did not go unnoticed by Rhys. "You okay now?" he queried, seeming to take Rupert's entire behavior as having been some form of drunken madness.

"Yeah . . . yeah," Rupert mumbled on a deranged note. His dazed eyes never left Lizzy. Instead, they were to acquire a misty haze, as though he had suddenly plummeted back into a moment in time.

"You didn't know I was here, did you?" Lizzy surmised crudely. "I've been watching you for over an hour now."

"You've cut your hair," Rupert noted, bemused. "And you've put on weight." He gave her the once-over. "Can we talk?"

"That depends," Lizzy said astutely. "Paige is an old acquaintance I did some work for and I think you owe her an apology."

"Me?" Rupert scoffed, stifling a snort.

"She's been filling me in on what you've been getting up to over the years," Lizzy announced quite candidly. "Still the serial womanizer with the roaming eye! I'm glad to hear Paige didn't fall for it."

"You did, though." Rupert smirked.

"And have the baby to prove it." The triumphant answer rang out as Lizzy watched with sheer satisfaction as that same smirk fell just as quickly from Rupert's face. "So I'd apologize if I were you because we definitely need to talk."

Paige wondered if she had heard correctly. Everyone speculated the same thing. That Rupert King's sexual peccadilloes, while no doubt interesting to the tabloid press, had sired him a child out of wedlock. A secret of secrets so buried, not even Fleet Street reporters digging in his garden, so to speak, had unearthed it.

"Liar!" Rupert bellowed, staring at Lizzy, sobering up at record speed. "You've got no reason to be telling me this now!"

"Revenge," Lizzy seethed, hearing the gasps that shook the room, "Only I've never been able to get close to you until I saw Paige and was told you'd been invited to her party. I offered to give her a helping hand and that's how I came to be here. It was the only way to see you and I'm going to make you pay."

Francine immediately interceded with her business card, surmising the ugliness of the situation. "Naturally, you'll be wanting a lawyer," she said shrewdly, "and the legal arrangements made for a DNA test to confirm paternity."

"Naturally." Lizzy snatched the card, schooling her eyes carefully on Francine. "I'll be wanting back payments for maintenance, too, adding to the sum of millions."

Rupert laughed sardonically. "You're trying to pull a fast one. Your baby isn't mine."

"You're a narcissistically self-delusional love rat to think you can deny your own daughter," Lizzy squealed hotly, determined to unfold every sordid detail about their turbulent relationship among witnesses. "You had no right to dump me when I got pregnant."

"You weren't pregnant," Rupert protested severely, ignoring the repeated gasps he heard resonating across the room. The music had stopped, and he suddenly became aware he had the privilege of an avid audience. "You were just saying that to ruin my career chances just when it got started, when I was working hard to get on the team."

"I haven't touched your lifestyle in any way whatsoever," Lizzy challenged, staring at Rupert in amazement. "I've kept quiet these past few years while you abandoned your financial and parental responsibilities. I didn't pin you down or harass you. I remained in the background and accepted you walking away, although I always hoped one day you'd come back. I didn't even approach the Child Support Agency."

"I abandoned nothing," Rupert dismissed, waving his hand disregardingly into the air and disliking the fact he was being seen and heard by all of Paige's guests as a man who fell into that primordial instinct of conserving his energy to inseminate as many women as possible, leaving the equally powerful nurturing instincts to the mothers left behind. "You were the one who told me if a man won't say no, then why should you."

"Because you don't see casual sex to be a crime," Lizzy screamed in reminiscence of their troubled past. "You seem to think that the desire for a mate, even serial mates, is just an expression of basic human need, while I needed some expression of commitment. I wanted you to share the budgeting, the home-making, nurturing, feeding, decision-making, teaching, even discipline. And all you did was let me down and put my life at risk by spreading yourself around. You left me alone to fend for myself and your child." Lizzy was shaken by her own revelation of what she had lived through. "I was hurt, insulted, and so ashamed, I couldn't tell anyone until now."

"And I felt trapped," Rupert screamed just as harshly in his own confession.

"Lizzy," Paige interceded, not knowing how she could stop this.

She had been on the receiving end of Rupert's gentle art of seduction, his paying great attention to detail as if his only purpose for existing was to study obsessively how to get women and keep all the relationships alive at once. Such philandering, such constructing the once dying breed of playboy with panache, required a lot of time and energy that would naturally exclude the desire to look after one's own child. Paige could not even fathom how Rupert found gusto to train and play football amid his extracurricular activities.

"Don't worry, Paige," Lizzy returned. "I'm sober. I've been sober long enough to pick out the three women he's enticed tonight already. Nothing's changed."

Three! Paige pondered in amazement, hardly believing she had missed a third person. "You're upset," she wavered, trying to place a consoling arm around her friend. "Let's go and sit down."

"You once told me you loved me." Lizzy pounced on Rupert again with venom, ignoring Paige's plea to calm down. "Then you left me to have your baby by myself. You didn't even come to the hospital to see her being born. You refused to visit afterward, even when I discreetly contacted your parents to tell them the good news. I can't imagine why they haven't tried to get in touch either, unless you told them it wasn't true. You don't even know what love is."

"And you would, wouldn't you?" Rupert mocked childishly. "So why now?"

"Because I read about your suspected engagement to Paige," Lizzy revealed.

"I never proposed to her," Rupert insisted.

"I know," Lizzy conceded, having been told the awful truth by Paige while they had wrapped up the arrangements for her party. "But it made me see clearly that you had forgotten about us, that the newspapers don't even know we exist. You hid us from everyone, and I'm going to make you pay for everything you've put me and your daughter through." Her threat was as steadfast as her refusal to spill one tear, though it was clear to everyone they were there behind the strength of her iron gaze.

"I . . . I—" Rupert stuttered, embarrassed by the umpteenth forewarning.

"Did not answer my letters, even though I'd been discreet," Lizzy interrupted sadly. "You fobbed me off with your publicists every time I called your club. If you think you've spent your life solely in the pursuit, capture, and attention of women, it won't be anything compared to the way I'm going to hound you. And by the time I'm done, the whole world is going to see you for what you are. Scum."

Rupert was not going to lie down and take his vilification. "You're not getting a penny out of me," he railed at the defamation.

"No, but your child will," Lizzy promised in an oath to herself. "I won't be silenced another year waiting for you to grow up. I'm going to have the CSA and a lawyer on your case."

"What do you want from me?" Rupert barked, his shock now worn to a tether.

"I want you to acknowledge you have a six-year-old daughter," Lizzy bellowed so loudly, the room echoed her pain.

"Yeah, right!" Rupert shot back, shrugging his shoulders.

What happened next took everyone by surprise. Lizzy's hand shot across the small expanse of space that separated her from Rupert and slapped him right in the face. He yelped at the pain caused by her nails. It sounded like a strip of leather against bare skin, and Paige was forced to cringe at the pitch the severe blow made.

"I hate you," Lizzy cursed raggedly, unashamed. "Don't you even want to know your child's name?"

"Lizzy!" Paige gasped again.

"For our daughter's sake, I want her to know you exist," Lizzy relented her sorrow on a much calmer note, not surprised Rupert had chosen not to retaliate, "even though you'll probably try to treat her the same way you've treated every woman in your life." Lizzy was shaking with emotion. "She has your name on her birth certificate—I saw to that, and I'm going to damn well make sure she knows who to call Daddy."

"Come on, let's break this up," Gwerfyl interrupted, sympathetic to Rupert's predicament. At fifty-six, discretion was still her forte in life and the hush-hush atmosphere surrounding Lizzy's altercation was a matter she considered involved the two people concerned and not an issue to ruin her daughter's big night. "This is a party. Let's get it on."

"I'll get you another drink," Rhys told Paige, seeing how commensurately astounded she had become.

Rupert was suddenly startled at seeing the harmful effects his past life had created to change the mood. "I'm sorry," he told Paige, relieved that the DJ had been instructed to start playing some party tracks pronto and that Paige's guests were beginning to disseminate. Everyone was instantly encouraged to dance and put the event behind them. Facing Lizzy, disturbed by the scratch that was visible on his chin after the blow she had given him, and flinging his hands into the air, he added quite cynically, "So whassup? Let's talk."

If Paige had thought revenge would be sweet, that she could actually see Rupert King squirm without going to the trouble of finishing the job herself, it did not feel so now.

"I feel sorry for him," she later confided to Rhys when her party was over and the final guests had left. They were seated in Aunt Elva's dining room, at the table where lay all her presents, which she had decided she would open in the morning. The time was 3:30 A.M. and Paige was tired.

"You're sorry for him because I suspect at one time he had power over you," Rhys returned with his internal wisdom.

"I thought he did," Paige admitted. She trained her eyes on Rhys and told him with sincere honesty, "Once upon a time, I liked him. I can see you already know that."

He nodded.

"He's the kind of guy who's reluctant to commit, but would gladly allow a woman to have his baby," Paige said quite absently. "I didn't even know he knew Lizzy Chadwick." Her eyes narrowed. "She also said something before she left about Francine."

"Are you trying to tell me something?" Rhys asked, confused.

"What?"

"Have you slept with either of those two men?"

"What two men?"

"Rupert King."

"No!" Paige told him emphatically.

"And your boss?" he asked.

"No!"

"Then why did he look at you like that when he left?"

"It's a house I'm trying to sell at Holland Park," Paige tact-

Accepting the four introductory books for FREE (plus $1.99 to offset the cost of shipping & handling) places you under no obligation to buy anything. You may keep the books and return the shipping statement marked "cancelled". If you do not cancel, about a month later we will send 4 additional Arabesque novels, and you will be billed the preferred subscriber's price of just $4.00 per title. That's $16.00* for all 4 books for a savings of almost 40% off the cover price (Plus $1.99 for shipping and handling). You may cancel at any time, but if you choose to continue, every month we'll send you 4 more books, which you may either purchase at the preferred discount price. . . or return to us and cancel your subscription.

* PRICES SUBJECT TO CHANGE

THE ARABESQUE ROMANCE CLUB: HERE'S HOW IT WORKS

PLACE
STAMP
HERE

THE ARABESQUE ROMANCE BOOK CLUB
P.O. BOX 5214
CLIFTON NJ 07015-5214

fully deviated. "I haven't clinched a buyer." She paused. "I'm sorry about Rupert."

"Why are we still talking about him?" Rhys asked her, annoyed. "Wouldn't you rather I were kissing you right now?"

His voice was as soothing as a lick of golden syrup when he bent forward and took her lips. Suddenly Paige was consumed by a passion she had never known before. She closed her eyes and gave herself over to the contemplation of her birthday wish. She had longed for this, that they share a kiss alone without prying eyes. Rhys's inquisitive tongue began licking the base of her lips with a light flicking motion that had Paige squealing with delight until she coaxed him to take more of her mouth into his.

He obliged her, too. They kissed like two fervent animals. Nipping, licking, panting, devouring . . . There seemed no end to this kiss. Paige felt as though her heart had burst forth from her rib cage and slammed into the very column of male flesh that was breathing erratically next to her. She was electrified. Her blood flow quickened, her pulse raced, a deeply intense feeling throbbed between her legs. And still the kissing did not stop. At any moment, she felt sure she would be swallowed whole.

The tongue delved deeper and twisted against her own. He nibbled her lips until they pulsated. Paige lost all thoughts of sanity as her breath was pulled from her mouth and taken into Rhys's. This man wanted her and she knew it. He was kissing her in a way that eloquently told Paige he knew what he wanted to happen next. For now, he just wanted to kiss her. And it was all good. She liked his breed. All male, soulful dark eyes, perfectly sculptured teeth, the rangy smell of his lust for her, and especially those large pink lips that were so invitingly kissable, she could not bear to tear her mouth away. Yet she had to gasp for breath.

"Come here, you ravenous vixen," Rhys panted, retaking her lips.

His hands roamed. His fingers caressed. He inquisitively

traced an invisible line down her neck to her collarbone while their lips, still locked, rotated a sensual motion that signified a much deeper stirring. It was so deliciously erotic, Paige thought she would melt on the spot. And then, suddenly, she was left bereft when he removed his mouth and stroked a heady finger across her cheek.

"I have a present for you," Rhys told her, reaching into his jacket pocket.

Paige's heart was still thumping madly when she was presented with a green box, embossed with the word SOTHEBY'S on the front. She had no idea what was inside, only that it appeared slightly weighty, looked expensive, and had been acquired at auction. Paige gazed at Rhys, finding a smile on his face as he urged her to open it. When she did so, she was surprised to find, embedded in lashes of yellow satin, the most adorable six-inch stone statuette she had ever laid her eyes on.

"It's an official nineteenth-dynasty," Rhys added, pointing at the date detail that had been inserted into the box. "Excavated in 1950, and I happen to be told on good authority it once belonged to the goddess Aset, who was renamed Isis."

Tears welded Paige's eyes as she recalled this being the moniker she had used on the Internet when they met. She gasped, unable to take her eyes off the tiny Egyptian artifact, notably once carved with such verisimilitude as to pass for true beauty. It had suffered some erosion, but the stone was marginally still intact, and was etched into an adorable maiden on her knees with her arms folded and hands clasped together as though in prayer. She had painted wings folded around her body, the fantasy of a tomb angel or priestess perhaps, Paige discerned from the slightly chipped headwear on the maiden's head. It was old, but had worn well over the centuries, and she would find it a suitable place by her bed.

"Such handiwork and hardly marred." She transferred her gaze to Rhys. "It's beautiful." *You're beautiful,* she mused, starry-eyed. "You've been a good friend."

Rhys smiled. "It still retains all its original pigmentation, too," he continued in explanation. "I think there's a legend to this piece. I need to look into it, but it is said whoever owns it will find true love until old age."

Paige nodded like an amiable priestess. "I can see why," she said, before realizing the implication of what Rhys had just said. When the significance of it filtered, her eyes widened in surety. "You gave this to me because you want me to find such a love?"

"Only if you want it," Rhys answered with noble reverence.

Paige leaned forward and kissed his nose. "I do."

"Then show me this house in Holland Park on Monday," he told her on a decisive note, knowing he wanted their relationship to move beyond friendship. "Because if you want me to stay, I'll stay."

Eight

Paige was drifting on a cloud when she awoke from her hazy dream. *I wish I could be with Rhys Langston forever more.* That had been her birthday wish. As she rolled over, the body lying next to her roused her attention.

His short, slick black hair was slightly ruffled, his smooth, golden-brown complexion now needed a shave, and his mocha-colored eyes were shut, closing him off to the world. Paige smiled, reminding herself that she had invited Rhys to stay the night. Aunt Elva had giggled most jovially as she had watched them tiptoe upstairs before departing herself. Paige was mindful that her entire family were in the guest rooms down the hall, and would, no doubt, want a report on whether she was happy with her new beau.

She dared not touch him, but Paige wanted to. He had gone to sleep the moment his head hit the pillow, and she had cuddled up next to him and slept, too. But it was now 6:30 A.M. and her body was beginning to speak in a way it had never done before. Paige closed her eyes and breathed deeply, desperately attempting to quell the bout of tension. What woman could deny herself a sense of arousal when such a sexy body was lying next her? And Paige was not beyond comprehension of such denial.

When she opened her eyes and was suddenly met with the wild yearning demand from the soulful eyes that were now open and facing her, her sexual awakening spiraled. Paige could not help herself. She leaned forward and stole those very pink luscious male lips that had danced around in her dreams like a wild fantasy until she had awakened, wanting them pressed against her own.

And now that they were, Paige was lost in a world of ecstasy. The real world disappeared the instant their lips met. It was magic. Sheer bliss. Rhys was alive in front of her, fired up and ready to be adulterated. His kiss deepened and his eyes closed, and Paige felt a renewed sense of excitement course through her veins. It was the certainty that they were going to make love. It was knowing that it was going to happen that very morning that made Paige unable to curtail the rising fever at the pit of her stomach.

I wonder if you're as wild in bed as you look raced through her mind. She had thought this on kissing Rhys for the first time at Heathrow Airport. And as he kissed her now, Paige almost felt arrogant in her yearning to discover whether her suspicion of him would prove to be true. That this man's untamed, passionate nature was due to the hunger he had for her, to take her, dig deep into her, and force her to scream his name.

Paige sighed as her head sunk into her pillow, weighed down by Rhys at her side, his playful lips now taking full possession. His tongue delved deep, craving to taste more. His appetite seemed heightened by Paige's favorable response. He liked that in her, that she was keeping pace. Urging him on until he felt himself rise with ardent need. Her tongue was like a whip, lashing his teeth, gently flogging his inner mouth, binding itself to his until he knew not whose tongue was whose.

And Rhys loved it. He loved this woman's sense of sexual fun. It turned him on like nothing he had imagined could ever have done. And he was a man who could not deny he had spent some wild days in his youth. But this woman was different. Paige's animalistic mysticism redefined anything he had known. And she was baiting him with that same aura. She knew how to do it, too. Nipping his ear, licking his chin, sweetly biting his neck.

In an instant, Rhys had rolled over and was on top of her. Paige was dressed in a flimsy nightdress and he had slept in his underpants, but right now he wanted to rip away both impediments. But not yet. He wanted to just watch . . . see . . . savor . . . the fire dancing in Paige's eyes. It was for him. All for him. He was smitten that such desire could exist in a woman who wanted him so.

Paige was incited by the male dominance that gripped her. Rhys had lifted her hands over her head and laced his strong thick fingers through hers. An aggressive excitement shot through her like a bullet. And he saw it, too. Paige saw his eyes widen, watched as his wicked smile deepened, and then her heart melted as he waited. Simply waited until their eyes locked . . . and the heat singed between them like a flicker in the air. . . .

Tears rose into her eyes. Rhys lowered his head and kissed each eye in turn. Gently brushing his soft wet lips across each lid, and then down to her cheek, until he felt her entire body rise up to welcome him. He assaulted her mouth with delicious fury. Paige was shaken by the sheer magnitude of it. No one had ever kissed her like this before. No one. This was what she had waited for. Not the flippant meeting of bodies with someone who could never care for her, but a soulful bonding of body and mind, where emotional feelings could overflow to abundance. This was such a union.

And Paige could hardly believe it was happening to her. She had gone on the Internet to find someone who would help her come to grips with the advent of her birthday, and instead had found what was seemingly turning out to be the love of her life. Could birthday wishes come true? If so, the best was yet to come. But for now, all Paige wanted was to be even closer to her omega, for she indeed was his alpha, *ad finem*.

They kissed until they were bruised, and then Rhys felt the urgency to venture and sample what was his for the taking. His fingers began the slow exploration while their lips, still locked, kept the momentum as he moved along Paige's thighs to her panty line. He pulled at the lacy fabric until it felt taut and rigid, before releasing it against the soft, satiny brown skin that bore a burnished arousal beneath its honeyed complexion.

Paige wriggled beneath Rhys's touch, aware that his soft fingers wanted to delve further to where her need was at its strongest. She wanted more. The hunger was strong to feel those very fingers against her naked flesh. But as she looked at Rhys and their gazes held, it was clear they were both aware of something. It was too early in their relationship for such intimacy. Though they were clearly enjoying each other and wanted to take their emotions further, both instinctively knew that there would be a better time and a better place. That their minds had not yet gelled and if they were to pursue this, something could be ruined that would not be so easily repaired.

And so when Paige felt the soft, final kiss Rhys pressed against her collarbone, she knew. He wanted to wait. In the most uncanny of circumstances, she could have felt disappointed. But Paige saw the glimmer in those deep soulful brown eyes. It told her that Rhys was a man who respected his physical needs and was discerning about whom he shared them with. It spoke volumes to her about his self-worth as a person, and she touched his cheek, knowing—as a woman—she shared that same feeling of self-worth, too. She would indeed be worth the wait.

"Good morning." She smiled wickedly, her heart thudding madly.

He touched her lips with a shaky finger. "I must remember to say good morning more often, Miss Wonky Tooth."

"Hey, less of that." Paige elbowed him.

"I like it," Rhys told her, not having noted the slight misalignment before.

They both chuckled, and he rolled over and snuggled beside her. It was true amity personified, holding each other, savoring the climb down of their emotions to a more sated stage. "Enjoyed your party?" he asked.

Paige nodded, hardly believing she had invited him to stay the night. "I don't know what my family is going to think. On second thought, yes, I do actually." She sighed.

"Will they mind?" Rhys was concerned. He rubbed a consoling finger against her right ear.

"Be shocked probably," Paige admitted, taking ahold of one of Rhys's hands and squeezing it affectionately. "They've never seen me this reckless before. It must be because I'm thirty."

"There's a lot of advantages to being thirty," Rhys told her, kissing her forehead. "You can now think about taking out a pension."

"Don't tease me." Paige laughed, snuggling deeper into the warmth of him.

"Seriously," Rhys ventured, thrilled at how soft she felt next to him. "Don't you have one?"

Paige giggled. "I think pensions are fine for most people. They're part of our system and reflect the insecurity of our collective consciousness, but I don't believe in them. I can make any amount of money. All I have to do is sell and own property."

"And you have property?" Rhys asked, casting her a brief inquiring gaze.

Paige felt her body quiver as their eyes met, and was stirred to clench his hand tighter. "Not yet," she answered truthfully. "But I am thinking of buying houses as investments and renting them out."

Rhys quietly absorbed the information. He in fact owned a house in Monaco that cost two million and was now worth three. Of course, it was information he wanted to tell Paige, but not yet. There were certain aspects of his life he wanted to retain until he knew for sure that this woman could like him for who he was as a person, and not someone with a fat wallet attached.

"That's a good idea," he acknowledged with a wry smile. "And in your business, you should do quite well."

"I intend to," Paige ventured, her heart shaken by his grin.

"As soon as I buy into the realty agency and become a fully fledged partner."

"You're very ambitious," Rhys noted, a business tone now attached to his voice.

"In this day and age, a girl has to be," Paige told him. "It's too risky for a woman to rely on marriage to provide her with everything. It's no longer a guarantee."

Rhys's antenna rose to the bait. "When we first chatted on the Internet," he reminded her, "I suspected you were a person swamped with gender vulnerability. How does a man break through that?"

Paige's eyes widened. She did not understand. "What do you mean?" she wavered.

"You don't want to be dependent on a man for anything, it's as simple as that," he concluded. "To merge with someone is a frightening prospect to you. Why?"

"Because . . . because . . ." Paige hated the shift in the conversation. "It doesn't work."

"What doesn't?"

"Marriage."

"And you know, do you?"

"Yes, I do."

"How?" Rhys taunted.

"Because I just do."

"No, you don't."

"I do," Paige insisted.

"Then tell me." It was a demand.

"Because my parents are divorced," Paige blurted out.

Rhys was silenced. He raised his head and looked across at Paige. He could feel her attempting to distance herself from him beneath the sheets, and immediately clasped his hand around her waistline. The soft flimsy fabric of her nightdress tickled against his fingers, making him aware that beneath the fabric were the shaking nerves of a woman who had, perhaps for the first time in her life, revealed some inner truth.

"How old were you when it happened?" he asked her quietly.

"Fifteen." Paige closed her eyes and desperately fought back the pain.

"And?" Rhys asked, sensing more.

"They've lived a lie ever since." She sighed deeply. "You saw them last night. All happy and all smiles. But right now, they're in separate rooms. At breakfast, they'll put on an act of togetherness, but when they leave, Mum will be going home alone and Dad will be going back to *her*."

"His new wife?"

"His mistress," Paige confirmed. "But he still has a room at home, in Nottingham," she went on, refusing to allow the tears to build. "We moved there from Wales, where I was born. As a teenager, I was confused. You see, in our family, understandings are reached. There was no sitting down with us children and explaining the situation. It's a united front for the grandchildren. Penny tolerates it, but I still find it very hard. That's why when I was eighteen I came to live with Aunt Elva. She's a romantic fool really."

The cynicism was not intentionally aimed, but Rhys felt the sting of it all the same. He saw Paige as a woman who was afraid to acknowledge the separation that had occurred. That her parents had lost touch with her life in a way she had not been able to admit to herself. That such childhood memories had left her feeling so insecure, she needed someone lest she would be alone at her own birthday party. It was all making sense to him now. Paige needed to draw out the best sense of herself.

"I think your aunt has a spirited heart," he acknowledged, sensitive to the mood that cascaded through them both. "I think she'd like you to have the same."

"How can I when—"

"The hunter shouldn't lie with the prey." Rhys repeated the earlier remark she had made when they had been seated at Elva's dinner table. "You're lying with me now, in your bed," he reminded her, gently squeezing her waistline until he felt her quake beneath his fingers.

Paige felt her face redden as blood rushed into her cheeks.

Had they not paused to savor the moment for another day . . . She closed her eyes, dismissing the sweet, blissful moment from her mind. She felt Rhys's brief kiss across her lips and the stabbing urge between her legs. Paige longed for him to touch her there, but suddenly felt vulnerable and weakened that Rhys should now know how really frightened she was. How she saw herself as a woman who aspired to be loved, but did not want the heartache of believing she could sustain such a love only to have her partner leave her, as was the fate of her mother.

"I'm wondering whether I've made a mistake," she muttered, looking deeply into Rhys's eyes, hoping to dear God that she would see something there to give her hope.

"You haven't made a mistake," Rhys whispered against her lips, ensnaring her with such a meaningful gaze, he felt another shudder beneath his fingers. "I want you and I'm going to stick around until you realize how much you want me."

He was so self-assured, Paige hardly knew how to react except to kiss Rhys again. He put his arm around her and held her close. With her head nestled into the nook of his shoulder, Rhys closed his eyes.

"You remind me," he began, "of home."

"Monaco?"

"No, Leland, where I was born."

Paige immediately raised her head from his shoulder. "Oh?"

"Everyone's childhood sucks on some level," Rhys continued, turning his head slightly to throw Paige a misty gaze.

"What was yours like?" Paige asked, fascinated, replacing her head back into the nook of his shoulder.

"I remember my father's radio repair shop and my mother cooking black-eyed peas, greens, and cornbread on Sundays," Rhys began, running a finger down Paige's arm. "And her wooden house which once belonged to my grandmother." He sighed. "My mother used to work the tenant farm that my grandmother owned when she was younger, and on Saturdays, she would turn the kitchen stove to making money by hot-combing people's hair."

Paige exhaled a hot breath. "When was the last time you saw her?"

"When I was twenty," Rhys confessed, his finger now tickling Paige's neck. "She had diabetes, and two strokes had worn her out before she died. The house got taken over by her cousin, who sold the furniture and kept the money. My brother had just graduated from high school and we didn't know what else to do, so we went northeast to New York."

"What did you both do there?" Paige croaked, shifting uncomfortably as a deep tingle began to invade her system like an epidemic.

"My brother Clyde started work as a short-order cook and immediately met a girl." Rhys chuckled, hugging Paige closer. "They have five children—all girls. Me, I had ambitions to make money, and began working for a pensions and insurance company."

"What happened to your father?" Paige rasped, curious.

Rhys's hand stilled and he grimaced. "He died, too. He was shot. That's how my mother got her first stroke."

Paige heard the resonance in his tone, and instantly knew that whatever had happened, it was bad. She also suspected Rhys did not want to talk about it. In the recesses of her mind, she tried to conjure what little knowledge she had about Mississippi. She decided the place probably still represented a backlog of history: the Black Codes, Jim Crow laws, and lynchings. If there was one area of her life where she felt deep, fundamental regret, it was the whole issue of race. She knew what it was like being on the receiving end of prejudice, and realized that although she and Rhys were cut from a different cloth, their characters were shaped in a similar pattern.

"But you have memories of him?" she probed, gently placing a consoling hand on his stomach.

"He was someone who worried constantly about providing for his family," Rhys recalled, making soft feather strokes with his fingers on Paige's temple. "Not a penny was wasted.

He would switch off every light in an empty room because he hated wasting electricity. I needed a role model to progress, which was why I liked my Uncle John. He was the richest person in our family."

Like Aunt Elva, Paige mused. "What was he like?" she asked, relaxing to the soothing rhythm of Rhys's fingers against her forehead.

"He owned a barbershop," Rhys explained with a determined edge to his voice, which took on a more pronounced Southern American tone. "I used to glean everything from him about making money. He got that shop by picking up scrap paper and selling it to the scrap merchants. He hustled and worked hard, and that was an ethic which stuck with me."

"What was your father's name?" Paige inquired, chagrined to find herself feeling much closer to Rhys than at any time since their first meeting.

"William," he told her in recollection. "I was given it as a middle name. My mother's name was Bea."

"Do you still think about your parents?" Paige probed, her deepening emotions encouraging her to rub a compassionate hand across Rhys's stomach, soothing the ache, abating the pain, while her head noted what the W represented in his full name.

"I wonder what they'd think of me now," Rhys answered, unsure. "I don't think they'd understand what I've achieved. If my father was here, he'd still be going around switching off all the lights."

Paige chuckled lightly. "I remember my father applying for a higher position at the engineering company where he worked," she commented on reflection, knowing that issues had been far easier in England. "He was very disappointed when he didn't get the job. When he asked why, he was told that the union members weren't ready for a black foreman. Ten years later, after applying for it the first time, he got the job. It's nice to see that progress has been made now, but we haven't established a paradigm."

"Will we ever?" Rhys inquired forlornly. "Here maybe. In Mississippi, I don't know."

Paige could see that Rhys had bridged some emotional distance between his earlier life and the life he lived now. Although time might have shifted, she imagined how hard it must have been for him to move beyond the pain of the wounds he had endured. To shut down a part of memory that was still riddled with the bad times of history was not easy for anyone, and she wondered whether this had some bearing on his work.

"I'm wondering if what you went through in Mississippi is what has made you interested in researching black history," Paige guessed, turning the subject.

Rhys's hand stilled on her brows for one brief moment. "It's a hobby," he admitted, smiling wryly. "Do you not believe me?"

"We met on the Internet." Paige chuckled, not wishing to tell him that she had run his name through the search engines. "You could be telling me just about anything."

"I'm a mad ax murderer." Rhys giggled at the reminder.

"Did I really say that?" Paige said, appalled she could ever have been so suspicious of such a handsome man.

"You were being careful," Rhys assured her, hugging her to him once more. "I like that about you. It tells me you wouldn't have just run off with anyone."

Paige smiled at the reassurance. "Only you."

She earned a soft kiss against her lips for that remark before Rhys sighed. "Actually, what I used to do was sell insurance and pensions on a commission basis, and I worked my way up," he began in explanation. "There was a scandal at my company. I didn't want to get involved, so I came here to London and met up with an acquaintance who I had met in New York on one of his financial visits, and began working for him."

"And then what?" Paige breathed, her senses reawakened and trembling at the power of his kiss.

"We made good investments in various company stocks,"

Rhys told her, his voice husky and gruff. "We also took risks which I wouldn't take now. I hustled with the big boys on higher stakes than my Uncle John. It's the same game as selling scrap paper. Then I set up my own venture capital company to fund projects of my own interests. My excavation in Egypt is one such personal interest area."

"I was just curious," Paige said, apologetic.

"It's okay," he responded, planting a kiss against one of her eyelids, piqued that he should be telling her so much. "I've been funding my personal interests for sometime, which include African diasporic studies, African archaeology, and anthropological research in Africa and America."

Paige was absorbed, and began to make circle motions with her fingers around his navel. "Which was the most exciting for you?"

Rhys relaxed and sucked in a ragged breath. "Providing the necessary line of credit that my friend, Dr. Darren Warrington of the University of Florida, needed to complete his research for his current book about the black Seminoles. It's about the discovery of Peliklakaha, where slaves gained their freedom before the Civil War."

"He must be very grateful," Paige said, recalling having seen the name when she had run a search for Rhys's credentials on the Web.

"He's a very dedicated man." Rhys looked at the bedside clock. "And as much as I'd like to continue this discussion, I'm going to have to love you and leave you."

Paige stared at the clock. It read 7:34 A.M. "You have to go now?"

"Sorry, sweetheart." Rhys planted a kiss on her forehead, fearing that if he stayed in bed a moment longer with this desert princess, she would soon be finding herself out of her nightdress. "I have things to do."

He pulled back the sheets and jumped out. Paige sucked in an amorous breath as she caught sight of his strong chiseled torso, the sturdy build of his thighs and legs, the soft dark curly hair on his chest, which she had failed to run her hands through, and more ardently, the bulge that protruded from his underpants. A tremor danced along her limbs. God, Rhys Langston was gorgeous. She jumped out of bed on his trail.

"Let me at least make you breakfast," she tempted, running up behind him to wrap her arms around his waistline. She kissed his back, then pressed her warm cheek against it. "I can make a very good fry-up."

Rhys turned in her arms and faced her. Paige looked so adorable, he wanted nothing more than to return back to her bed. "I have some work to catch up on and phone calls to make. Why don't I call you tomorrow to take a look at that property in Holland Park. After then, we can do lunch."

"Sounds like a great idea." Paige smiled, feeling another flutter run down her limbs.

Rhys looked deeply into her midnight-blue eyes and kissed her again. "You're on."

Nine

"Have you slept with him yet?" Blanton Blake demanded on entering Paige's office at precisely 10:44 A.M., finding her seated at her desk. He appeared unsettled and a little nervy, and Paige's eyebrows rose as she watched him close her office door.

He was dressed in his usual formal manner, but his tie was slightly askew, indicating he had already undergone a busy morning. With the fresh burst of spring just around the corner, the property market would soon see a new influx of houses ready to be placed for sale or to let. Paige knew that with the advent of March, the increase in workload would be a testing period for them both. Nonetheless, that did not mean her boss should delve into her personal life to take his frustration out on her, no matter how close they had become as friends.

"I don't think that's any of your business," Paige relented immediately, squeezing the pencil she held in her right hand between her fine-boned fingers.

After staring at the stone statuette Rhys had given her until her eyes begged for mercy, she had dressed that morning in a pink flimsy dress, and complimentary mauve-colored mules, to bolster the renewed feelings of hope that had uplifted her since Rhys had departed her aunt's house before breakfast the day before. He had saved her the embarrassment of explaining events to her family, who had thrown her a mixture of pensive, curious, and excited glances while she downed orange juice, toast, and scrambled eggs.

Her new rekindled spirit had sustained throughout the day and was carried in the sway of her brown hair, was reflected in the way her makeup was so decisively applied—a touch of pink above her eyes, brown brows and eyelids, lushes of gloss to her lips—and played across the smile on her lips, which would signify to the most lay of persons that she was thoroughly happy. Only one person saw differently.

"You ought to know better," Blanton counteracted, seating himself among the cushions in her sofa, "especially after parading around with him at your party."

Paige slammed down her pencil. "Just exactly what is your problem?" she argued in a venomous tone, her euphoria suddenly thrust into suspension. She was a woman who considered herself virtuous to some extent, and she now wondered what he saw. "Ever since I found Rhys Langston, you've been nothing more than a splinter in my brain persuading me that I should not attempt to find love wherever I can find it. Luckily, things happened to have worked out for Rhys and me, and you can't even be happy for me."

"I'm not happy for you because you know nothing about this man," Blanton chided, schooling his charcoal-colored eyes in her direction. "He could be a totally unscrupulous character and you're none the wiser."

"I know he's planning to stay in England," Paige expanded. "He told me so. In fact . . ." She stared at the brochure in front of her before throwing Blanton her most arrogant midnight-blue gaze. "He's put in an offer for that house at Holland Park. I've contacted the vendor this morning and will be taking him out for viewing just before lunch."

Blanton's face registered a high level of shock. "He's yanking your chain," he mustered with a snort. "That house costs a whisker just under two million. Where does he have that kind of money?"

"If he didn't have it, he wouldn't be viewing, now would he?" Paige snapped back, the thought now occurring to her that Blanton did have a point. She had not considered it before, such was her joy that Rhys had decided to buy somewhere to live in London so they could be together, but now the dawning question as to where the money was coming from was beginning to sink in.

"And you believe he's really going to buy it?" came Blanton's retaliatory remark.

"I'm sure he has adequate finances to cover his offer," Paige defended. "He is a client and as his realty agent, I have to treat him as such."

"You know," Blanton began harshly, "I thought you were a better person than this. I actually believed you were responsible enough to become a partner at this firm. Instead, I'm finding you're on some flight of fancy with a man who is successfully convincing you that he has a place in your life. When are you going to wake up?"

Paige was stunned. She did not expect Blanton Blake to understand any of her motives for attempting to find a suitable lover in her life. He had already stated as much when he had caught her logging online. His suggestion that she was living a fantasy, an adventure that would surely run its course until the bitter end, had her blood heated to a frenzy.

"Get out of my office," she blazed.

Blanton's eyes widened. "Don't get bitter with me," he said, faintly shocked. "It's unbecoming."

"Really?" Paige chided, his remark adding more fuel to her fire. "I'll tell you what's indecorous. It was having to listen to the indiscreet, improper, and offensive remarks you made to me and Rhys Langston at my party on Saturday. He happened to be my guest, not yours. And you and Rupert King did nothing but try to ruin the night for me."

"I'm only trying to look out for you," Blanton related wildly. "You're insecure right now and—"

"Spare me the lecture," Paige interrupted, finding herself searching her desk for a suitable object she could clutch onto.

"You don't know what goes on in my head, but you would like to think that you do. All I've ever heard from you is how *you* want me to conduct my life. I believe you'd like to see me end up an old spinster."

"That's not true." Blanton rose to his feet, arrogantly throwing down a lilac-colored cushion in the process. "I just want you to take your head out of the clouds."

"How dare you," Paige fumed, reaching for her filing tray, which was full of papers, and throwing the entire ensemble across the room. "I'm wide awake. My feet are firmly on the ground. I have no illusions about what is going on here. What do you take me for?"

Blanton dodged the flying mass of items, shaken by the mad fluster he could see on Paige's face. He had not seen her this angry before. This side of Paige Alexander was seemingly a surprise to him. "What the hell—"

"You should concentrate on your own relationship," Paige ranted, snapping up a tube filled with pens and pencils from her desktop. "Poor Latanya must've been wondering what you were playing at. Does she know?"

"What do you think?" Blanton railed. "I'm breathing, aren't I?"

"Not for long if I have anything to do with it," Paige threatened. "I saw her face on Saturday, so sort your own affairs and leave me alone with mine."

"Paige!"

"And if I want to sleep with Rhys Langston," she continued, unabashed and amazed she had survived her party unscathed, with nothing having actually gone wrong—not affecting *her* anyway, "I will."

"Let him use you if that's what you want," Blanton yelled with jealousy. "See if I care."

"He's already pipped you to the post," Paige bragged, sucking in a deep breath at the heady recollection that they had nearly made love. "So you needn't worry."

"There's a word in my country for a woman like you,"

Blanton objected with resentful scorn, "but I'd rather not say it."

"Get out," Paige rasped, and for good effect, she threw the damned tube.

"It's all going to end in ashes," Blanton taunted.

"And don't count on me becoming a business partner at this firm either," Paige blazed.

Africans, she seethed, forcing the tears back as Blanton left in a huff. So much for friendship. Theirs had just ended. It had all gone horribly wrong now. There was no restraint, no halfhearted caution, no vestige of discretion in their words. Her stomach was now filled with knots as she thought how best she could make herself immune to the ineluctable assault that was sure to follow in the days ahead.

Paige sighed miserably and gazed at the chaos she had created across her office floor. Paper littered the carpet, pencils were scattered, and her innards were in an equal state of dishevelment. It now seemed possible to her that Francine was right. Blanton had harbored feelings for her, feelings that they had never shared in spite of her own crush on him. Though she could not stifle her joy that she had now met Rhys Langston, she could scarcely expect Blanton Blake to share it. Had he been more forthcoming, had he not so easily taken Latanya Folasade and proposed marriage, then perhaps her mood would not have swung so readily toward Rhys.

Was it cruel? Not really. He had moved on and so had she. What did he expect, after all? She blinked, and the tears dissipated as Paige assured herself that this transient unpleasant period would soon pass. They were all grown adults. Rupert had his cross to bear, Blanton no doubt had his with the task of repairing whatever damage he had created with his fiancée, and she could indulge in her wonderful affair with Rhys Langston. The game was now over. Set and match. And that, she told herself, was that.

"I see your temper has been played out on someone today."

The sudden greeting took Paige completely by surprise as Rhys Langston entered through her office door.

Paige was on her knees, on the floor, picking up the over-spill caused by her little altercation with Blanton Blake minutes before. As she turned her head, she found Rhys looking quite handsome in a pair of tailored blue trousers, a black knit jersey, and black blazer-cut jacket, towering above her. It was casual enough for spending the day browsing through a house, but not quite the model of a tycoon she would expect could afford a near-two-million property. Embarrassed, Paige rose to her feet, her heart skipping a beat.

"My boss," she scorned, shedding her sated fury.

"What'd he do?" Rhys probed, concerned, enjoying the view in front of him.

"Accepted my rejection of his partnership offer," Paige slurred in partial truth, "not that it bothers me any."

"So you've decided against it?"

"You were right," Paige exclaimed, walking over to her desk to place the items in her hand on the desktop. "It's not a validated investment."

"I'm sorry."

"I'm not." She seated herself. "How did you find me?"

"I rang your mobile," Rhys proclaimed, looking at her dead center between the eyes as he faced her from across her desk. "Your Aunt Elva picked up and gave me details on how to get here."

Paige sighed, feeling her body tremble beneath Rhys's steady gaze as she realized she had left her personal mobile phone on the kitchen table. "I'd forget my head if it wasn't screwed on," she intoned lightly. She rose out of her chair and reached for her jacket behind it. "Let's go."

"Wait a minute." Rhys restrained her as she came around the desk, and forced her to face him. "Are you all right?"

His soulful eyes presented a more smoldering effect to her, and Paige was at a loss as to how she could begin. Since meeting Rhys, everything felt as if it had spiraled out of control. She had thought she could multi-task three men—make one jealous, teach another a lesson, and make do with one for her party. It all seemed so childish and wrong now. It was not a case that anything was broken, that she felt herself to be a bad person. Paige's shift in mood from being ecstatically happy to being unsure of herself had more to do with what she considered to be her true ethics and principles in life.

"I'm feeling out of sorts," she told him in typical English.

"The big Three O," Rhys surmised. "Your youth hasn't separated from maturity, you know. You're just as gorgeous as you were when I last saw you."

Paige felt the blood rush into her face as Rhys took ahold of her hand and pulled her toward him. The last time they had seen each other was in her bedroom, where they had kissed and cuddled and talked until she finally waved goodbye to him at the front door. It all still felt like a dream too real to be true, and Paige was beginning to think she needed time for intense morbid reflection on whether it could all go wrong, too.

"Do you like me?" Her question was sudden and unescapable.

Rhys was shocked to hear it. "Of course I like you," he gushed, moving a strand of hair away from Paige's face. "I'm here, aren't I?"

For how long? Paige quietly panicked. "I know you're here," she accepted, running a reassuring finger along his shoulder, "but . . . well, I was wondering, do online relationships really work? You see, I've been thinking—"

"You've been thinking too much," Rhys interrupted wryly, dismissing Paige's fears. "Do you know what the most difficult truth to uncover is?" He held her midnight-blue gaze until he felt sunk in the pool of Paige's glare. "To know thyself."

Paige felt her heart tremor with expectation. She could not speak. All she became aware of was Rhys's lips as they met hers. She was smothered with something that went beyond tender. Paige knew not how to define the way in which Rhys was kissing her. It was gentle . . . provoking . . . considerate . . . arousing . . . kind . . . tempting . . . Her legs were weakened on the spot by the intensity of it.

She closed her eyes and acceded to his every wish. Rhys's arms closed around her waist, and her own arms rose up to lock his neck between them. Paige's fingers tickled the soft hair at Rhys's nape as she, too, kissed him in earnest. She caught his breath in her mouth and savored it, felt his tongue lick against her own and reveled in it, took the full pressure of his lips pressed against her own until, finally, they both gasped for air.

"You know how to kiss," Rhys panted heavily.

"That's reassuring." Paige giggled on a hoarsely breath.

"C'mon," Rhys encouraged. "Just imagine what the fourteen year old you would think of you now."

"She'd have certain reservations," Paige murmured.

Rhys laughed. "Let's go and take a look at this house," he suggested, dropping a brief kiss on her nose. "Then I'll take you to lunch, as promised."

He smiled, and Paige's heart was uplifted.

"Do I need to hire a private detective to vet my potential neighbors?" Rhys joked as they departed the taxi and he threw a careful eye at the imposing house in front of him.

Paige returned the chuckle. "Hardly necessary," she assured. "The vendor is a Jordanian-born property developer who has an Islamic art collection worth at least one hundred million. He bought this property seven years ago and has spent a lot of money refurbishing. If it was good enough for him, then it's worth a look." She reached for the key as they embarked the steps that led to the front door.

"Why is he selling?" Rhys queried curiously.

"It's not because of the neighbors," Paige claimed, convincing him. "He's recently purchased a much larger property at Kensington Palace Gardens, once the former Egyptian embassy. His neighbors have now elevated to King Fahd of Saudi Arabia and the Sultan of Brunei."

"Snobbish vendor," Rhys rebutted.

"I'd say," Paige agreed. She opened the front door and entered the three-story whitewashed house. "It's west eleven and quite enchanting."

Rhys followed behind and looked around. "It looks bigger on the outside."

"That's because we take our photographs at an angle of twenty degrees so you think you're looking at something bigger," Paige explained, tapping the brochure Rhys held in his hand. "It's a trade secret."

"I can see you're quite skilled at your job," Rhys admired. "What else do I need to know?"

"We haven't overvalued to create an urgency, though that is common practice." Paige chuckled on a serious note. "But there are two other clients who have placed offers. One's for the asking price and another is just a shade over. The vendor is looking to close the deal, and I think he'd rather it was more than a shade over the asking price."

"So I have to outbid the highest offer?" Rhys probed, narrowing his brows.

"If you really like it." Paige smiled, then added, "And provided you can afford it."

Rhys brows lifted. "Oh?"

"Under anti-money-laundering legislation, we must have details about the origins of the money a client is offering for any property. It's the law, I'm afraid."

"Of course." Rhys nodded in acceptance without elaborating. "Okay, let's take a look around."

Paige's smile widened, but she was not immune to the shadow that had crossed Rhys's face. She had seen something akin to this before on once showing a property to a Botswana doctor. He had claimed that he had made his fortune from selling medical supplies to the Third World, but it was suspected he owned casinos in Russia and Macao and had bought small banks in the Caribbean. He was also suspected of having involvements in the arms industry, and other claims from credit sources included owning a Boeing 767 jet.

Needless to say, it was difficult to check out his background, and so she had little choice than to suggest to the vendor that they deny his bid for their property. Certainly Paige did not believe Rhys Langston had an equally unscrupulous background, but she was curious in spite of and beyond the **virtue** of liking him.

"Main door, lobby," she began, moving forward to where a marble-floored reception hallway faced them. "The ground floor boasts a spectacular double reception room with direct access onto a private garden. On your right is a beautiful bow-windowed drawing room overlooking the front garden, and further along the hallway, you will find a very bright and well-presented dining room."

A wry smile crossed Rhys's face. "You're good at this," he relaxed. "I'm interested already."

"I've been selling property for over a year," Paige warned him on a chuckle as they made their way toward the kitchen. "I'm giving you the usual spin."

"And enjoying it," Rhys remarked, smiling and following in her footsteps. The kitchen was larger than he had expected, and he immediately glanced at the brochure. "It says there's a patio area back here."

"There is," Paige confirmed, pointing with her finger. "There's access from the kitchen door."

"And upstairs?"

"There are five bedrooms on the two stories above, three en-suites, and a family bathroom."

Rhys dipped his head and gave the brochure a once-over. "An immaculately presented freehold house that has been completely refurbished and interior-designed to the highest standards," he repeated. "Does that include light fittings, curtains and drapes, carpets and other accessories?"

"Everything is included in the price," Paige confirmed, "except the murals. The vendor will be extracting those from the walls upon completion of the sale. They're from his country apparently, but he will be leaving the walls in good repair and undamaged."

"Right," Rhys breathed. "I'll take a good look down here, then you can show me around upstairs."

The viewing took just over an hour. Paige was in awe at how thorough Rhys was. He had checked all the closets for space, the central heating system, garden, and garage. Even the electric circuit breakers did not escape attention. When, finally, Paige was closing the front door and turning the key in the lock, she was surprised when Rhys planted a kiss against her cheek and seemed in approval of everything he had seen.

"You're a master saleswoman."

"Just doing my job," Paige exclaimed, smiling.

"I like it." Rhys nodded. "And it's house number four, my favorite number."

Paige remembered. "A little too large for you, I think, though," she responded more seriously. She was still in her role as realty agent, and thought perhaps she should be suggesting something more suitable. "We have some penthouses on our books at the agency I could show you."

"Ah, but I'm a family-minded sort of guy," Rhys countered lightly. He looked at the house with a twinkle in his eyes. "This is for long-term prospects."

"Quite an ambiguous remark," Paige returned, intrigued. "I wonder who the lucky lady is."

"Only time will tell," Rhys declared softly. "I'd like to invite a friend of mine along for a second viewing, if that's all right?"

"Anyone I know?" Paige wavered lightly, not trying to pry. Rhys had not been in the country for very long, so she was more than bemused that he should have any friends in London, aside from his investment banker.

"Just someone with an astute eye," Rhys answered. "I'm starved. Ready for lunch?"

Paige nodded, but did not want to leave the subject. "Of course, I'll gladly give you both a second viewing."

"Actually, I'd like to arrange that with your boss," Rhys ventured, making his way down the few short steps toward the sidewalk. "Can you leave me his number so I can arrange an appointment with him?"

Paige swallowed. "I don't understand—"

"Don't take it personally," Rhys suggested, wondering whether he could trust Blanton Blake with the knowledge of his true earning power. "It's a lot of money and I would feel better if I were dealing with your boss."

"A man," Paige boomed in comprehension. "You're treating me as though I'm incapable because I'm a woman. I *know* how to do my job."

"No doubt you do," Rhys agreed, "but this is not about you."

"Damn right it's not," Paige revealed. "This is about you and your problem in dealing with me as a successful woman who's in control."

"C'mon," Rhys began, hailing down a black cab. "Let's not argue. We're going to enjoy today, aren't we?"

Paige stood motionless on the spot and stared blankly as she watched Rhys run over to the black cab. Rooted to the sidewalk, she hardly knew how to react. Her suspicions had moved swiftly from wondering about Rhys's liquid and bankable assets to his inability to deal with her on her own status level. She had not noticed it before, but now when she thought back to their initial conversation on the Internet, and their later ones about her self-sufficiency and independence, the dawning was there. Rhys Langston was a born leader who had no wish to be underpinned by a woman.

"I think I'll walk," Paige rebutted, turning quickly on her heels.

"Paige, wait!" Rhys yelled. He grimaced as the taxi refused to wait and sped on its way. Cursing an oath beneath his breath, he followed quickly on Paige's hot trail. "Why are you running away?" he asked on reaching her. She refused to stop. "Paige?" He restrained her arm until she was forced to remain still. "It's just a house."

"Which I should be closing the deal on."

"And I want your boss to do it."

"Why?"

"Because . . . it's a man thing."

"Yeah, right." Paige broke free and was on her way again.

Rhys ran after her. "Okay, call me a chauvinist pig."

"You're a chauvinist pig."

"I like to do things my way. What's the big deal?"

"The big deal as you call it," Paige began, "is that things have changed. Times have changed. Women now oil and turn the corporate wheels as men do. As a New Age man, you shouldn't be having a problem with that."

"I don't," Rhys proclaimed, wanting to tell her the truth, but still determined to wait. "It's just that . . . I'm a man with certain philosophies in life."

"As you've told me when we chatted on the Internet," Paige reminded him. "And?"

"I choose to live by them."

Paige continued walking. "I don't."

"I'm not asking you to," Rhys argued.

"Good."

"Fine," he spat out. "This all goes back to you never wanting to feel dependent, vulnerable, or helpless. You don't ever want to give yourself up to anything or anyone. Why do you feel so threatened by men? It can't just be about your parents getting a divorce and living a lie."

Paige stopped in her tracks and stared at him. Her heart lurched sickly. "Don't you dare try to turn this around," Paige relented angrily. She continued walking with her shoulders straight and her head held high. "I'm a woman who does not fool herself with empty dreams of things that are beyond my capabilities. At the same time, I do not waver in the face of those tasks for which I am competent and which I am prepared to take on, like closing the deal on this house. This has nothing to do with being threatened by you or any other man."

"It has more to do with how afraid you feel when you are not in control to do things your way," Rhys agreed, knowing she might well have a crisis when she learned how rich he was.

Paige stopped in her tracks again and faced Rhys head-on. "Afraid. Of what? Having fun? Letting go? We've been through this before. Why are you still harping about it?"

"Because expressing the part of yourself which feels weakened and vulnerable isn't a sin," Rhys told her. "You're allowed."

"So that a man can demoralize me." Paige fought back with hard-hitting words. "I am not the kind of girl who thinks a man is some kind of coat rack that I can hang my needs and dreams on."

"But a part of you would like to do that, but you don't want to admit it in case it shatters all your dreams of who you are," Rhys concluded.

"That does it." Paige clutched at her handbag until she felt her knuckles were about to break. "I don't want lunch."

This was to be their first argument, and she was sickened at the subject matter it involved. It was running the spectrum from her being commitment-phobic—that she had trouble relating positively to men—to her basic feelings of insecurity should she lose any modicum of superiority. And it angered Paige that Rhys should remove the mask so eloquently. That he could see behind the camouflage of her self-sufficiency to the frightened girl that lay behind it.

"C'mon, you've got to eat," Rhys taunted, touching her shoulder.

"Move the hand or lose it," Paige snarled.

As though bitten, Rhys not only removed his hand, but took an exaggerated step backward. "I'm sorry." He gestured.

Paige suddenly became professional. "If you wish Mr. Blanton to deal with your purchase, then here's his number." She reached into her handbag and pulled out a card. Handing it over, she blinked. "As for us, perhaps it would be best if we just remain friends, as we were. That way, there will be no confusion between who's being courageous and who's vulnerable."

"Paige!"

She had sabotaged the relationship, but Paige seemed not to care. Instead, she turned on her heels, waved good-bye, and walked away. The directness of her decision caught Rhys off guard. He watched her go with a mixture of fear and longing in imperfect silence. The sound of her voice seemed to echo with an aching kind of intimacy that chilled him when she spoke about her dreams. Something had made her deeply bitter. Perhaps it was her parents' divorce, or that she felt the only person she could rely on was herself. Whatever it was, her burning desire to succeed did not escape him, but Rhys was more concerned as to what the real driving force behind Paige Alexander was.

"I'll give you one million things she sees in you, and you've got them sitting right there in the bank," Franklin mocked as he watched Rhys close the office door behind him.

"I've told you, she knows nothing about me like that," Rhys chimed emphatically.

"But she's got you thinking about buying a house which will just about part you from over half your investments," Franklin jabbed unhappily.

"Just how quickly can you liquidate?" Rhys asked, seating himself in the chair facing Franklin's desk.

"A few days." Franklin shrugged.

"Good." Rhys was relieved.

"So when are you going to tell this desert princess of yours?"

Rhys raised a brow, confused as to how Franklin knew this was how he'd seen Paige in his dreams from the moment he had laid eyes on her while in Egypt. Deciding Franklin's Middle Eastern origins had influenced a lucky guess, he ignored it and continued. "That's the tricky bit, he breathed. "She's not talking to me."

"That's good news," Franklin elated. "You can go back to that excavation site you got going on without feeling bad about anything. Where's the location anyway?"

"Dhashur," Rhys said absently. "I can't forget about her," he appended.

"You said she's zero publicity," Franklin rambled on, "so there won't be a problem, and your money can stay right where it is, gaining twenty percent."

"I don't want to leave," Rhys intoned madly. He ran an exasperated hand through his hair. "I like this girl. I want to get to know her. I want to break that hard shell of hers and get right to the core to see if there's a heart there."

"This is heavy," Franklin drawled in an unusual Arabian slur. "She's really got under your skin. Which property agents are you using?"

"Blanton's." Rhys transferred his dark eyes to the business card Paige had given him, then glanced at his watch. "I'm going to go back to the hotel," he murmured, "to shower and change. I'll call you in a couple of days about the transfer to a new bank account. I'd also like you to take a look at this house with me."

"What about the house in France?" Franklin queried as Rhys rose out of his chair. "You can't afford to keep both."

"I'm going to have a think about what to do," Rhys acknowledged.

"Don't think for too long," Franklin warned shrewdly. "No woman is ever worth that much." The moment Rhys left, Franklin was on the phone. Speaking into the mouthpiece, he said firmly to one of his henchmen, "There's been a change of plan. I have an idea. Listen very carefully."

"So, he's one half of a whole and not the more exciting half at that," Paige accused hotly at the breakfast table, while Francine glared at her murderously.

"Say one more thing against my husband and I'll swing at you," her cousin railed back. "Tell her, Aunt Elva."

"I'm staying out of this," Elva revealed, staring at her younger niece in concern. "What's wrong, sugar plum?"

"Nothing," Paige returned harshly, staring at the plate in front of her, where fried eggs and tomatoes invigorated her senses. It had been two days since she had last seen Rhys, and she had not so much as received a phone call from him.

"It's Valentine's Day," Francine announced, "and she's jealous because Mervyn's sent me a card and she hasn't got one."

"Is your beau still here or has he left the country?" Elva softly inquired, detecting the tears in Paige's eyes.

Paige did not know where Rhys Langston was. He could be just about anywhere. "I don't know," she confessed sadly.

Aunt Elva shook her head. "At least you have your work," she compensated. "You're a beautiful girl. I'm sure another young man will come along."

Paige was not convinced. She looked at her eggs and felt positively sick. She was right back to where she had started before visiting *www.totallyblackdating.com.* Only now, there existed new revelations that brought further bitterness, cynicism, and depression. At that precise moment, she felt like her life had run out of promise and was instead stacking up disappointments. Looking back seemed suddenly easier than looking forward. She no longer cared, at least not in that finely calibrated way she used to when she was much younger.

Now that she was thirty, Paige felt she had racked up enough turmoil in one way or another. It occurred to her that she might want to eschew that lifestyle, and think about doing something completely different that would not bring about a period of confusion and despair. Perhaps a new hobby like flower arranging, dressmaking, painting. Maybe pottery. Working with clay, she could sculpt a statuette of her own into something that would take her mind off the dreaded subject of sharing her life with someone.

A long sigh escaped her lips. "I'm not hungry." She wanted neither her breakfast nor another young man.

"You're not dressed for work either," Francine broached, displaying her disapproval that Paige was still in her nightgown with her hair uncombed, while *she* was sporting a well-cut designer suit with her hair and makeup in place for taking on the law office that day. "So what you going to do, stay at home and mope all day?"

"Maybe," Paige chided.

"Has the property market gone belly-up?" Francine goaded. "Or is Blanton becoming too hot to handle?"

"No," Paige affirmed sternly, not missing her cousin's teasing tone. "I need to move all my birthday presents upstairs, and then I'm going to go into the office."

"What's all this about Blanton Blake?" Elva immediately demanded.

"Nothing," Paige wavered. "Only, I've decided not to take him up on his partnership offer. I don't think it's what I want to do after all."

"I wonder what's changed your mind," Francine derided with sarcasm. "It can't be that he's going through with his wedding plans after all, can it?"

Paige rose out of her seat, annoyed. "I sincerely hope that he does; then maybe he and you can both leave me alone."

"Francine!" Elva scolded as she watched her niece tearfully leave the breakfast table. She instantly left her own chair and followed in hot pursuit. "Paige?"

Paige was about to climb the stairs. "What is it, Aunt?" Her voice was trembling.

"Me know what it's like to be unlucky in love," she said compassionately. "I've lost three husbands, but even at my age, me still live in hope. In life, there's good, there's better, and there's—"

"The best," Paige finished unhappily. "I know."

"Just hang in there."

Paige smiled and kissed her aunt on her left cheek. Later, she walked into her office, fully dressed, with her hair styled and makeup applied in a precise manner. She carried her briefcase loaded with work, and her mood had changed marginally, but Paige was more surprised when she caught Blanton rushing toward her with a full, sweeping smile.

"We've sold Holland Park." He beamed brightly, taking ahold of her arm and leading her into his office. "For one million and seventy-five."

"But that's below the asking price," Paige noted, closing the door behind her.

Blanton walked majestically toward his desk, in full glee that they had shifted their first big property. "The vendor was adamant we take this offer. Who are we to argue when we're making a cool ten percent from the sale. We should celebrate."

"You celebrate," Paige remarked, trying to sound chirpy.

"Look." Blanton paused on seeing the frowning expression on her face. They had practically ignored each other over the past two days, and he could see she was not intending on changing her position that morning. "If this is about what I said, then let's put it behind us. Things between us are sweet at the moment and now that we can mean more to each other, maybe—"

"Blanton, don't," Paige interrupted, running an exasperated finger across her brow. She was still plagued with the worry over whether Rhys would ever contact her again.

"Just think about it," he went on carefully like a wise mogul. "That's all I'm asking. You're going through a braver and more foolhardy period in your life right now. I can wait."

Paige sighed heavily. "Why would you want to do that?"

"Because sometimes a man doesn't see what's in front of him until he wakes up," Blanton confessed. "I'm awake now."

"And engaged to be married," Paige reminded him.

Blanton grimaced as he seated himself behind his desk, appearing aggressive like a Zulu warrior. "You'll soon know what it is I am saying."

Paige winced at his determined tone. "Listen," she began

with total honesty. "What I share with Rhys Langston is not a flicker, okay? It's oxygen, it's energy. He's like an ache I've never felt before. Can't you see that?"

Blanton grew annoyed. "Kill it."

"I can't," Paige protested in earnest, clutching her fingers around her briefcase as the sheer bolt of lust for Rhys shot through her body in reminiscence of him. "I have to know where it's going."

"Don't let him stoke the fires that lay dormant," Blanton warned, scrutinizing Paige carefully. "You'll only get burned."

Paige glared at him, totally uncomprehending the situation. "Haven't you enough consideration at all for your fiancée not to be playing me like this?"

"I can take care of Latanya," Blanton croaked, "and I am not a player. Don't put me in the same rank as your last lover. You Englishwomen pride yourselves on dating the wrong kind of men, like Rupert King, who always have the occasional fracas with the law and God knows how many children, and then deny protection from a good educated man."

"Like you," Paige blurted. She shook her head in denial. "I don't need this right now." She began heading toward his office door, then braced her hand on the doorknob. "By the way, who bought the property?" She had expected Rhys's name to drop from Blanton's lips, hoping this would give her an excuse to talk with him again, but Paige was in for another shock.

"Someone called Mr. Coates-Davis," Blanton returned loudly. "His name sounds familiar." He pondered. "And he's paying in cash."

"Cash!" The shock rendered her immobile. Her heart dropped. "What about Rhys Langston's offer?"

"That's the damnedest thing," Blanton harangued, leaning his back into his chair and digging both hands into his tailored trouser pockets. "He called me two days ago and put in above the asking price. I did relate it to the vendor, but he declined. Seems you'd better look into who this boyfriend is of yours because something's not right."

Paige scoffed. "You wish."

"He's waiting for you in your office, by the way," Blanton revealed on a dry note. "I tried to break the news to him gently."

Paige's heart stopped. "Rhys is here?" She felt a cold tremor run along her limbs as she read the knowing expression on her boss's face. "You've told him, haven't you?"

"I'll be right here in my office," Blanton informed her, prevaricating the issue, unable to digest the sparkle that lit up and just as quickly died in Paige's midnight-blue eyes. "This is your package. You bought it and wrapped it up for your birthday. Guess you'll have to untie it yourself."

Ten

Things were getting to the point where Paige surely began to think events were beginning to formulate a past she could look forward to retelling in her old age. "Rhys," she gasped, closing her office door behind her. "I should have you arrested for trespassing." Naturally she was nervous and a little apprehensive to find him seated at her purple-colored sofa, and thought injecting a little humor would help the situation.

Paige did not know what to do. She felt awkward. She did not know what to say either. What had Blanton done exactly? Tell Rhys the truth? That he was initially a pawn in a game strategy that had now seemingly become ever more unpredictable? Yet Rhys seemed comfortable, and reacted with a smile on her arrival. He was even holding a pink envelope in his hand, which Paige knew instantly to be a Valentine's card.

"Hi," he greeted her kindly, glancing at his watch. "I've been waiting—"

"I was busy at home," Paige interrupted, throwing a bewildered gaze across the room to find him dressed immaculately in black jeans, a pale cream-colored jersey, and the brown camel-skin jacket he had been wearing when they first met at Heathrow Airport. "I thought I'd come in late."

The sound of his voice left her stumbling and flushing. Paige was mesmerized by his presence. She felt just like the fourteen-year-old girl she had once been and which Rhys had been curious about, dizzy and confused, lost in the middle of the girl stuff without yet having grown to develop certain reservations. But Paige held doubts now, knowing she was no longer fourteen. Knowing now she was facing a grown male adult who had a man's reflections and magnetic sensations.

"This is for you," Rhys offered, rising out of the sofa and taking brisk steps toward her to hand over the pink envelope. "With an apology," he added.

It was for not having contacted her over the last two days. Rhys had been otherwise engaged in matters of his own. He had been attempting to liquidate his assets, and was beginning to suspect that things were not as they should be with his finances. Franklin had been unusually protective with his answers, and seemed to present plausible explanations for everything. But Rhys wanted a full overview, and had begun to dig for some facts of his own. Information that was leaving him disturbed at his findings. But he was not going to plague Paige with his problems. He was just happy to see her again.

He felt starstruck as his eyes gleamed at her appearance, finding her attractively dressed in a white Bruce Oldfield jacket, black pin-striped trousers, and a white silk camisole finished with a few choice pieces of ethnic jewelry. Her short brown hair fell into place quite easily, projecting the elegance of her style in a more modern way that he admired immensely. Rhys imagined he would always be attracted to this woman, with her fiery temper and vulnerable gaze.

"This is very . . . sweet," Paige relented, placing her briefcase on the floor to tear open the envelope. "And I never expected to find you here."

"The property fell through," Rhys sighed. "You were right. I should've made you take care of the purchase. I think your boss has something against me."

That's true, Paige mused, her heart trembling with nerves. She stole a gaze at Rhys to find him looking at her with yearning mocha-brown eyes. His sensual hunger was evident in the soulful depth of his lingering gaze, and Paige wanted nothing more than to be kissed by him again. "He's very ambitious when clinching a sale," she prevaricated in a throaty tone. "Ruthless, in fact. But we have other properties."

Rhys seemed unconvinced as he stood facing Paige. He did not touch her. Instead, his gaze scanned her honeyed complexion, feminine-shaped figure, and the arched slanting brows he considered marked some mystery behind her façade. There was something he did not know, but intended to. "Are you having problems with Blanton Blake?"

"He's . . . not happy that I've declined becoming a business partner," Paige lied, glancing at the brightly decorated Valentine's card she had pulled from the envelope and held between her fingers. A flutter of butterflies caused havoc in her stomach as she viewed the picture of a cupid's bow on the front and saw how beautiful and marginally expensive it was. Just the type of sentiment that would, no doubt, brighten a girl's day. "I like this." She held it up to him.

Rhys's concern shifted to her approval. "Am I forgiven?"

Paige nodded and held his gaze.

He ventured a step further and stroked a line across her cheek. "I haven't stopped thinking about you since we argued." He kissed her lips. Sucked them right into his and held on for a long, lingering taste. "It was petty of me." He released her lips and licked her tongue. "I was just being stupidly protective."

"Of what?" Paige whispered, confused and shaken by the sensual onslaught.

He wanted to tell her the truth about his burgeoning assets, hoping she would still recognize him for the man she had grown to know, but Rhys restrained himself with a prevarication of his own. "Of dealing with an independently minded woman such as you."

Paige's mouth fell into a wry smile as she lifted her lips to him for the taking. "Have I bruised your ego?"

"A little." Rhys returned the smile, pressing his mouth against her own. "Perhaps you can soothe it tonight by joining me on an excursion to Monaco."

Paige was dazed. "What?" Rhys took the pink envelope

from her hand and pulled something Paige had missed from its interior. It was a plane ticket to the south of France, with flight details printed and ready for use. She gasped. "You want me to visit your house in Monaco?"

"I'm sure your boss will see it as a business trip, if you tell him I'm looking for an agent to advise me how to sell it," he suggested, running a shaky finger across her cheekbone. "But the truth is, I want us to spend some time together alone."

Paige's eyes filled with tears as the suggestion caused a deep throbbing sensation in the pit of her stomach. She did not know what to say. The last time she had been invited to take a trip with a handsome man, Rupert King had let her down so badly, she was to find herself returning to England with bountiful feelings of rejection. Could she really risk repeating the cycle with a new man, new destination, and with the same expectations?

"I don't know," she told Rhys, unsure.

"You need a break," Rhys encouraged, taking ahold of her hand. He knew he needed to return to France because there were matters he should double-check on, but not wanting to be parted from Paige, he thought it would be a nice idea that she join him. "You'll love the place and maybe you can give me a valuation on the property." He kissed the inside of her palm. "C'mon."

It was certainly tempting. The coaxing effect was positively putting Paige into a frenzy. She had never seen the south of France. Her only trip to Europe had been to Greece for a ten-day holiday when she had been a teenager. The idea of going with Rhys seemed just as exciting. A little sun, a little sea, a little time away from the humdrum of her troubled life. Now that her birthday party was over, she could afford to recuperate from the big event. It was the perfect tonic she needed. And with a man such as Rhys Langston in tow, how could a girl refuse?

"I'll have to let my boss know how long I'll be away for," she said with mirth, closing her eyes as Rhys began to slowly brush a kiss across her neck. "I can't just leave."

"Until the weekend," Rhys appraised her on a whispered note, nipping her earlobe with promises that she surely needed the break. "Four days."

Paige could hardly imagine Blanton complaining, though the way in which he resented her relationship with Rhys Langston could not rule out his likelihood to protest. They were already into midweek, and were not quite pressed under for her to escape two days off work before the real flood of properties piled in. But she was sure Blanton would find some excuse to prevent her from leaving and having the two days spill over into the weekend, and she was resolved to be firm and decisive.

"I'll go and ask him now," she told Rhys on a positive tone, exhaling a labored breath as she handed him her Valentine's card to hold. "You wait here."

Paige threw Rhys a reassuring glance as she left her office. Her pace was quick and her heartbeats much faster as she rushed into Blanton's office. She found herself instantly rooted at his door when she saw him standing arrogantly behind his desk. Latanya was with him. It was clear to Paige that she had just entered—midstream—into a heated altercation, and she paused to shelve the amorous feelings Rhys had already evoked in her, undecided what to do.

Miss Zimbabwe looked equally flustered, only hers was not caused by excitement, but a flurry of tears. Mascara had washed from her eyes down her elfin features, and her rosebud-shaped lips were quivering with grief. Her tall imposing slim-line figure was almost drooped in sorrow beneath the African-styled green and gold garb she was wearing, bearing the tradition of her country. And the distance between her and Blanton was a clear sign that he did not intend to console her. Paige did not know what had happened, though judging from the frustration clearly etched on Blanton's face, she knew it was not good.

"I'm sorry for barging in," she apologized, shifting her gaze from Latanya to her boss. "Blanton, can I talk to you for a minute?"

"Yes, you talk with him," Latanya spat out in her rich Zimbabwe accent. "He say he not marry me. He say it is too soon. He tell me this today on Valentine's Day. I tell him he is to shame me in front of my family."

Paige gasped. "I . . . I—"

"This is private," Blanton insisted, glaring at Latanya. "I will talk to your parents."

Latanya sniffled like a woman in mourning. "What do you tell them?" she scorned. "I know you want English girl, but I say you come back to Zimbabwe with me. This"—she pointed around his office—"is nothing for what you can do back home. You are woman. What you think?" She aimed the question at Paige.

Paige's brows rose at the direct confrontation. She pondered the news that Blanton came from Zimbabwe, too. It was a minuscule piece of the jigsaw that told her a little more about him, certainly not enough to give her a full picture to go on. Still, to say she had known him a year and was only making such discoveries about the man now led Paige to contemplate with rapid relief that she was grateful to have met Rhys Langston. He was much more open and honest. If Latanya had been presented with the same veil of blankness about Blanton as *she* had been, then Paige more than understood the confusion and suspicion that stirred more deeply than what lay behind the eyes of this foreign woman.

"You shouldn't rush into anything," Paige said, then bit her tongue. Paige knew it was not her place to give advice to a woman who wished to be married when she felt so against the institution herself because of what her own mother had gone through.

Clearly, the shock was stamped on Latanya's face. "Why you say no?" she chided, hurtful.

The old memories caught up with her. Suddenly Paige found herself thrust into a situation where she was forced to provide an answer. It was a case of looking at two people with stable lives and firm goals, suddenly reacting against all the preconceptions they once held dear, and thinking of what would be the best thing to say. "I think you should first have someone in your life who is your friend," she began, shifting her mind-set to the task of taking care of others. "He should understand your past, believe in your future, and accept you today the way you are. You should not expect a man to rule over what he hasn't earned. Let him respect you first, earn your trust, then see how you feel later." It sounded like good advice, she hoped.

The silence that fell on the room was almost tangible. Then Latanya spoke. "You are right." She nodded profoundly, wiping the tears from her eyes. Suddenly, her solemn vows to marry seemed less solemn. "This way, I do not have to love him. There will be no pressure for sex and I will not be frightened of him leaving me. I have seen the American program. We can be friends."

The sweeping statement shook Paige to the core. Such thoughts had entered her mind long ago. When she had heard her mother cry into the night because she was in her bed alone. The times she had heard her father tiptoe up the stairs after spending most of the evening with another woman. And the occasions when she wished her father would explain himself, tell her whether marriage meant anything at all. But he had made the rules—they were not to speak of this. Each moment of concealment turned the family into a group of strangers living under the same roof, until she was happy to move in with her Aunt Elva.

The best outcome for her mother, she supposed, would have been to have stopped caring for her father. To have stopped loving him. To wake up one morning and find that while she respected him for being the father of her two daughters, she could not love him anymore. But that would never happen. Her mother's heart belonged to one person. Her bitterness had hardened both her daughters. Penelope had married, but out of loyalty more than love for her husband. And Paige, she just wanted to run.

"I . . . I think you need to talk this over with Blanton," Paige wavered, swallowing hard as she saw the drained expression on her boss's face. His deep charcoal-colored eyes had darkened, and the boyish dimple she had grown to know so well had deflated into his oval face. "I . . . I only came to ask if I could have a couple of days to go into France on business."

"Go," Blanton exclaimed, his voice weakened.

"I'll be back by the weekend if you need me for . . . anything."

He was slowly retaking the seat at his desk, digesting with blatant regret Latanya's bolstered spirits and lively understanding at this new lease of Westernized standards. "Go."

"Yes, I go shopping," Latanya enthused, mistakenly assuming he was talking to her and undeterred by the dejection plainly masked across her fiancé's face.

"You will be all right?" Paige inquired, seeing the blank stare in Blanton's eyes as he failed to look at her.

"Go."

She left his office with a heavy heart, feeling she had said too much. When Paige reentered her own office, Rhys had retaken his seat in the sofa and was browsing through the air ticket he had given her earlier. He noticed immediately that Paige's complexion had paled, and wondered frantically what in God's name had happened.

"Paige?" He rose to his feet.

"I've just done a terrible thing," she acceded solemnly. "I think I've just liberated Blanton's fiancée."

"You're not making sense." Rhys chuckled at how ludicrous her suggestion sounded.

"I've just dashed all her dreams of ever being married," Paige wavered, certain, judging from the expression she had seen on her boss's face, that there was sure to be a revengeful throwback on his part.

"What?"

"I'm so aggressively in control, it rubs off on other women," she derided unhappily. "What was I thinking?" Paige rolled her eyes heavenward.

"Look." Rhys crossed the room toward her, placing the air

ticket, the Valentine's card, and its envelope on her desk as he passed it by. "I don't know what has happened, but no doubt you will tell me on the way to Monaco. Can you come?"

"Yes." Paige nodded. "But I can't do this."

"What?"

"I can't go to Monaco with you."

"Why not?" Rhys's disappointment echoed the room.

Paige decided it was time she came clean. After seeing the demise she had caused with Latanya, fearing that it might now force Blanton to spill the beans on her, she resolved that Rhys should know about her motives for locating him on the Internet in the first place at once. At least it would be better coming from her than to have him hear the truth third-hand from someone else.

"I have something to tell you," she began just as the telephone at her desk shrilled loudly into action. Paige squealed on a sickly breath. "I'll be right back."

Rhys stared in wonder as he watched her reach for the handset. He did not feel unduly worried. He suspected Paige was feeling insecure about herself in some way again, and it triggered his initial panic at the consequences. He wanted her to shed her helplessness, her anger, and the pain of her childhood. Lord knows he'd had to take the same journey once and had never looked back. He had never returned to America, but had spent his life traveling, first living and working in London, then moving on to Monaco.

Perhaps it would not be such a good idea to invite Paige to his home after all, he thought on reflection. It was too soon, though he felt eager in his wanting to get to know her better. A simple evening on the town was probably more suitable, he mused, reevaluating the situation. Standing facing Paige at her desk with his hands shoved into his trouser pockets, overhearing her while she recounted her farewells to her friends from India, Rhys changed his mind. He waited until she replaced the handset, then reached for her wrist and pulled her into his arms.

"You don't have to come to Monaco," he amended, rubbing

both his hands up and down her arms in reassurance. "Why don't we go out to the West End instead? I can pull in a favor from someone and get us two tickets for a musical; then we can go somewhere for a nightcap."

"But—" Paige protested, wanting nothing more than to explain the torturous thoughts running havoc in her head. Then her train of thought shifted. "Who do you know?"

"I have friends," Rhys coaxed. "C'mon. It's Valentine's Day."

Of course, Paige recalled, closing her eyelids. She felt Rhys's kiss brush across her lips, and the tears that mounted behind her eyes. Paige was weakened. She was fatigued with sensual yearning that she could want this man so much. That his kisses could affect her so easily she felt able to just about promise him anything. Her eyes were liquid when she opened them and lifted her hand to his cheek, rubbing the back of her fingers against the bone. She would wait. She would tell Rhys the truth another day.

"What time would you like to pick me up?" she whispered, disguising well the edge to her voice.

Rhys smiled. "Be ready for eight and dress to be wooed."

Paige flung herself into his arms and felt the strong hug that enfolded her. From despair to hope in one week. She could hardly believe it. So why was the pressure still building?

Francine popped her head through Paige's bedroom door and caught her applying the final touches to her makeup. Paige was classically dressed in a short black off-the-shoulder gown, revealing her shapely legs beneath dark-brown sheer panty hose. Her feet were crowned in a pair of black high-heeled sandals, and a black and gold sequined bag was on the bed, indicating to Francine that her cousin had a hot date.

"Anyone I know?" Francine probed in surprise.

"Rhys Langston," Paige answered, as though it should have

been plainly obvious, blushing her cheeks with a shade of burnished copper.

"Oh!" Francine ventured into the room and closed the door. Paige was seated comfortably at her dressing table in front of the mirror, seeming a little edgy and nervous. "You've seen him then?"

"He came to the office and invited me out to a musical tonight," Paige informed her brightly. She picked up her Valentine's card from among the clutter of her makeup and displayed it to her cousin. "Nice, isn't it?"

Francine swallowed. "So you guys are dating?"

"Why wouldn't we be?" Paige asked, replacing her card and continuing to apply her blusher.

"I just thought after sleeping with him—"

"What?" Paige was taken aback. Shaking her head in disgust, she briefly glanced at her cousin's reflection in the mirror, too annoyed to confront her directly. "We shared a bed, but not in the way you think," she sputtered, offended. "Why would you think I'd do a thing like that with you, my parents, and my entire family staying in Aunt Elva's house?"

"After the way you've been behaving lately with this Web-surfing, Internet romance thing," Francine conceded, embarrassed, "I just thought—"

"He wanted to get his socks off, hit and run," Paige concluded, beleaguered. "We kissed and talked."

"And then what?"

"Nothing."

"Is he gay or something?"

"No!" Paige snapped, offended. "Tonight is dinner."

"I'm sorry for thinking the worst." Francine backed down.

"You two doing anything tonight?" Paige queried, swiftly changing the subject before she got angry.

"Mervyn's taking me out to dinner," Francine declared comfortably. "I was about to get dressed."

"Well, enjoy yourself," Paige breathed, reaching for a stick of red lipstick.

Francine eyed her cousin with a sense of trepidation, feeling perhaps she had not been as supportive as she should have been when Paige was at a low ebb. “Paige.” Her mind searched for what to say. “About this morning.”

“What about it?” Paige quipped, smoothing her lips in a furious shade of crimson.

“I didn’t mean to have a go.” Francine flinched. “I suppose you know what you’re doing.”

“I do.”

“He looks like a nice guy.”

“He is,” Paige agreed.

“He obviously likes you,” she approved, having seen him at Paige’s party and now knowing the man had not taken advantage of her cousin.

“He does at that,” Paige confirmed.

“And you like him?”

“Yes.” Paige replaced her lipstick.

Francine nodded in acceptance of what she was hearing. “Good,” she gushed. “Guess I don’t have to check that an abduction clause is written into your Internet dating contract.”

“But?” Paige turned from her dressing table to face Francine, anticipating there would be a further addition. Her cousin had remained standing by the door, with her hands crossed together, appearing calm and yet slightly uncomfortable. For a top-notch lawyer who broached war every day and was hard to faze, Paige could hardly believe her cousin could be easily shaken.

“Nothing,” Francine denied, studying her manicure.

Paige remained unconvinced. “Francine?”

“I was with Lizzy Chadwick today,” Francine bristled. “The DNA test results were disclosed this morning at a private hearing in the family division of the High Court. It proves that Rupert King is the father of her daughter, and his publicists are going to make some sort of statement.”

Paige shrugged. “I don’t see what that has to do with me,” she debated, turning back to her mirror to smooth her hair into place. She had swept it up into a tight chignon, and pulled strands from around the sides and her forehead to accentuate the shape of her face.

"Your name might get bandied about a bit, that's all," Francine returned, "Rupert is refusing to cooperate, so there may be a lot of mud-slinging."

"*My* name." Paige was aghast. "But Rupert and I are finished. We're no longer in a relationship."

"I know," Francine agreed. "I'm just warning you that I think Lizzy is going for a no-holds-barred spillage to the press. She's spitting revenge, and you and this new guy might have to cope with the wrath from one of Rupert's formidable ex-girlfriends."

"And as an ex myself," Paige expanded, "I can either keep a stony silence as details of our liaison unfold, or get pulled in knee-deep when Rupert's love life threatens to overshadow his football career."

"It's just as well you met Rhys Langston," Francine intoned. "At least this way you can look like the cat who got the cream."

Paige rose from her seat. "Well you've changed your tune," she gasped, annoyed. "Is this you finally giving me your seal of approval?"

"Let's just say I'd rather this than watch you get dragged into something ugly," Francine bridled. "If Rhys Langston is making you happy, then you've won a fantastic battle with yourself. I'm glad you've listened to your heart and moved on."

"We're not talking marriage," Paige scoffed, aware of the deeper implications of her cousin's statement. "He may be my protector . . . my desert prince, the man who will rescue me from myself whom you said I would never find, but don't go there with talk about us cementing what we have. I'm not interested."

"You've got to get over your parents' divorce sooner or later," Francine chided, folding her arms arrogantly beneath her breasts. "You can't allow it to affect your life forever."

"Who says I'm letting it get to me at all?" Paige croaked,

walking toward the bed, where she reached for her gold sequined handbag. She threw a pensive glance at the Egyptian statuette Rhys had given her, recalling the significance of what it stood for, and felt her heart warm in confusion, knowing she would be seeing Rhys again.

"Forget I said anything," Francine rebutted. "I don't want to fall out with you tonight." She turned and reached for the doorknob. "Enjoy your evening."

Paige watched her leave, and grimaced. She was annoyed that her cousin should plunge her into a further malaise. Just how on earth had her life become so complicated? Paige could not begin to guess. All she wanted was someone she could go out with. Someone who could be classified as a boyfriend and who wanted her. A man she could talk to, revealing things about herself without feeling demoralized. He would listen, pay attention to her feelings, and make her feel special. Why should it be more difficult than that?

You can't force a man to like you, lust for you, or love you. Paige amplified Francine's remark in her mind as she broadened the subject while seated in the limousine that arrived for her outside her aunt's home. Elva had been absolutely delighted when she saw the white stretched car that arrived for her niece, and Francine had been noncommittal, though her eyes had lit up when Paige waved her departure. But the thoughts that plagued Paige as to exactly where her life was leading were still forefront on her mind as the driver took her toward Claridge's to pick up Rhys.

Was he the man for her? Paige questioned. He possessed all the hallmarks of being such a person. And if so, Paige knew she needed to tell him the truth about Blanton and Rupert. The matter of Lizzy Chadwick courting the press about her love child could force matters. Paige even pondered the irony that while Lizzy sought the sort of commitment that equaled marriage, *she* did not.

And with Rupert King being a well-known footballer, it

was likely Paige could be confronted for a statement about her own falsely suspected proposal from him, which had only served to underline her belief that such commitments from men did not exist. Their affair had been broadcast in the press, though their breakup had been conveniently omitted. Paige was at a loss as to what she would say should she be approached for comment.

It dawned on her that this could mean Rupert's spin doctors had chosen to keep it quiet until an opportune time so focus could be kept on his game play—scoring goals and not girls—which posed a dilemma for her. The entire circumstance of how she came to be with Rhys Langston, having acquired him from the Internet, could then be exposed, ridiculing them both. Paige swallowed hard at the sheer nightmare of it all. She reminded herself that Rupert did not know anything about Rhys, and calmed herself instantly. Rupert might well be a master player, but she was the student who had outstripped her mentor.

There was a different taste of victory that felt sweet on her tongue when the limousine pulled up outside Claridge's and she sensed the languid wormth that spread throughout her body when Rhys appeared at the car door. The volcano activity in her body erupted when the driver left his seat and accommodated Rhys's entry, and her heart almost stopped as she heard his footsteps sink into the limousine's carpeted interior.

The scent of his aftershave—the potency of frankincense and myrrh—was the first thing to invigorate her senses as Rhys seated himself beside her. Paige was in awe at how handsome he looked in polished black crocodile lace-up shoes, a black tuxedo and tie, a yellow band around his waist, and white ruffled shirt with the addition of gold cuff links. He was fresh-shaven, and must have used the hotel's barbers that day, after he had left her at the office, because his hair was also neatly trimmed and clipped at the sides.

"Hello again," Rhys whispered, planting a soft kiss against her cheek as he handed her a single red rose.

"Hello to you, too," Paige responded, accepting the Valentine gesture with a smile dancing on her lips. "Where are we going?"

"Don't you want to be surprised?" Rhys teased.

Paige linked her arm over his as they both leaned themselves into the plush burgundy-colored leather seats. "I need a clue." She chuckled.

The driver revved the engine and pulled away from the hotel. "I don't like providing clues," Rhys temporized softly. "I just want you to relax and enjoy tonight."

He reached to the side of the car and tapped a button. Paige was amazed when a total in-car bar unfolded itself behind the car's leather interior. There were two crystal flute glasses and two bottles of champagne, and she stared in amazement as Rhys pulled one of the bottles from its ice bucket and began to do the honors. The last time she had seen a bottle of champagne in an ice bucket, she had flung both items across the small interior of a private jet. It was the mother of coincidences she should find herself again in similar circumstances replayed with a much nicer guy having the best of intentions. When the cork popped, they both laughed profusely before he handed her a filled glass.

"To friendship," Rhys announced.

"To us," Paige answered, totally smitten.

It was Disney's spectacular production of *The Lion King* at the Royal Albert Hall in the heart of London. It also marked a new phase in the already luminous period of the star dancer and choreographer.

Paige was bowled away by the unforced acting, natural-sounding symphonies, and most surprisingly, a delightfully modulated singing voice that stood out from the seasoned singers in the cast. It was a landmark in the genre for being a musical that was actually about Africa. The title number was especially a big success, with its exhilarating, interweaving swirls of primal paradise, scenic ingenuity, and breathtaking costumes and designs. And the dancing was so intricate and speedy, Paige had to wonder how the dancers avoided falling into the orchestra pit, which was a slot in the stage.

"There is simply nothing else like it," she told Rhys, still enchanted as they both returned to the haven of the limousine after the show. "I'm totally sold on seeing it again."

Rhys chuckled. "It reminded me very much of Africa," he said charismatically. "The colors, the scenes . . ."

"What's Egypt like?" Paige asked, intrigued, as the limousine sped away.

"Hot, noisy, polluted," Rhys answered, leaning his full, tired weight into the leather of his seat. "But full of history," he added with passion. "I enjoy learning about the cities through the very buildings and tunnels that make them up. I get a rush of adrenaline—how I would imagine delving into the belly of a beast must feel—where nothing is hidden or censored."

"You visited the pyramids?"

"And the tombs," Rhys affirmed, reaching for the second bottle of chilled champagne. He uncorked it easily and continued. "I like it mostly when the gateway to heaven is opened."

"The sunrise," Paige exclaimed, recalling how he had described the emergence of a new day to her on the Internet.

"Uh-huh," Rhys acknowledged.

"Are you going back?" Paige asked, accepting more champagne.

"I've funded a project out there," Rhys explained, filling a flute for himself before replacing the champagne bottle. "There's an archaeologist in charge, but I need to return sometime soon to take a look at the excavation site. He's found a main shaft which might lead to a tomb."

"Oh." Paige had not realized, but of course she could not expect Rhys to stop his life just for her. "When are you leaving?"

"I don't know," Rhys told her truthfully. "I'd like to fly back to Monaco this weekend, though."

She nodded in acceptance and took a large, fortifying gulp of champagne. It was what she feared—Rhys leaving. It was why she refused to have a heart full of hope and dreams and the promise of a future. It was also why, deep down, she felt so bitter. But at least she could console herself that he had been at her birthday party and given her a wonderful Valentine's Day. She could hardly complain in view of his honesty. He was not going to intentionally leave her a disillusioned woman as Rupert had done. After all, they were friends, even though they had both been hopeful an ensuing romance might have developed.

"Where to now?" Paige tried to smile.

Rhys noted her disappointment, and read it accurately. "Do you want us to be more than just friends?"

Paige was flustered. "No," she lied.

"You said it's been a while," he recalled from their initial conversation in the chat room.

"I . . . I . . ."

Rhys removed the champagne flute from Paige's hand and leaned forward to replace it on the bar. Returning to his position, he inched himself a touch closer. "Am I dealing with your sexual frustration right now?" he asked her again.

Paige could not deny the truth when she searched the smoldering depth of Rhys's soulful dark eyes. "Yes," she whimpered, clearly hopeless at seduction.

"Then it's time you made me take care of that," he whispered, allowing his gaze to drift slowly downward, stopping only when he was confronted with the plunging cut in the cleavage line of her black dress, where the soft swell of her breasts tormented him.

This was reckless. It all felt so reckless, this dry-mouthed, heart-pounding, Isis-and-Omega-getting-it-together stuff without a thought for sense or reason. But it was happening. For a moment Paige thought she would faint from her desperate need for this man. It was as though she had been waiting for him for a lifetime. Could it always be like this—him bringing love, excitement, and adventure home?

"I don't know," Paige whispered, unsure that she should follow the dictates of her heart. "I guess the only way I can knock you out is with a kiss, right?" she joked.

The slightly anxious note in her voice pulled Rhys back from the brink of his own sensual madness. "Only if you stop identifying with a man and be yourself. Be a woman," he murmured, sensing that her entire body had stilled, that her skin looked flushed and the huge black pupils of her eyes seemed rimmed with topaz-gold that bounced from the yellow streetlights that invaded through the tinted glass windows.

"Rhys . . ." Paige breathed, unable to deny herself what she truly wanted.

"Still running?"

"No," she admitted, sinking fast into the deep abyss of Rhys's bewitching, mesmerizing soulful eyes. She felt as if the word had been torn from her throat, as the desire to be held by Rhys swept through her like a forest fire. "I want to know how you're going to take care of my ache for you."

How could he resist? The words clamored in Rhys's head and almost blinded him. It took everything that was good in him to hold him back, briefly, so that he could replace his own glass onto the bar. And then he had Paige in his arms, smothering her with kisses, feeling primitively murderous that this woman could belong to anyone else except him. He groaned as he gathered her to him and held on tighter, her own kisses matching the leaded weight in his loins.

Paige burned for him. She called out his name like an impenetrable caress on a whisper, and Rhys held on even tighter until the limousine pulled up outside Claridge's. . . .

Eleven

She was lying against the bubbles, her damp short brown hair tumbled about her face, her naked honey-colored shoulders against the whirlpool of warm water, her throat begging that the kisses should repeatedly and endlessly go on and that the man who shared the Jacuzzi with her would never stop.

They were in the steamy en-suite that led from Rhys's hotel room, their clothes providing a telltale sign on the floor that led a path directly to where they could be found, adoring one another in a deep spa. The bathroom was lit with four aromatic candles that flickered a warm and hazy glow against their brown skin, and Paige and Rhys were lost to the world in their own sanctuary of pleasure.

The bubbles were hot . . . soothing . . . calming, like Rhys's kisses. They were touching every area of Paige's neck, pleasing and exciting her so that, on impulse, her wet hand roamed around his neck, pulling Rhys off balance until he slid into the tub. Water heaved over the side onto the tiled floor, and Paige giggled as he surfaced, wiping bubbles from his face.

"You did that on purpose." He laughed, deliberately reaching for her to keep from submerging again. Aiming for her bare legs between the water, he tangled his own through hers and pinned her to the side. "Not this time."

His hair, wet and shining, dripped water down his face, making him look so tantalizingly adorable and sexy, Paige was smitten again. She traced the outline of his mouth with her tongue. "I would dare myself anything," she whispered confidently, the hot words sizzling from her throat into the damp air.

"Really?" Rhys was amused. This woman was certainly changing before his very eyes. She was not quite the one he'd suspected held traditional values whom he had initially spoken with on the Internet.

"And I'm not afraid to let go and have fun either," Paige tempted, relaxing at a stroke when she felt Rhys's hands slide up her back and pull her closer.

It was all the encouragement Rhys needed as their lips met. His mouth was hot and hungry. His pulses raced, his heart thudded madly. It was not anything new. Women always made him react this way in bed. But as Paige's body arched and stretched beneath the hot steaming water, welcoming his further advances, Rhys experienced a sensation so new, it bolted through his brain like lightning. The en-suite swirled about him. Their sensual vapor amid the steam almost blinded him. What was this woman doing to his senses?

His best defenses were down, his primitive urges were roused. He wanted nothing more than to take this woman and make sweet love to her until she was limp with exhaustion. His lips were wet with her pulsing desire, his eyes were languid with the hot dew from the Jacuzzi, and the heavy drag of his need for Paige became so intense that the bubbles pulsating against his manhood were torture. He was not going to deny this woman tonight as he had done at her aunt's home. Tonight was special. Tonight it would be all right. Tonight, he had grown to know this princess who had come to him, as an image on his laptop, in the desert under the guise of Isis, and captured his heart.

Paige let her mind go. She was no longer in control. She was experiencing lovemaking as it was meant to be—mindless, liberating pleasure with no boundaries. It was what she needed. What she wanted, to surrender her mind to someone who would understand her needs. Flesh against flesh, hot heat bubbling between them. Paige tasted and touched like she had never touched a male body before. It had been a while, but it did not feel so now. Rhys filled her heart, mind, and soul with such wondrous delight, it hardly felt like she had been in abstinence for so long.

She could not compare what she was used to feeling to what she was experiencing now. Rupert had never evoked such desire. Her crush on Blanton had certainly not stirred her in this way either. *There's good, there's better, and there's the best.* Paige understood and accepted. Until now, she had never known the full madness of need. The kind that made you think you had lost your mind because pleasure, intimacy, and vulnerability were so entwined. But there was no fear of merger. No fear of being joined. On the contrary, something inside Paige almost begged for it.

Naked, agile, ravishing, she wrapped her legs around Rhys and allowed him to hold her closer, enough for him to poke his member against her. Paige's eyes shot open at the merest sense of it beneath the water. It was real. It was there. The bubbles made her feel dizzy and light-headed, knowing she wanted it buried in her, hot and throbbing. She almost lost her mind, giddy with the tormenting thought.

"Rhys," Paige gasped, in a voice she scarcely recognized.

He made the kind of soft noises that would gentle a sleeping baby. Paige was incapable of movement, but Rhys's perception was all-knowing. He gathered her up, lifted her into his arms, and carried her out of the heated water, leaving a wet path to the bedroom. Despite the heat steaming from their skin, by the time Rhys placed Paige onto the large expansive bed, they were both shivering uncontrollably. The fuse was on a slow burn only long enough for Rhys to reach for the new packet of condoms he had purchased earlier and then hurriedly join Paige beneath the sheets.

"Come here," he said, folding Paige into the comfort of the cotton, wrapping his large arms around her. He wanted to keep holding her, but his body was protesting with a new urgency of its own. "Kiss me."

Paige was his in a heartbeat. Their lips met and the onslaught was resurrected. Paige melted into him, warm, soft, affectionate. Her hands began to freely roam. This reacquainting herself with the male body was as magical as it was exciting because she was with a man she wanted to make her own. He was not someone who saw her as a fling or fancy, a bit on the side, or a challenging prospect like a one-night stand as Rupert had tried to treat her. This was a man who, in spite of how they had come to meet, wanted more.

Taking her time, she ran kisses down his forehead to his cheek, his neck, nose, chin, and mouth again. Rhys answered her smile with his own before closing his eyes to accept her amorous attentions. Paige's elegant, exploring fingers slid down to his hips and held him loosely. It was more than Rhys could take. He wriggled beneath Paige as her grip tightened, and then his eyes shot wide open, unable to swell anymore. He held Paige's wrist and stalled her, his other hand clinching the packet of condoms.

"Take one," he ordered gently.

Paige did his bidding and eagerly ripped open the packet. She handed the slim sachet to Rhys, and watched as he quickly applied the latex. In an instant, he had her on her back, returning the pleasure she had given him. Rhys licked the wet bubbles from her skin, nipped her earlobe, planted kisses against her neck, all the while gently stroking with his fingers—featherlike caresses against the honey of her skin.

It was Paige's turn to wriggle when he parted her legs and began to playfully tempt her with his tongue. Her eyes closed and her mind was gone again, as she moaned, squealed, and whimpered in a language totally alien to her. She felt the ecstasy like running hot water, trickling down every vein and artery within. Her gasp was almost deafening as her lungs exploded with the release. But it was not over.

Rhys's eyes lit up as he went on his knees and plunged into her. He filled her in one fell swoop, and moaned his entry like the hunter who had caught his prey. His face was dappled with sweat, remnants of water, and was a picture of blissful agony at how sweet his life had just become at that precise moment. Paige matched him stroke for stroke, measure for measure, gasping as Rhys's well-endowed member filled every inch of her.

Another heat built, much deeper, more agonizing. She was not aware she could feel ecstasy again, but it was coming like a tidal wave. The speed escalated, the impatience whirled. Paige felt an aggression rise within her from an unknown entity between her legs where Rhys was probing. It bordered out of her control. As her thoughts began to tumble and skid, her last rational flash was sharp as her temper.

"Stop now and I will kill you," she shrieked on the tether of something frightening.

Rhys answered her brazen plea with a powered craving of his own as his thirst to escape into a bliss took over. His fingers laced themselves between hers and held fast, his yanking delved deeper into her, and his mouth ensnared hers until she told him with her tongue that she had reached heaven. In that moment, Rhys was lost. A soulful moan like the roar of an animal left his lips as he planted his head in Paige's shoulder.

"How . . . how did you know how to do that?" Paige labored, catching her breath, lest she would die.

"I can feel you," Rhys gasped, his heart pounding like a sledgehammer. He planted a satisfying kiss against her neck. "I can feel every bit of you." They held on tight and closed their eyes. Then Rhys made another startling admission. "I think I'm also falling in love with you."

Paige could not answer. Instead, her head spun. She was more than surprised when one word loomed into her mind and tormented her. Marriage.

"I thought you were against that sort of thing," Francine told her cousin the following day as they had lunch in the canteen at her law firm. Paige had telephoned Francine early that morning to meet her at noon, and seemed to be in glowing spirits as they faced each other from across the table.

"If I could consider a business partnership with Blanton Blake, then I'm wondering if being married is all that bad."

Paige swallowed lightly, delving her spoon into her soup bowl and trying hard to forget she had been haunted all night with giggling spooks dangling wedding rings, a friendly apparition brandishing a horseshoe, and a kindly ghost, dressed like an absent-minded vicar, reciting a love sermon.

Paige looked the picture of health with her hair freshly washed and blown dry, a new layer of makeup applied to her face, and wearing a neat set of clothes, having returned to Aunt Elva's to shower and change. The crimson-colored trousers, pink knit angora jumper, white jacket, and an adornment of pearls around her neck projected the classic image of a woman who had regained control of her life once more.

"You know there's the small print," Francine warned, lighting up a Marlboro cigarette, herself sporting a finely cut blue checkered suit that made her seem less doll-like than she was. "Thou shall pick up his dirty socks from the floor, wash his smelly underpants, turn a blind eye when he doesn't put up that shelf you've nagged him about a thousand and one times, smile kindly when he belches at the dinner table and when he passes wind in bed at night. That's what you have to put up with if he's not an optional extra."

"Francine!" Paige laughed out loud, before swallowing a mouthful of soup. "I was thinking about the *smaller* print. You know, thou shall make love to me twice a week, father me two children, make enough money to keep a roof over our heads and see the kids through university, afford early retirement to a villa in Spain, and provide a ninety day cruise into our old age."

"Wow!" Francine broached, her hazel eyes widening in amusement. She brushed back a curl of auburn hair with manicured fingers. "You have been thinking. Giving you a headache, is it?"

"Only if Wesley Snipes becomes available, in which case all the above is null and void," Paige joked.

The two cousins laughed again. "What's brought all this on anyway?" Francine inquired, puffing smoke from her cigarette and, in her usual manner, waving it away with her free hand so the gray odor would naturally not dim the light shade of her honey complexion. "Are you in love?"

"Maybe," Paige answered secretly, remembering the Egyptian statuette Rhys had given her and the symbolic promise it held that she would find such a love that would last into her old age.

"You and Rhys Langston have . . ." Francine's face broke into a smile. "And there I was thinking you'd be a lost cause."

"I know it's been nearly two weeks since we've met," Paige added with conviction, swallowing more soup, "but I feel like I've known him a lifetime. We've still got a lot to learn about each other, and we don't mind taking it slow."

"Good for you," Francine approved. "When are you seeing him again?"

Paige held her soup spoon in midair. They had not arranged anything. She had left Claridge's by taxi that morning, after spending the dawn reacquainting Rhys with her body, which he had studied with immense amorous scrutiny until she screamed for mercy, and he had made no mention of when he would be calling her next. The last thing Paige remembered, as she reluctantly tried to steal her way out of his hotel room, was his lowering the cleavage of her dress to suckle at her nipple in hopes that he could coax her to stay while she was on her way out the door.

Now, Paige felt it was an oversight not to have asked. "I think he'll be calling me later." She nodded, sealing the confirmation by plunging the spoon into her mouth.

Francine's brows rose in speculation. "Of course," she uttered, in a tone unconvinced. "Working today?"

"Yes," Paige croaked, detecting the tone.

Paige looked into her soup, but felt the flash of disappointment. She could not shake the feeling that, somehow, she had done something wrong. Her judgments had not been too hot in the past. What if she had made a bad judgement now? *No,* she told herself firmly. She had run with her instincts. Last night in Rhys's arms had been the best time of her life. Even if he were to leave her now, she could never regret Valentine's Day and what sharing the night together had meant to them both.

Francine extinguished her cigarette into an ashtray nearby. "I've got to run." She breathed out her last puff. "Tough case today. Lizzy Chadwick and Rupert King."

"Again?" Paige intoned.

"I'm hoping they can reach a compromise," Francine exclaimed, "but don't hold your breath. This may go to court."

"As bad as that?"

"It's getting ugly." Francine nodded. "Lizzy wants to backdate Rupert's financial obligation toward his daughter and force his involvement in their child's upbringing. He's still in denial, but he won't be able to escape digging into his pockets. I'll see you later."

"Yes." Paige nodded.

She watched her cousin leave, then looked at her mobile phone. *I could call the hotel and have them patch me through to his room,* Paige thought, knowing she needed reassurance. But she decided against it. She was not accustomed to chasing men, even if he was the right man, just so she could make herself happy. *I'll keep myself busy,* Paige mused instead. And her first thought was to return to her office.

"I thought you were in France," Blanton chimed, watching Paige breeze her way into his realty firm, just as he was handing over some typing to their secretary for processing. "What happened?"

"Change of plan," Paige told him. "Things okay here?"

"I'd like to see you in my office, now," Blanton countered, turning his back on Paige to lead the way ahead.

Paige felt slightly alarmed as she followed him in. Blanton was not smiling. He did not even look friendly. Like the sunset, he had shifted and changed before her very eyes to someone quite distant. His chilling presence was still with her as she closed the door to his office and silently walked over toward his desk. She watched as Blanton seated himself behind it and expected her to do the same on the other side. It almost felt like the first day they had met, when he had conducted her interview, only this time Blanton was not offering her coffee, and she was not replying that she liked it dark and sweet, like her men.

"What is it?" she asked him on a light note, hoping it would not be a question of him firing her or worse, flirting for her affections again. The last time they had spoken, she had overstepped the mark by intervening in his personal affairs. It was no less than his interference in hers, with his prejudicial assumptions and tainting of her character. If a tally had to be reached—they were now even.

"This." Blanton reached for a Xerox on his desk and handed it over. "I thought Coates-Davis's name sounded familiar, so I called a friend of mine who works in the City and also does dealings across the pond on Wall Street. He faxed me this over last night. You can keep that. It's a copy."

Paige stared at it. The truth was most revealing in print. *A man at the center of a one-million-pound insider-dealing probe into the trading of shares is a thirty-two year old American with a criminal past now living in the sunny planes of Monaco. Rhys Langston bought five hundred thousand Rail Lines shares just days before the transport secretary made an unexpected announcement which dramatically increased the value of the stock. The suspicious trade is now the subject of an insider-dealing inquiry by the Financial Services Authority, the City regulator.*

"I don't understand," Paige wavered.

"That was two years ago," Blanton confirmed, pointing at the Xerox Paige held limp in her hand. "And it gets worse. There was an announcement that the government would guarantee shareholders a minimum of two pounds and fifty pence for every share they held. It made your boyfriend a paper profit of nearly one million overnight. He placed the order through a London stockbroker who now works for Adabi Mercantile Investment Bank. His name is Franklin

Coates-Davis, the client who has just successfully acquired the house in—"

"Holland Park," Paige finished, seeing the connection. "Oh, my God. What's going on?"

"I don't know," Blanton reeled, shaking his head, "but you're up to your eyeballs in it and better get out."

"There must be an explanation," Paige protested, staring at the copy, the words looming to frighten her while she continued to stare. "Rhys doesn't have a criminal past."

"It says there that he does," Blanton debated. "I wouldn't be surprised if the shares your Internet lover bought ended up in a nominee account controlled by Adabi Mercantile. I'm told Adabi were, and still are, main advisers to government officials and so may have had advance warning of the transport secretary's announcement."

"This is all speculation," Paige peeved, tossing the Xerox copy onto Blanton's desk. "You're only saying all this to break me and Rhys up. You're jealous, and you always have been."

"I agree I've never liked the way you went about finding him," Blanton challenged, "but not even I can invent this sort of stuff. I told you he may not be all that he pretends to be. I see now that I am correct."

"Then why was he never convicted?" Paige pounced, a reflection of Rhys's adorable face formulating in her head. "Answer me that."

"Because . . . I don't know," Blanton hollered. "I'm waiting to hear from someone about his criminal past."

"Who?" Paige demanded, her fingers trembling.

"A friend in New York," Blanton informed her. "I'm doing this for your own protection."

"Get lost." Paige rose out of her chair, her heart pounding miserably. "This is about you trying to discredit Rhys because I happen to be falling in love with him. If you want me, you can have me, but strictly on a business basis. My interest in you goes no further."

"You think by taking this man to pitch against Rupert King that you have made me jealous?" Blanton accused with uncharacteristic arrogance, his eyes hard. "I am an African. I can have many wives. I do not need to waste time on Englishwomen and their games."

"Fine." Paige snatched the Xerox copy from Blanton's desk and walked briskly toward the door. "You can prove it by apologizing to your fiancée." Throwing Blanton a derisive glance, she stormed out of his office.

Paige sniffed inelegantly. Twisting her fingers, she paced the floor of her own office until she was forced to remove her white sandaled shoes. Throwing herself into her sofa, she hugged her lilac-colored cushions nervously. She was not in control again. Something had happened beyond her capabilities to solve. She had no idea how to go about smoothing away the creases or straightening the wrinkled lines. Her troubled midnight-blue gaze fell onto her laptop, and she immediately reached for it and placed it on her lap. Switching it on and fighting back the tears, Paige waited until the operating system loaded.

Plunged into finding answers to justify her life, she logged on. Her modem whimpered a cacophony of sounds, and she fell silent and stared at her screen. Paige did not know what she was searching for. All she knew was that she was back online. . . .

"It's eating up the news," Francine announced, displaying the latest headlines to Aunt Elva and Paige across the breakfast table. "Lizzy one, Rupert zero," she broached, bending the morning's newspaper in half to read the small print. "Lizzy is really out for the kill."

Paige kept her head down and sipped her tea, deferring from mentioning she was embroiled in a scandal of her own. A whole month had passed since she had severed ties with Rupert King, and while it may now be news to everyone else, it felt like ancient history in comparison to the new predicament she was now facing.

Silently contemplating Francine over her teacup, she

replayed in her head the awful details Blanton Blake had told her the day before. The melodrama had never left her mind from the moment she had departed her office, continuing to work its satire long into the night. When Rhys had telephoned her to coax her to come for dinner, she had gracefully declined, to give herself vital time to process the information she had acquired.

It was with a heavy heart that she had decided she would confront Rhys that day with her findings, certain he would have a valid explanation that would make her feel safe and secure again. It all had to be a terrible mistake, she even told herself, while Francine began to relate more details about Rupert's liaisons, half of which Paige was listening to, the other half she chose to ignore.

" 'The footballer vows not to dessert the team as evidence of his love child is likely to add strain to his current tryst with Blanton's real estate agent Paige Alexander,' Hey, you got mentioned," Francine drawled, not detecting her cousin's silent mood. " 'The couple have not announced their engagement, and recently postponed a trip to Portugal amid rumors of an alleged paternity suit which was cited by Lizzy Chadwick of the London party planners Chadwick & Co., where a verdict of paternity was proven at the High Court.' "

"Do you really have to read that now?" Paige protested, having heard enough gossip, clearly polished and plugged by Rupert's personal bagpipers and spin doctors. "Can't you see this is all publicity for the shoot-offs at the Millennium Stadium in Cardiff this week."

"Aren't you concerned that your name is being passed around like a football for sport?" Francine challenged, annoyed.

"Of course I am," Paige returned hotly. "But there's absolutely nothing I can do about that when Rupert's the one who's signing large advertising contracts since he became household goods after playing in the World Cup last year. Everything will die down in a week or two."

"What's the matter?" Elva asked, homing in on Paige's tone. "You don't sound well."

"I'm not," she admitted. That much was the truth. "I'm just sick of hearing about Rupert all the time. He'll set up a generous trust fund for his daughter eventually."

"Is it just Rupert?" Francine probed deeper.

Paige faked innocence. "What?"

"Why you're upset," Francine croaked, concerned. "It says here that you were seen nursing your wounded heart with a mystery lover, while Rupert King was left holding the baby. Have you spoken to Rhys this morning?"

"No," Paige remarked sternly, rubbing a ragged finger across her brow. "This is all old news."

Francine's brows furrowed. "You mean you have *new* stuff to tell us?"

"Yes. I mean no." Paige wavered, confused. She rose from the breakfast table. "I'm not hungry."

"Paige, sit down," Elva ordered. It was a demand. Paige sighed weakly and returned to her seat. "Whatever you have to tell us, just say it. If it's something you don't want your mother to know, we can discuss it here and now."

Paige pursed her lip into an hard line. "I think I'm in love," she affirmed, shaken, "but it may be with someone who . . . has lied to me."

"I knew it," Francine chortled, shaking her head vigorously in the negative. "What's he done? Killed somebody?"

"Don't be ridiculous." Paige flinched, knowing her cousin's lawyer brain could sometimes run away with her. "It's not anything like that."

"He's married," Elva responded softly.

"No, he's single," Paige told them both.

"He's got a secret love child like Rupert," Francine relented, still caught in the whirlwind of current newspaper events.

"No children," Paige breathed, unsure how much she wanted to reveal. "It's nothing personal," she elaborated slowly.

"Then what is it?" Francine pounced, her patience worn in anticipation.

"I think he's conducted some unethical business dealings," Paige divulged finally.

"Is that all?" Francine railed, unmoved, having dealt with far worse scenarios. "A dead body would have been far more exciting."

"Francine!" Elva warned.

"I see it in court all the time," Francine proclaimed, as though it should have been evident to her aunt and cousin both. "Men in business don't stick to rules. They rise to the challenge and kick dirt in the process. If you've ever seen a herd of vice presidents stampede, it's because someone's gone for their throat, choked them, cut off their air supply, and found out their deepest secrets to expose them. They make the best candidates for selling TV and movie rights, I think."

Paige's lips quirked at Francine's demeanor on the subject. "So you think I'm overreacting?"

"Only on the *being-in-love* bit," Francine crooned. "You haven't known him long enough for that."

"Love doesn't have a time and place when it comes," Elva debated, fixing Francine with a determined glance. "It just happens."

"Does it now?" Francine seemed amused.

"Didn't it with you?" Elva inquired suddenly.

Francine wished she had a cigarette. She could see from the expressions marred across her aunt and cousin's faces that she had missed something relevantly important. "I *love* my husband," she responded quite candidly.

Paige recalled having heard this admission before, in the same lull, matter-of-fact sort of way as when Francine had told her the first time, when they had lunched in the canteen at her law firm the day she had logged onto *www.totally-blackdating.com* and found Rhys Langston. Nothing had changed in Francine's tone now. It was devoid of affection, emotion, and meaning. A notch of ambiguity in her remark even resonated the room.

"You're not *in love* with Mervyn, are you?" Elva quavered, unsure why she had not seen it before. "That's why you're living here with me and only go and see him in Birmingham on weekends."

Francine laughed nervously. "Don't be silly, Aunt Elva," she protested. "I like my job and I like the prospects it offers for me here in London. Mervyn understands that I can't find the same kind of work in Birmingham."

"You could if you really wanted to be with him," Elva insisted. "I don't understand you young girls today. Me no understand the men either. In my day, things did not go on so. A man see you, him like you, him marry you. We old folks, we know about love."

Paige lowered her head. She understood. She had listened to her aunt in fascination that she could have felt such wondrous feelings, not once, not twice, but three times in her lifetime. To find it once was a hard feat in itself. And Paige had found it with Rhys Langston. He was her fire. She burned for him every time his image conjured up a picture in her mind. She'd wanted to see him last night, too, but she needed time to think. Sort out in her mind how she could best ask him about Omega Private Equity Funds Ltd. Why, when she ran a search on the Internet, it revealed that its latest profit margins had exceeded four million, listing Rhys Langston as the company's chief executive. Was it all legal? She did not know.

"I'm going to my office." Francine rose out of her chair, and smoothed the crease in her expensive checkered suit. She looked the picture of judicial England, warranted to present another leading case, and it was hard to see behind the hazel color of her eyes whether she had been fazed by her aunt's piercing interrogation. "Do I make a statement on your behalf?" She turned her attention to Paige.

"What?" Paige asked, suddenly lost.

"About your status with Rupert King," Francine explained. "The press will be asking, if they're not outside the house already."

Paige was alarmed. "Just tell them this relationship is dead and buried."

Francine left the kitchen and Paige stared at her aunt. "What should I do?" She needed advice and quickly.

"Has he told you how he feels?" Elva asked with a smile breaking on her lips.

"He thinks he's falling in love with me," Paige revealed, her heart melting at the repetition of his sweet endearment. "That's what he's told me."

"Then talk to him," her aunt advised. "Find out what he has to say. If he has nothing to hide, he'll tell you the truth."

Paige nodded, but still felt like she was walking on a path fraught with hazards.

"I thought you said Miss Paige Alexander was zero publicity," Franklin Coates-Davis bellowed as he faced Rhys Langston from across his desk. A copy of the morning newspaper was in front of him, and he picked it up and handed it over to Rhys before reaching to his cabinet for a bottle of bourbon. "She *is* the girl who works at Blanton's?"

"Yes." Rhys nodded, glancing across at the headlines.

"Paige Alexander?"

"That's her." Rhys was confused. "How did you know?"

"She's right there in paragraph six."

Rhys saw it, only he could not believe it. His desert princess, linked to one of Britain's most renowned football strikers, with the headline citing Rupert's greater interest in Paige's D cup than in the latest Cup finals. His blood ran cold at the derision, especially when he saw mentioned that she had been seen with a mystery man. It was him. And Rhys could not afford the unwanted publicity. "I didn't know about this."

"You're going to have to get out of the country for a while," Franklin advised immediately, handing over a glass of bourbon. "You've come out on top after that Rail Lines scandal.

You don't want to risk it resurfacing over a skirt. Go back to Monaco."

"But I want to talk about my latest transactions," Rhys exclaimed shrewdly. "That's why I'm here. I've noticed some discrepancies."

"There were a few things I couldn't liquidate as you would like," Franklin began, pouring himself a glass of bourbon. "It's nothing I can't handle—I've told you this already."

"I'm no longer buying the house in Holland Park," Rhys informed him sadly. "I really liked it, too, but another buyer came in and gazumped my offer."

"That's too bad," Franklin wavered, sipping his liquor slowly, hiding his deceit well.

"As I was saying." Rhys returned to the main subject in hand. "There's a large consignment of money that doesn't seem to have been transferred. You don't think this Internet hacking business had anything to do with it, do you?"

"I'll look into it," Franklin assured him, downing more bourbon. "Did your real live goddess like her birthday present?" he instantly deviated.

"The Egyptian figurine?" Rhys schooled his eyes on Franklin, puzzled at how this randy, middle-aged, Middle Eastern man, with his receding hairline and puffed-out cheeks, had come to acquire with such cool perception his choice of names for Paige. "She loved it. That was a great tip. Thanks."

"Did it have any markings on the bottom?" Franklin prodded flatly. "Numbers, dates, anything?"

"I didn't look." Rhys shrugged, puzzled at the interest. He drained the last of the bourbon from his own glass. "Look, I have to go."

"What about your excavation project in Dhashur?" Franklin reminded Rhys as he remained seated and retook the newspaper Rhys handed over before watching the younger man rise from his chair. Likewise, he retook the empty glass. "Don't you want to check if they've found anything?"

"A main shaft," Rhys divulged, glancing at his watch. "It

was discovered before, but the lead archaeologist thinks it might lead to the tomb of Atum."

Franklin's eyes widened. As though in shock, his mouth fell agape. "What?" He swallowed. "I don't believe it."

"I'll know more when I'm out there," Rhys explained, taking a second glance at his watch. "I really have to go."

Franklin shifted uncomfortably in his seat. "Did you discover the legend about the—"

"I need to call Miss Alexander and see if I can meet her for lunch," Rhys insisted.

"Keep it very low-key," Franklin warned, suddenly shaken, resting a stern finger on the newspaper in front of him. "You don't want your name added to this piece of garbage."

That much Rhys agreed with. But he really needed to see Paige, and there was an urgency for him to do so. She had declined seeing him the night before, and he now suspected it had something to do with the announcement he had just seen in the newspaper. She probably thought he would be angry with her, or perhaps there was more to it than she had let on. Maybe she was still involved with Rupert King and had not told him the entire story. He could not be sure.

All Rhys knew was that when he had phoned, she'd sounded elusive, upset, and a little on the nervous side. It had kept him awake wondering what was wrong. Now, it seemed the answers had stared him right in the face. Whatever matters he needed to sort out with Franklin would have to be shelved for the time being, even though he quite rightfully heeded the warning.

"If I'm going to go down," he declared before making his departure, uncaring what lay ahead, "it will be with someone I love."

Twelve

Paige did what any young, spirited realty agent would do under the circumstances. She went to the gym and then shopping. Before her workout with Georgia Bagnoli and her retail therapy blitz on Oxford Street, she had turned to the pack of reporters and photographers camped outside her aunt's house that morning and delivered the ultimate putdown on the man she had come to despise for making her life so problematic.

"He's loaded with loyalty, but for the most part, it's been misplaced."

Then she picked herself up, dusted herself down, and went about her merry way. She knew Rupert's international celebrity managers were probably undergoing contractual renegotiations, which in turn would lead to his book, CD, and computer game. Or more importantly, lucrative promotional deals with car manufacturers, mobile phone makers, and any other coveted brand name looking for a high-profile personality to sell their goods. She was not about to partake of the publicity wheel by endorsing or adding kind sentiments to the process.

"Any comments about his love child?" a reporter had vigorously persisted, despite her having given her assertion before entering the taxi that had blessedly arrived outside her home.

"I'm not talking about it today, tomorrow, or ever!" Paige answered simply.

It was quiet dignity. Not that she cared. Not that she was

not enjoying the silent revenge either, but all Paige could think about was Rhys Langston. She had missed him, despite her refusing to see him, and in her bedroom that morning, had stared at the Egyptian statuette he had given her, as a reminder of what they had meant to each other, before she left for the day. Now, after she'd spoken with Aunt Elva, it seemed everything would be just fine. She would talk to Rhys and he would, no doubt, explain the awful insinuations her boss had made about him.

It was the one thing that had kept her away from her office that morning—facing Blanton Blake. She did not want a repeat performance of what he had told her. Paige felt she would rather speak with Rhys first, then weather the storm with her boss later. But she could not delay any further. Her shopping therapy was over, it was now nearly lunchtime, and she was reminded there was work on her desk to be done. There was also a property to show at two o'clock, and another at four. The office was becoming busy as the new properties for sale were beginning to flood in, and so, grabbing a sandwich and a plastic cup of takeaway soup from the nearest delicatessen, Paige hopped into a taxi and arrived at her office.

Dressed to fit the bright, breezy day in February in a dark green cashmere suit, cream-colored heels, and a suitable beige blouse, Paige entered Blanton's doing a balancing act with five shopping bags and her lunch. Her hair had been swept by a mild wind, which also roused color in her cheeks. It made her look slightly flustered rather than calm when she walked into her office and off-loaded everything onto her sofa. She was on the point of placing her hot soup on her desk when she heard the knock at her door, seconds before her boss walked in.

"Do you want to hear what I have to tell you?" he announced, staking residence by the door, dressed formally in tailored gray trousers and a pale yellow shirt, his gray silk tie firmly fixed, like his expression.

"What now?" Paige cringed, knowing from his tone it had

to be worse than what he had told her the day before, and what she had endured on her doorstep that morning.

"Aside from the fact that you're making news coverage as the ex who dumped Rupert King," he began scathingly, "and can't be bothered to utilize your office desk when I had expected you four hours ago," he added, briefly glancing at her shopping, "your Internet lover and prospective client was a colleague at a New York firm who were part of a pensions and investments bond scandal."

Paige's blood ran cold. "And?"

"According to my source, he was paid off," Blanton revealed, "to keep quiet."

"This is all speculation." Paige refused to be swayed as she shook her head, placing her soup on her desk. "Rhys Langston is not that sort of man."

"No?" Blanton persisted. "Where is he now?"

"Right here," a voice intruded, seconds before Rhys Langston materialized and ventured into Paige's office. "Who's asking?"

Blanton's expression changed to one of almost disbelief when he found himself faced with the very person he was attempting to discredit. Rhys looked measurably taller at the side of him, and was smartly dressed in a black pin-striped suit, with a clean white pressed shirt, a dark-blue tie, and his short black hair slick and smoothed away from his face. He appeared in total contrast to how Paige remembered him, a person casually attired and, for the most part, in jeans. Now Rhys looked like something that had walked off the pages of *Esquire* magazine, and Paige's heart skipped a beat as his smile revealed his perfectly sculptured teeth.

She was happy to see him. Her body reacted with instant alert, warming to his presence, the very sight of him, sensing the faint smell of his aftershave. She was trembling at how handsome he appeared, how she could so easily find herself wanting to rush into his arms and smother him with kisses. It was a magnificent, exhilarating feeling to be in such a love-struck state, and equally dilapidating to have it easily spoiled by Blanton Blake.

"I was telling Paige that we needed to know more about your . . . business transactions before we can show you any further properties," Blanton prevaricated immediately, with prejudice.

Rhys did not miss the hesitancy, and narrowed his brows. "Is there a problem?"

Blanton was unmoved. "I was considering there could be."

"Really." Rhys walked the span of the room and leaned his back against Paige's desk, then proceeded to dig both hands into his pockets to contemplate Blanton with an inquisitive stare. "I'm sure you're going to tell me all about it."

"We don't need to go into this," Paige said, slicing her gaze between both men nervously, her heart held on a thread. "It's all been a misunderstanding."

"Two years ago," Blanton overrode, "investigators at the FSA tried to establish how a certain share deal you made was executed."

"And?" Rhys asked, narrowing his eyes so that it was not made clear what dark secret lay behind them.

"It's alleged you took information from a government's main adviser on Rail Lines PLC, therefore having advance warning of the transport secretary's announcement in order to buy shares while they were not being actively traded," Blanton transpired. "All buyers of our properties have to reveal how they are to fund any purchases and—"

"Is this about me or something else?" Rhys interrupted, his mental antenna raised

Blanton fell silent.

"If you had done your homework," Rhys continued, "you would've discovered that the FSA concluded their findings six months ago, ruling me out completely. You see, rather than waiting for the full two-pounds-and-fifty-pence compensation share price offered by the government, which would have netted me nearly one million, I sold my shares soon after I purchased them for two pounds and ten, creating less profit. If I had insider information, I would've held on to them and claimed the remaining forty pence per share."

Paige was immediately relieved. "I told you there would be an explanation." She aimed that at her boss, feeling confident enough to take a seat among the cushions in her sofa. She threw Rhys a smile, and felt her heart somersault as he returned one to her.

"You're falling for this?" Blanton harangued, aiming his plea at Paige, noting the flirtatious glances they exchanged before turning to level an accusation at Rhys. "What about your criminal past in New York?"

Rhys raised a brow. "What's supposed to have happened there?"

"You being bought off by the company you worked for because of a pensions and investment bond scandal," Blanton revealed impatiently.

"There was a scandal," Rhys admitted, keeping his gaze fixed. "I nearly got caught up in the investigation because it was a pension I had sold. A colleague of mine illegally transferred it to an investment bond to liquidate the funds so he could save the client from bankruptcy, and I became implicated. We had a fight. He gave me a bruised lip, in fact, less than what I gave him. The firm compensated me on the provision that we both resign and I keep my mouth shut."

"Happy now?" Paige told her boss, annoyed that he should take matters so far. She turned toward Rhys while removing her cashmere jacket and offered him an apology. "I'm sorry about this."

"No need." Rhys shrugged off the matter, an excited nerve shifting in his groin as he watched Paige shed her outer garment. "He's just doing his job."

"You're really falling for this," Blanton pressed on, his face now enraged as he attacked Paige. "You pick this guy up off the Internet and choose to believe everything he's telling you?"

Rhys's eyes widened suddenly as the blow came down, hard and brutal. He pushed himself from Paige's desk and pulled his hands from his trouser pockets. His brown gaze swiftly moved from Blanton to Paige, amazed that this man knew so much about him. Not only did he know, he was elaborating further on details Rhys had no knowledge of at all.

"Pitching him against Rupert and then me," Rhys heard the male voice continue. "It's all some kind of game to you, isn't it? And when that wasn't enough, you decide to coerce my fiancée into adopting similar liberal Westernized standards."

"That's not true," Paige spat out, alarmed and thoroughly shaken.

She looked at Rhys. Her heart plummeted. He did not seem the quietly comfortable man he had been on entering her office. His face had now become like stone, his soulful brown eyes had hardened, and his large pink lips were no longer invitingly kissable, but were pursed into a firm line. Paige had never seen him look so callous. Her image of Rhys had always been that of a desert prince, rescuing her from afar. Now, it seemed Blanton's cruel revelations might dash all her hopes and dreams for a second time.

"What is he talking about?" Rhys demanded of her.

"It was supposed to be uncomplicated," Paige blurted out, slowly rising to her feet, feeling at any time she would faint.

"Am I missing something?" Rhys questioned again.

"I just wanted to teach Rupert a lesson," Paige whispered, the stinging tears now threatening to spill over in a flurry of embarrassment.

"You're her temporary lover," Blanton rasped to Rhys, relating the truth as only he knew it. "She wanted to try the escort agencies first, but going on the Web promised instant results."

"I tried to tell you," Paige implored Rhys, her voice shaking in tune with her body. "It's not like how he paints it."

"She wanted someone for her party," Blanton accused hotly, adding relish to his tone. "When she ditched Rupert, that left her manless. Somewhere along the line, she even tried to play on me and I nearly fell for it, but I'm engaged to be married."

"And that's where I come in?" Rhys intoned sternly.

"I thought . . . ," Paige croaked, taking two paces forward, her legs shaking with such overwhelming humiliation that she dared not take another step should they give way. "I thought—"

"That I could be used as some form of bait?" Rhys gushed, his pained eyes boring into her midnight-blue ones.

"No!" Paige contradicted emphatically, the tears now rolling down her cheeks with shame and mortification. Trembling like a leaf, she turned and almost lashed out at Blanton. "Get out of my office."

"You're still putting him over me—someone who knows you—your friend?" Blanton drawled in amazement at seeing Paige's flurry of tears. When she did not answer, but instead clenched her hands together, he stared at Rhys Langston. "And you're still going to believe whatever she tells you?" When Rhys remained silent, Blanton was at a loss. "You two deserve each other," he rebutted, turning and bracing his hand on the doorknob. "I don't know who's the spider and who's the fly," he flung out at Paige, "but one of you is going to be gobbled up." He stormed out of her office.

The silence was unbearable. Paige was rooted to the spot, disbelieving she had just witnessed what had happened. Blanton had made it all seem so ugly. So unspeakable that when the pieces of truth began to drop from his lips, she felt as though she despised herself, that she could be capable of such deceit, that no man could ever trust her again. But it had not been like that. In her mind, Paige had simply wanted company. She would never have guessed in her wildest dreams it would come in the shape of someone as gorgeous as Rhys Langston. She needed to explain. She needed him to understand. But when Paige dared to look into Rhys's dark eyes, the pain that reflected back tore her in two.

"A lie is always halfway across the world when the truth is just getting its shoes on." She panicked, folding her arms across her bosom. "It's not like how he tells it."

"Even if we had a map," Rhys flinched, feeling as though

his heart was breaking in half, "neither you nor I could find the moral ground."

"I thought—"

"You could play a big boy's game by little girl rules," Rhys exclaimed, angry that he had not seen it before. It explained why Rupert had been so worked up at her party, why he had said she was playing some kind of game to get him back. It accounted for why her boss had behaved so bestially and given her a predatory gaze on departing. It even defined in his mind why he had thought she had slept with one or both men. And now he was witnessing the tears of disgrace. This woman had never felt anything for him at all, except to use him selfishly for her own aim.

"Rhys . . . " Paige wept, daring to take another step toward him.

"You cry like a child for what you cannot account for as a woman," he derided, feeling more pained at seeing her tears. "I thought you were my desert princess, but I was just dreaming. None of it was real."

"Yes, it was—still is," Paige crooned. "That's what I've been trying to tell you. I've never felt this way about anyone before, not until I met you."

"And I'm supposed to believe that?" Rhys reproved, closing his eyes briefly for fear that tears might threaten to break his composure, too.

"It's the truth," Paige sobbed, venturing another pace in his direction and clenching her fingers to keep her stable. "Believe me—"

"How could you play with our lives?" Rhys objected angrily, his eyes re-opening to find that Paige suddenly seemed closer. He longed to touch her, feel her lips against his, but his treacherous thoughts saw her only as a threat. "You couldn't clinch your boss, so that made me fair game?"

"No!" Paige whimpered, overwhelmed by the deep pinning pool of emotion she felt for Rhys, but was unable to share with him at that precise moment.

"You treated me like some sort of commodity?" he yelled.

"Rhys, listen to me," Paige pleaded, deciding to walk completely over to him. She touched his hand, but he pulled it away and retreated a step backward. "However this all began, it changed the moment you kissed me at the airport. It grew into something more when you took me to dinner. It blossomed when you were with me at my party and gave me such a special gift, which I stare at it every night before I go to bed. It bloomed when we went out to the theater. It deepened when we made love, and now, whatever it is, it's out of control. I *need* you."

Rhys was not convinced. "I'm going back to Monaco in the morning," he said, his forehead creasing with the confusion spinning around inside him. His innards were torn to threads, his guts felt as though they had been wrenched out. His heart was weeping. "I don't know if I'll be back."

"Rhys, don't do this to us," Paige begged, fresh tears tumbling from her eyes. She tried to touch him again, but he pulled away and walked toward the door.

"I came here today to tell you . . ." *How much I've fallen in love with you,* Rhys thought. "That I didn't want my name added to the garbage I read in the newspapers today," he told her coldly. "Please see to it that I stay out of it."

Paige was mortified that Rupert's spillage should now be staining her. "They say a man doesn't go very far in life without leaving some raw edges," she nodded, pained as the knife dug deep. "I don't know what you and Mr. Coates-Davis have got going on, why he is now buying the Holland Park property and not you, or why you have so much money in Omega Private Equity Funds Ltd., but whatever it is you're both up to, please see to it that I stay out of it."

Rhys's face drooped in surprise, and Paige noticed. Her heart swelled with a confusion of regret and sorrow that she should reveal he was not the only person who held secrets. If he was working for Mr. Coates-Davis, that was of course his business, but she wanted Rhys to also realize there were paths to his life that he had not allowed her to venture on, so he should not be holding her entirely accountable because she had not opened the gateway to her own.

"I wish you all the best in sorting yourself out," Rhys said, bracing his hand on the doorknob, keeping to the subject that accounted for his fraying emotions and refraining from passing comment about what she had just told him. "Good-bye, Paige."

With that final remark, Rhys was out the door and gone from her life.

It had all ended in chaos, confusion, and disaster, just as Blanton had told her it would, and she was left feeling much worse. The fantasy adventure had indeed run its course to the bitter end. That night, Paige bawled into her pillow. The lamenting ran into the morning and kept her in bed. It was Francine who knocked on her door around noon and quietly ventured in to see what was going on. Paige was hidden under the sheets, feeling every inch a woman in mourning.

"Paige?" Francine sighed, her petite figure still dressed in her long nightgown and her auburn curly perm covered with a head scarf, having just awoken and not yet ventured downstairs for breakfast.

"He's gone," Paige wailed bitterly into her pillow. "As I knew he would be."

"Oh, Paige." Francine immediately sat on the edge of her cousin's bed, and instantly rubbed her hands over the sheets, feeling it to connect with one of Paige's legs beneath. "I'm so sorry."

"I've been a fool," Paige murmured, her head still hidden. "It's all ruined. Blanton squealed. He told Rhys everything."

"Blanton Blake, your boss?" Francine crooned, pulling the sheets back so she could see whether Paige was telling her the truth for real. She found her cousin with puffy red eyes and the most forlorn expression she had ever seen in life. Her hair was disheveled, the rich honey brown of her cheeks were pale, and she seemed fragile, like something that could be easily broken. "The jealous bastard. I told you he had the upper hand."

"I know." Paige nodded, weakened by a further series of tears. "I should have listened to you. He wanted it to end in ashes and made sure it did."

"Where's Rhys now?"

"Gone. Back home to Monaco."

"Monaco?"

"He has a house there."

"He's not coming back?"

"No," she sobbed. "He'll probably go on from there to Egypt to oversee his investment."

"Egypt!" Francine was silenced. Then she tried to inject a little optimism. "It was all too bizarre anyway," she said, compensating for the situation having gone awry. "There's a psychology to these Internet dates. They always start off brilliantly, full of butterflies, sweet adoration, and plenty of lust, but statistics reveal they never work out."

"They have statistics on this sort of thing?" Paige choked on her tears.

"These kind of relationships are a new phenomena," Francine revealed quite candidly. "Someone's got to tote up the points and weigh the pros and cons."

"Any pros?"

"There have been," Francine admitted. "But they're far outweighed by the cons." She sighed and elaborated. "Only last week I had a case in court where I had to explain to the defense that e-mail isn't private, but is the most exposed form of communication on earth. It leaves electronic footprints as the message is stored and forwarded around the Web system. It's not tangible, just like Web relationships. The guys always live abroad. You don't get to see their friends or families. Dating is done by e-mail, jpegs, and videocams, and sex is in cyberspace. None of it's real."

"But I met Rhys," Paige breathed on a hiccup. "He was tangible, here, in my arms. We kissed, we hugged, we made love in the flesh."

"Made love," Francine chimed, as though unsure of the words. "Look," she reasoned logically. "Meeting a person in this way is unrealistic. It usually takes six days for the relationship to get serious, twenty-one days for the man to propose, and 0.6 seconds for the woman to say yes. The ideal of making love doesn't even factor."

"It was beautiful!" Paige sobbed, ignoring her cousin. "And he gave me this." She pointed at her Egyptian statuette, sitting comfortably on a table by her bed. "He said it belonged to the goddess Isis. That's the name I used on the Internet. Don't you see? It's all symbolic and whoever owns it will find true love into their old age. It's a legend. And he gave it to me." New tears surfaced. "By having this, I know it was all real." Paige dug her head into her pillow, dejected, as the tears flowed. "I don't expect you to understand. You're not even in love."

"Don't turn this on me," Francine repeated for the umpteenth time. "I *love* my husband."

"Oh, knock it off," Paige cried, raising her head slightly to throw red glazed eyes across at her cousin. "You said something to me once about having an old love you can imagine going back to and one who reminds you how far you had come. That's when it suddenly dawned on me. Mervyn is a love that reminds you of how far you have come, that's why you married him. You didn't think you would find someone who could truly love you, so you settled for him."

"Don't you ever say that to me," Francine snarled, removing her hand from the mold of Paige's leg beneath the sheets. "You've no idea what you're saying. He's my best friend. We share everything."

"He makes you feel special, does he?" Paige moaned in recollection of something else she remembered. "Shares your ideas, opinions, and dreams, does he? That's what you told me, right? Then why did Lizzy Chadwick see you sneak off with Rupert at my party?"

"What?" Francine gasped as the bustle of questions threw her, before the last one hit home.

"She told me," Paige lamented. "Only you didn't know he had Claudia and Tina before he got around to you."

Francine's lighter shade of honey complexion seemed much paler suddenly. "That's a lie."

"Deny it all you want," Paige spat out. "But you're as bad as my father."

"Your father is only giving your mother back what she deserves," Francine uttered, before covering her mouth, knowing she had divulged information that was far better left alone.

"What's that supposed to mean?" Paige croaked, suddenly suspended between tears.

Francine shrugged her shoulders. "Your mother cheated first—so I heard on the family grapevine at our house."

"What?" Paige was stunned.

"He was a spare tire, came and went, while your dad was doing the night shifts," Francine went on. "Your father found out and divorced her, but has kept up pretenses ever since."

"I don't believe you," Paige railed, her mouth falling open at the sudden revelation that love had never left her mother, but rather Gwerfyl had found it somewhere else.

"The women in our family have never been lucky with men," Francine informed her, rising to her feet to brush down her nightgown. "We've never found our protectors, our princes, the ones who would rescue us from ourselves. Just the Godfreys. They're the men who know how to keep a marriage together, but they never bring love, adventure, and excitement home, not the way we would like it. Now you know."

"But Aunt Elva—"

"Lost all three," Francine appended. "Wake up to reality, cuz. I tried to tell you the easy way, when you kept harping on about waiting to meet someone special, and then confusing yourself about marriage as though it's a jail sentence where a woman hides everything, including herself. Meeting Rhys Langston is as juicy as your past is going to get. You need to move beyond that now. That's the way it is." She looked at the Egyptian statuette situated on a side table by her cousin's bed. "At least you have something to remember him by. Just do yourself a favor and pop by the church sometime."

"And listen to the religion of slaves?" Paige dismissed, narrowing her tear-glazed eyes like a viper about to strike. "The ideal Christian, according to his own doctrine, is a weak, adulterate, self-despising little worm. His only hope is to pray that he will be one of the chosen few and everyone else will be shoveled into the hellfire. It's a doctrine of self-morality for guilt-filled people like you and Mum, and Dad and maybe even Mervyn. If things are no different among the people in church, as you now seem to be telling me, why should I go there?"

"I want you to be with someone reliable," Francine concluded finally.

"What I *want* is the scorching heat I felt when I was with Rhys," Paige blurted, amid a fresh bout of tears, her heart mourning her loss. "The burning ache that almost scalded me, the deep blister his kisses left on my lips, the way his body nearly singed mine because we were so hot for each other. The flame we kindled until it flared out of control. If that's the hellfire, show me the way."

"Oh, Lord," Francine breathed, as though she had heard true blasphemy as never before.

"Say your own prayers," Paige cried, the taste of salty, bitter tears spilling down her cheeks and onto her lips. "I only pray Rhys comes back to me so I can tell him how much I've fallen in love with him."

Francine solemnly closed the door behind her as she left Paige crying, and cast her eyes heavenward. Something inside her was filled with remorse. Slowly walking away with fresh thoughts that told her she needed to reevaluate her own life, she whispered an impassioned "Amen."

Three weeks later, Paige heard a knock at her office door. She was seated at her desk, immersed in work, having survived her recent ordeal. There had been no word from Rhys since he had left her. No phone call or e-mail sentiments. On one occasion, she had thought to go into *www.totallyblack-dating.com* to try and locate him under his moniker, Omega, but decided against it. Too much damage had been done, she judged from the way she had handled his departure.

There had been the tears, the absences from work, the depressing lapses into solitude where she had reminisced about how good they had been together. Rhys was, after all, a fun guy to be with. Though they had shared only very little time together, he had been good for her. But it was all behind her now. She had developed a much deeper understanding of the pitfalls of finding love, especially after broaching the subject of her father with her mother. The sore conversation had taught her a vital lesson. She had learned that modern life was full of such brief interludes, encounters, and fleeting dates. It was foolhardy to even think she could be expected to find true love on the Internet, when in real life it was an equal impossibility, according to the testimony of her parents.

Returning to work was not an easy feat either. Blanton had apologized for his interference into her private affairs, she in turn had apologized for her intrusion in his, and they had both reached a tacit consent not to raise the matter again. It was professional conduct at its subtle, two-faced, conniving best. Paige even decided that the whole romance with Rhys and its consequences had been a mad blip in her life that was meant to happen to create bounce and energy in her very existence, putting her back on track. And with that resolve firmly implanted in her mind, she had detached her attention from her feelings and gotten on with life, surmounting herself in work. Now, as she shifted her gaze from her computer laptop, her head rose expectantly to observe the person at her office door.

"Come in," she announced, staring in anticipation at the newcomer—a foreign man—who entered. His obese figure registered in Paige's mind immediately, as did his tall frame, expensive suit, and the way he strode into her office as though he were presiding over a royal feast. "Can I help you?" Paige smiled easily.

"I'm looking for Mr. Blanton Blake," he remarked with an Arabian accent. "We have a scheduled appointment."

"For what time?" Paige asked, glancing at her watch before flicking through her diary, where she listed both her own and Blanton's calendar of business activities.

"Eleven o'clock," he told her.

"Oh, dear," Paige returned, her tone professionally pitched, as her watch told her it was two o'clock. "You're late. He's been called away on another appointment. Can I help you?"

The newcomer's eyes lit up and he seemed eager to seek guidance. "Actually," he began, venturing further into the room, placing both hands into his trouser pockets as he did so, "I have just bought a house with you, subject to contract, and have to sign the papers."

"With your attorney," Paige advised.

"Of course." He nodded. "But I wondered if you had keys for access so that I may take measurements for curtains and carpets, that sort of thing."

"I don't think that will be a problem," Paige told him curtly. "When would you like to see the property?"

"Today," the newcomer announced. "I was expected to be taken along by Mr. Blake, but hadn't realized I had overlooked the time."

Paige raised an annoyed brow. She hated when clients took liberties like this, expecting realty agents to drop everything and accommodate them at the slightest whim. It was one of the liabilities of the job, she mused on reflection on the numerous times she had had to put work on hold to take a particular buyer to measure up at short notice. But she kept her smile fixed and offered her usual courtesy.

"I don't think we have anyone available today to take you along," she rebutted kindly, far too loaded with work to accommodate him herself. "It's the new season. We're very busy. Perhaps—"

"I've paid cash for this house, Miss . . .?"

"Alexander," Paige divulged, curious as to who he was. "And you are?"

"Mr. Franklin Coates-Davis," the newcomer announced. "If you look me up on your computer, you'll find that the house on Holland Park Road was sold to me—cash."

Paige's heart skipped a beat immediately. She almost gasped knowing she was facing someone who had connections with Rhys Langston. Yet he looked worlds apart from the man who had stolen her heart. She could see Mr. Coates-Davis was a native Arab, and she was curious as to why he had an Anglicized name. Equally curious to her was the reason why he was buying the house she had suspected would have been an easy sell to Rhys Langston. As far as she knew, Blanton was dealing with the paperwork, but there had been some delay. She suspected it was her boss's usual proficiency in checking that the sale was legit. She could not be sure, and Paige could not help wondering what exactly was going on.

"You know something?" she amended, falsely skimming a glance over her diary. "I do have an opening in fifteen minutes. Perhaps you'd like to wait in the foyer until I'm free."

"Of course," Franklin accepted politely. He threw Paige a smile, then left her office.

Paige rose out of her chair and for five minutes, paced the floor of her office. A myriad of thoughts suddenly shot through her mind. Maybe Mr. Coates-Davis knew where Rhys was. Perhaps he could pass on a message. Then it occurred to her that Rhys was probably with him in London. She overruled that option immediately when she thought back to Rhys having gone to Monaco. Maybe he was back. It suddenly filtered through her head, causing her to fluster with the possibility that she might in fact see Rhys again.

Paige wondered how she could question Mr. Coates-Davis without appearing nosy or in desperate need for news. Surely a simple inquisition would not look too suspicious? But as she nervously smoothed the line in her blue designer jeans, slipped into the red sandal-heeled shoes she had taken off earlier, and threw on a short red woolen jacket over the white silk blouse she was wearing, Paige had a rethink. Even if she found where Rhys was, would he want her to contact him?

When a resounding "no" entered her head, the old feelings of lost hopes and dreams resurfaced.

Paige braced both hands against her desk and inhaled a ragged breath. Seeing her again would probably remind him of how much she had deceived him. At least, that would be how he would see it. Never mind the fact that she had fallen in love with him within the short period of time they had grown to know each other. Others might accept the situation as folly, but she had lived it and it all still felt very real to her.

Reaching for her handbag, Paige delved inside and located her lipstick and pocket mirror. She applied the deep shade of red, then plucked at strands of her hair, which she had left combed around her ears with a playful fringe at her temple for added body. She tried to smile, but glimpsing her slightly wonky front tooth made her feel worse because she was reminded that Rhys liked it. She still looked pale, but the color was flushed into her cheeks artificially with a hint of blusher, and now that she had added lipstick, she could pass for a woman still in control.

She reached for her desk drawer and located two keys before switching off her laptop. When Paige arrived in the foyer, Mr. Coates-Davis was seated, waiting alone, and rose slowly to his feet on her approach. He suddenly looked much taller and certainly more foreign, and was now holding a Monte Cristo cigar. He took a final puff, then immediately extinguished it in a nearby ashtray.

"My driver is waiting outside," he revealed, leading the way toward the exit doors, expectant that Paige would follow. "I hope you can give me some ideas on color schemes," he added with a smile. "Rhys has told me so much about you."

"Rhys?" Paige gasped, her heart thudding suddenly as she followed him out into the daylight.

"I was the one who suggested he buy you the Egyptian figurine for your birthday," Franklin remarked. "Do you still have it?"

"Oh, yes," Paige enthused. She still stared at it the last

thing at night before she went to bed, and it was the first thing she looked at upon awaking in the morning.

"I was hoping to have seen it before he gave it to you," Franklin went on, allowing his driver to open the car door to accommodate them both into the limousine. "May I see it sometime?"

"Of course." Paige nodded, anticipating hearing news on Rhys. "Whenever you like."

"How about this evening?" Mr. Coates-Davis invited. "Perhaps you can join me for dinner?"

"That would be nice." Paige nodded in acceptance without hesitation. As she seated herself into the soft white leather, she was filled with renewed hope that this was Rhys Langston's way of contacting her again, hopeful that on making this new connection with an old acquaintance of his, she would soon find herself back in his arms.

Paige held on tightly to her gold handbag, and the six-inch statuette that Rhys had given her for her birthday, as the elevator took her upward toward the penthouse suite at Seacon Wharf. Mr. Coates-Davis had invited her personally to his home, and the plush surroundings she had seen on entering the lobby gave every indication of his status level, not so far removed from the rich clients she often sold property to.

She was bemused, however, that he did not seem so interested in measuring for curtains as she had expected on their visit to the house at Holland Park. Instead, he had excitedly asked her questions about her relationship with Rhys and the statuette he had presented to her at her birthday party. She had been equally excited in responding to his interest, thinking perhaps he was sure to tell her of Rhys's arrival back to England, or relay a message to her on his behalf. Sadly, that had not happened.

Still, it had not swayed her from dressing in something that would engender male approval, should she find herself confronting the man who had been a constant memory in the forefront of her mind since their first meeting. The long coral-colored dress swept up into an embracing rush of fabric and, clipped into place with a gold brooch at her cleavage, was just the sort of confidence-booster Paige needed to connect with her alluring feminine ego once more. With her hair equally swept into a tight chignon, and her makeup applied with tenuous care to bring out the glowing shades of honey in her complexion, she was again the brave new woman depending on herself, wearing the mask of self-sufficiency.

But as she found herself stepping from the elevator, and her three-inch gold Donna Karan heels were digging into the deep pile-beige carpeting beneath her feet, Paige became bemused. Exactly why Mr. Coates-Davis had invited her to dinner was now dancing across her mind. He had been polite with her. She was not suspecting that she might be in any imminent danger, but it was a mystery nonetheless to her why he wanted to see her statuette. Paige's mind was still riddled with curiosity when the door in front of her swung open and the expectant gaze of Mr. Coates-Davis met her own inquiring one.

"Thank you for accepting my hospitality," he immediately said on greeting her, extending his hand to invite her into his penthouse suite. He was traditionally dressed in an Arabian white ankle-length cotton *thobe* under a gray bisht robe. On his head was a *tagiyah* and its co-ordinating apparel of a *ghutra* and *agal,* and leather *khussas* were on his feet. He was also smoking a cigar, which made him seem almost regal. "Would you like something to drink?"

"Martini on ice," Paige nodded, dumbfounded as her gaze swept the huge space around her. The room was pleasant and held a wonderful aroma. There were plenty of ornaments, a Persian rug, several large cream sofas, and large green plants to bring life to what could otherwise have been a dull room, given the expansive area to fill.

"Please, take a seat," Mr. Coates-Davis advised from the cocktail cabinet across the room.

"I like your interior style," Paige commented, acknowledging her approval as she took a seat and continued her avid surveillance of the room, hopeful she would find Rhys waiting for her there. To her chagrin, he was not, and the disappointment resonated in her voice. "I don't think you need advice on your new home at all," she added with a hint of gaiety.

"You're right. I don't," Mr. Coates-Davis admitted, striding over from the cocktail cabinet to hand over the small glass with her drink.

"Oh?" Paige's well-marked brows rose.

"I placed an offer on the house at Holland Park to give myself the opportunity of meeting you," Mr. Coates-Davis continued.

"Me?" Paige was confused. She took her drink and stared at her client with wide, curious eyes.

"Of course I happen to know the person who was selling it and knew he would accept a cash offer," he went on. "It was the only way."

"I'm sorry." Paige shook her head, lost to the meaning of the conversation. "The only way for what?"

"To invite you here so that I can see the Egyptian figurine Rhys has given you." He took a seat next to her, and Paige became immediately nervous as to what he was implying. "You see," Mr. Coates-Davis enlightened her, "there's a legend to the making of the statuette you are holding. It once belonged to a collection of six. After talking to Rhys, I suddenly remembered a childhood story my grandfather told me in Saudi Arabia and made some inquiries."

Paige took a fortifying swallow of her Martini for stamina, not clear on what she was hearing. All she knew was that she had not been confronted with Rhys on her arrival and that she was with an old acquaintance of his who now did not seem so friendly. "Are you trying to tell me you are no longer buying the house at Holland Park?" she asked, keeping to the subject of how they had come to meet before taking another large sip from her glass.

"My only interest in you being here," Mr. Coates-Davis

confessed with smoke pumping from his lips, "is so that I can take a look at this wonderful figurine. May I?"

Paige stared at the object she held in her hand, not too sure why it should suddenly seem important to someone other than herself. It was indeed a beautiful statuette, carved with care and attention to detail, and still faintly retaining its colors as its maker had intended. Its sentimentality took her mind back to when Rhys had given it to her. *It is said whoever owns it will find true love until old age,* she mused. Paige could only imagine this to be the reason why Mr. Coates-Davis wanted it, and immediately held it to her breast.

"You can't have it," she told him. "It was a gift."

"I just want to take a look," he began mildly, placing his cigar into an ashtray on a marble table in front of her. "I want to see whether it has a marking beneath."

"Why?" Paige asked, defensive.

"Because the marking means something," she was told in a tone that bordered on irritation. "I need to see it now."

Paige closed her fingers more tightly around the statuette, and felt her body quake with sickly anticipation. Her head suddenly became dizzy and the room began to sway. She looked at her almost empty glass of Martini, and was immediately aware that she had been drugged. The statuette felt limp in her hand, and her fingers were quickly losing all sense of feeling. A nauseous attack hit her the moment Mr. Coates-Davis carefully pried the object from between her fingers. She dazedly saw the wry smile break across his lips as he upturned the statuette and read the marking beneath. Paige closed her eyes and touched her dry lips. Franklin's voice filtered into her lapsing consciousness as her head fell and darkness rose up to haunt her.

"Get Rhys Langston on the phone," he ordered. "Tell him we have his girl."

Thirteen

Paige awoke to the sound of horses. She could hear the scrabbling of hooves against what sounded like rough ground, then the noise abruptly disappearing like a faraway whisper into the night. It had gone so quiet, she felt as though the horses' hooves had found sand. It was dark around her, although she could see the faintest silvery shimmer against which everything else was jet black. She also knew she was unceremoniously on the floor, but her hands were not tied up and she had not been gagged.

She had no inclination of where she was and for a while, time seemed to stand still. Paige tried to recollect her thoughts, remembering where she had been last. Only the vague image of a man formulated in her head as she tried to clear the fatigue that muzzled her brain and that made it hard for her to come to her senses. She could smell the aroma of something cooking, and even heard the faint crackle of meat. She was not alone.

Weakly, she rubbed her nose as a shadow detached itself from the darkness. A charge of fear fixed Paige to the spot where she was huddled on the floor, and she quickly clasped her arms around her knees for protection against the unknown. The blackness was so dense she could not see his face, her only awareness being that it was someone who was not about to ask if she needed help and was most likely the person who had brought her to this place.

"Who's there?" she squealed, holding her breath in anticipation.

"I would be most grateful if you did not shout for help, Miss Alexander," he said quietly. "I have no wish to hurt you."

His voice was familiar and Paige blinked, forcing the image of the man in her head to materialize into something she could understand. She felt woozy and dazed, almost as though her body was fighting against an unnatural substance, and then suddenly the memory flooded like a tidal wave. The last person she had been with was . . .

"Mr. Coates-Davis," Paige blurted on a surprised note.

"Please, call me Franklin," he advised softly.

"Where am I?" Paige demanded, trying to focus her eyes in the dark, her tone bridged with confusion and bafflement.

"You're in Egypt," Franklin told her quite candidly.

"Don't be ridiculous," Paige chastised, gritting her teeth like an animal ready to pounce. "I'm in no mood for joking."

"We arrived two hours ago on my private jet," Franklin continued, undeterred at her tone.

"I would *know* if I had left London," Paige retorted sarcastically, thinking maybe she should try to stand on her two feet and face the shadowy figure head on. "The last time I looked, we were at . . . your penthouse."

"I brought you here on a false passport and forged documents," Franklin revealed, his voice echoing around her. "I'm afraid a little potency of your Martini allowed you to be quite cooperative."

A flurry of new memories instantly rushed Paige's mind as she recalled the world having disappeared into darkness that was much the same as she was facing now. Suddenly, as the disorientation began to wear off, she realized she had in fact been taken against her will. "Are you telling me that I've been abducted?" she raged, realizing she was at the mercy of a man she did not know at all well, whose motives were less than apparent and who had kidnapped her, but for what purpose, she had no idea. "What am I doing here?" Her voice was pitched in trepidation as the image of a stone statuette also fogged her mind along with the comprehension that she had been drugged.

"Don't worry," Franklin told her. "If Mr. Langston cooperates, you won't be harmed."

"Rhys?" His name hung suspended at the back of Paige's throat in disbelief. "Is he here?" she asked in stupefaction.

"Not yet," Franklin confessed. "But I'm counting on the way he feels about you to make him show up."

"Here, in Egypt?" Paige said, perplexed, shaking her head as though the idea seemed impossible. She was not afraid. She was not even hysterical. The primary emotion that ran the length of her body was not one of fear or even disillusion, but indignation that this man should believe in some romantic fantasy that Rhys Langston wanted her. She even snorted at the mere suggestion that Rhys should be the one chosen and predestined to jump to her rescue.

"Why not here?" Franklin asked suddenly, detecting the ambivalence in her tone.

Paige's brain was tormented with the fact that Rhys had not called her. He had returned to Monaco without a moment's hesitation, without even trying to understand what she had gone through. It occurred to her now that his incommunicado, his lack of contact to sort the matter out, was very unforgiving. His silence had left her aggrieved and feverish at the loss of him. It was as though he had been muffled to never speak with her again.

And she had tried to explain. She had desperately wanted him to know how much he had grown to mean to her. But Rhys's refusal to make contact said it all. He had severed all ties. He had considered her irresponsible and perhaps even childish. It was plain to Paige he wanted someone more mature in her outlook, who would be loyal and sincere. The stab of pain in her heart as she considered how stupidly she had behaved hurt more now than it had ever.

"You don't know what you're asking." Her voice shuddered in the dark. "If you think Rhys Langston loves me, you're very much mistaken."

"What do you mean?" Franklin demanded.

"He never wants to see me again," Paige divulged with a tremor in her throat. "So whatever this is about, you're going to have to find someone else to bargain with."

The situation felt very grave the moment Paige heard Franklin leave. She could not see him, but she heard the shuffle of his feet and sensed the short burst of chilly air against her skin before his breathing disappeared. She tried to think what possible reason Franklin Coates-Davis would have to kidnap her. Such practices were not uncommon in the Middle East, where women were often snatched for sex, ransom, slavery, or marriage. Panic shot up her spine as she contemplated the dangers that could face her. Without a considerate male family member to aid her—a father, a son, a brother—just about any sort of fate could befall her.

And it was hardly likely Rhys Langston would come to the rescue. There was only one thing for it. Paige knew she had to escape. Running her hands along her body, she sensed from the fabric she was wearing that she was still dressed in her coral-colored dress. Touching her feet, she was relieved to find that her high-heeled shoes were still present, but chagrined when she realized sand lay between her toes. Like a blind person, Paige ran her hands along the ground, and trembled in shock as grains of sand tickled against her fingers. Franklin had been deadly serious. She was indeed in Egypt.

Paige was able to brace herself on her knees, and slowly began to crawl in the dark. She thought she would follow in the direction Franklin had gone, where the cool air had approximated. It was so densely dark, Paige was loath to rely on all her senses, like an animal hell-bent on survival. She could hear voices outside, in the distance. She could still smell the cooking. Her fingers felt the footprints Franklin had left behind, embedded into the sand, which helped her along. When she finally reached what appeared to be an opening, Paige poked her head out and for the first time became aware she was in a tent.

Even the night looked darker in Egypt than it did in England. Across the way, to her right, she could vaguely make out the shapes of what appeared to be horses in a paddock. Further along were the shadowy images of what were men huddled over a campfire and the dark silhouette of more tents. To her left, she saw a large object. The smell of diesel told her instantly it was a car. Despite the prickly rush of fear that was running its way along her flesh, Paige decided she was going to run for it.

Her instincts were on red alert as she rose slowly to her feet and kept her head down as she left the tent. The sand beneath her feet did not make it easy, but as the car began to loom up like a huge bear in front of her, Paige could see it was a Jeep Cherokee, all power to take her to freedom. She tried the driver's door. It was locked. Stricken with panic, she made her way around to the passenger side and found the door open. Paige hesitated and looked around. She could not see in which direction the road was. She was not even sure whether she should go north or south, east or west. And she was doubtful on whether she would find the key in the ignition. Reaching across to poke her head inside, she realized it was not.

Her heart fell. Paige struggled to make out some semblance of where she was in the dark, but all she could see, aside from her shadowy adversaries, was the stillness of the desert. She felt the sudden tears at the back of her eyelids as her abandonment suddenly dawned on her. If she were to run now, she would get lost and quickly. She would need water when the sun rose. If her captures did not come to find her, she could die from dehydration if she had not found a safe haven and the vultures did not get to her first.

Escape was still on Paige's mind nonetheless, and that was when she remembered her mobile phone. The jolt it gave her forced her back on her heels in a hurry. She was not sure whether it would work from her location. There would be no harm in trying. She would return to her tent to discover whether she was still in possession of her handbag. But before Paige could budge, a hand clamped itself over her mouth and had her swallowing her fright in an instant.

"Still running?" the familiar whisper sounded against her ear. "Don't move."

With his free arm around her waist, he lifted her bodily off the ground and bundled her into the Jeep. Paige had precious seconds to contemplate a struggle before the large frame of a body joined her at her side, his grip still holding on tight. So tight that the nails of his fingers dug deep into the fabric of her dress and bruised her navel. Paige could hardly believe she was being snatched again. Only this time, she was not going to go down without a fight.

Tormented by the faint smell of frankincense and myrrh, she lashed out, thumping and scratching, ignoring the sound of her name. Hitting as hard as she could, she threw all her energy into the fight, until firm hands forced her down on her back and lodged her right shoulder beneath the steering wheel. Paige was panicked as one half of her became immobilized, but she soldiered on in an attempt to break free, until she began to feel she was wearing herself out unnecessarily. This man was much stronger than she was, and it was clear she was no match for him. She paused to catch her breath, unable to see his face, yet chagrined to find herself trying to see his eyes.

"Paige?" he repeated, a little louder.

Only then did she recognize the voice. His Southern American accent was tainted with a more international flavor, and Paige's heart lurched into her throat. "Rhys?"

"Irrational and aggressive as I've long suspected," came the reply. "I felt the sting of your fist this time."

Paige recollected her thoughts immediately. "At least it's not premenstrual tension," she rebutted, trying to break herself free so she could sit up. "You remembered me then?"

"This is the bit where you should be grateful I'm here," Rhys returned, releasing his hold on her.

Paige fumed. "Grateful! I can't believe you've just turned up out of the blue like this, behaving as though everything is just fine," she relented. "I've been abducted."

"So I see."

"And you haven't called me."

"I didn't think I needed to," Rhys sounded out, his tone wounded. "You shifted the goalpost the moment you started playing love soccer with my heart as a worthy ball."

"What?" Paige was in shock. After all the days of requiem, weeping, crying her heart out, this man was right here in front of her acting as if no time had passed at all. "Aren't you going to even ask me how I am?"

"You sound just fine to me," Rhys returned, releasing her in an instant. "What are you wearing anyway? Feels like a dress, and an expensive one at that."

"It is," Paige told him, wishing she could see at least a glimpse of Rhys's face to gauge the level of hurt that was evidently still there. But the darkness made it impossible, and she could only imagine that he still retained all the handsome features as when she had last seen him. "I wore it to dinner with your business acquaintance and suddenly found myself here."

She could hear Rhys searching the Jeep before he spoke. "What were you doing having dinner with him?"

"He invited me," Paige revealed, curious as to how Rhys had arrived there.

She was now able to position herself in the driver's seat and gaze through the window, detecting the men outside in the distance still hunched around the campfire. They were unaware that she had left her tent or that she was in the Jeep with Rhys, her desert prince who had, it seems, come to her rescue. She had once thought about fulfilling her own personal fantasy adventure in that regard when she had first seen Rhys Langston in the flesh, but Paige never expected it to be actually happening to her.

"And you went?" Rhys objected.

"He led me to believe you were not far off," Paige mouthed, annoyed.

"And you fell for his playful charm," Rhys jabbed on a note of jealous irony. He had been suspicious of Franklin for some time, especially where money was concerned, but it had never occurred to Rhys that the man he had always known as a conniving money-maker might pose the ultimate threat.

"I rather thought he was leading me to you," Paige said scathingly.

"He's certainly done that," Rhys sighed as he ceased his search. He could not find the Jeep keys anywhere. "He's used you as bait to get me here earlier than I expected."

Paige was exasperated. "I can't believe that you're so unapologetic," she railed in an alarmed tone. "Aren't you even going to say how sorry you are for treating me as though I no longer existed, or for the fact that I'm even finding myself here in this dangerous position?"

"I tried to call you before coming to your office," Rhys insisted, his voice devoid of emotion. "Where your boss decided to come clean about you, remember?"

"I'd switched my phone off," Paige confessed, her mind refusing to be taken back to that awful scenario.

"Why?" The question came at her in total bemusement.

"I needed to think."

"About?"

"Us . . . the things Blanton was saying about you."

"You didn't think to believe in me enough to ask?" Rhys's voice sounded so pained, Paige felt her heart absorb the stab of it.

"I'm sorry."

"Sorry doesn't mend everything in life," he told her mournfully. "Your boss was not the person I needed to hear the truth from."

"I know," Paige agreed on a whisper.

"I called him about you," Rhys continued blithely.

"Me?"

"The idea was not to alarm him after I got the call from Franklin," Rhys informed her, his tone low and tinged with a hint of anger. "I didn't have your Aunt Elva's number, and asked if he could pass a message to tell her that you're in Egypt. Unfortunately, he didn't sound too pleased, and he thinks you're on holiday with me. He said if you're not back pronto, then you're fired."

"Guess I'm fired," Paige peeved, shrugging her shoulders. Blanton Blake was a person she no longer felt she could work with anyway. Paige paused. "About what happened in his office," she began, nervously deciding it was perhaps best that they clear the air. "I want to—"

"Sssh," Rhys whispered. "Someone's outside."

"I don't care if—"

Paige was silenced as Rhys once again placed his hand over her mouth. The humiliating way in which she was feeling was swallowed with another bout of fright as she, too, heard the footsteps outside. Someone was walking around the Jeep. Maybe they had been seen. It certainly crossed Paige's mind as Rhys gently pulled her from her seat and they both huddled together beneath the steering wheel.

The shuffling of feet against the sand suddenly paused, and Paige felt her heart lurch, knowing that whoever it was outside the Jeep might have discovered she was no longer in her tent. She did not have to wait a moment longer for her suspicion to prove true. In an instant, she heard the key in the Jeep's door moments before it was flung open and Franklin's voice rang out in the air.

"I know you're in here, Miss Alexander," he bellowed harshly. "There is no escape."

Paige felt her body tremor, and was immediately reassured when Rhys placed his arms around her waist and held her comfortably against his hard, rigid frame. She closed her eyes and reluctantly savored the moment of being in his arms once again. Of feeling his warm breath behind her neck, soothing her, causing the ache to be close to him again to surge up inside her. It was like a wish come true, indeed not far removed from her birthday wish to be with this man forever more. But with all good things, there were complications, and this was such a time.

"Miss Alexander?" Franklin's voice sounded more stern. "Please do not tempt my patience."

"Go to him," Rhys whispered quietly, taking a firm hold of Paige's finely boned fingers and kissing each one in turn as he had done on first meeting her. "I'll follow. I have friends here."

Paige was mortified. She did not want to move. She did not want to leave Rhys, yet it was clear Franklin Coates-Davis was not going to budge either. He had obviously gone to the tent and not found her there. The Jeep was the closest haven in proximity to the tent, so he was correct in his assumption that she would be in there. Defeated, Paige turned in Rhys's arms and halfheartedly flung her arms around his neck. In spite of his dismissal of her, of his neglect in delaying contact, of the disagreements that existed between them now, she did not want them to part a second time with bad feelings.

She was surprised when, as she drew away, he pulled her back and brushed a kiss against her lips. It was brief, like the one at Heathrow Airport, but it immediately stoked up a wealth of feeling inside Paige as she hesitantly reciprocated, seconds before he pushed her away and she rose to her feet and stepped from the Jeep. Franklin heard her stiletto heels hit the sand and ventured forward, luckily finding her hand right away in the dark.

"I would appreciate if you did not try that again," he told her in the manner of an adult scolding a small boy. Franklin pulled her along, taking her back to the tent. "You will not find me as patient should you try a second time."

As Paige found herself being led away from the man she loved, her heart sank miserably, wondering whether she was ever likely to see Rhys again. She did not expect him to walk back into her life after everything that had happened between them, but hoped at heart they could remain good friends. Her only consolation would be the lingering pressure his kiss had left on her lips. It was all the memory she had of Rhys to keep. The other one, which had been the nineteenth-dynasty statuette he had given her, had been taken from her and was now, she suspected, with Franklin. Paige did not know why he required it, but Rhys's very presence in Egypt had to mean it had some connection with his excavation project.

As she seated herself in her tent, and heard Franklin station a man outside the gateway, Paige waited. She would await Rhys's return with all the hope in her heart.

The first thing Paige noted on awaking at daybreak was that she could not find her handbag. The second thing that dogged her mind was fear about whether Rhys Langston had been discovered. Having looked around her prison from her crouched position on the floor, where she had slept, she was to find that her coral-colored dress was sprinkled in sand, and that the tent she was in appeared much smaller than she had imagined it.

As she slowly rose to her feet and shook the sand from her dress, she could hear noises outside—the horses being mobilized, the engine of the Jeep being fired up, male voices conspiring with one another—and wondered how soon it would be before Franklin came to break hard facts to her on exactly what his motives were for bringing her there. Decidedly, she walked toward the opening in the tent, expectant on locating him close by, but when Paige peeped through, she was struck dumb by the horizon that met her startled gaze.

The skyline, merging exquisitely into the curvy shapes of brown sand that shaped the desert, was the most beautiful shades of blue-violet and yellow she had ever seen. Immediately Paige was retaken to when Rhys had described to her the streak across a sunrise. This must have been it. *When you see such a color, it's so beautiful, it's like finding the gateway to heaven.* She was enamored to discover such magnificence existed. Paige was still staring at it when Franklin approached.

He was dressed in native Arabian clothing, appearing more like a sheik of the desert than a businessman. Paige glared at him, feeling the pit of anger in her stomach rise up against him. He seemed unmoved as that same anger reflected in her gaze. Instead, Franklin surveyed her briefly through eyes that were dark and mysterious, then thrust a brown parcel in front of her.

"I trust you slept well," he remarked, handing it over.

Paige took the parcel, but supplied no comment.

"I'd like you to change into these," Franklin ordered, seeing the ravages of fatigue in her face. "One of my men has placed a pail of water over there for you to use." He pointed out a much smaller tent of brightly colored rusty-beige goat hair. "We'll be ready to leave in ten minutes."

"Don't I get anything to eat?" Paige seethed through clenched teeth.

"We only have dried dates, if that is acceptable to you?"

Paige let out a sharp, explosive sigh that expressed without exaggeration her outrage at being held hostage like this. "What is it you want?" she demanded scathingly. "What's so special about me to make you think you have the right to treat me like this?"

"This is not about you," Franklin revealed calmly, "but the Egyptian figurine you showed me three nights ago."

"Three nights?" Paige was shocked. Had so much time elapsed already? Having been drugged, she was hardly aware.

"You see, Miss Alexander," Franklin began, having now decided he would tell Paige the truth, "it used to belong to a goddess that we know in my country as Aset. She was renamed Isis by the Greeks."

"I'm aware of all that," Paige responded coolly.

"Are you also aware that Rhys Langston has been funding an excavation here in Egypt that his archaeologist believes may lead to the tomb of Atum?"

"Yes."

"Atum was also renamed Ra?"

Paige was confused. "Ra?"

"There is a legend in my country about the spell of the divine god, Ra," he continued. "Only Isis knew his secret name, and it is said that this name was placed on six stone figurines and kept in her temple."

"So?" Paige rebutted, finding the story tiresome and bland, almost to the point of grim.

"You had one of these statuettes, Miss Alexander," Franklin

informed. "If the tomb Rhys Langston is excavating is the tomb of Ra, the name inscribed beneath the figurine could lead us to his buried treasure."

"Treasure!" Paige was awed. "But . . . but I thought the statuette was about love."

"Indeed, the truth about the legend was lost and over time became misinterpreted," Franklin advised. "Isis believed that by placing Ra's secret name beneath each statuette, the spell of Ra would be bestowed on them. Over time, people began to believe she was talking about true love until old age. I was such a believer until I remembered an old story about the tomb from my childhood and checked it with a source."

"You're not going to get away with this." Paige swallowed at the enormity of what she was being told.

"Oh, but I am," Franklin contradicted. "I already know Rhys Langston has arrived here in Egypt. I am expecting him to contact me very shortly."

"I thought you were his friend," Paige debated on a shaky breath, knowing him to be speaking the truth.

"We are . . .business acquaintances," Franklin proclaimed wisely. "Over the years we've invested money shrewdly, and I would now estimate Mr. Langston's personal fortune to be in accumulation of five, maybe six million."

Paige was immediately dazed. "What?"

"Mr. Langston is a millionaire, my dear," Franklin announced. "He has a lot to thank me for."

"A millionaire!" Paige gasped. "Omega Private Equity Funds Ltd.?"

"His umbrella company which he used to invest in businesses that have a trading history," Franklin informed, "and which he occasionally uses to fund fly-by-night projects such as this little excavation he's got going on in Dhashur."

That explained why he had also afforded staying at Claridge's as opposed to a cheaper hotel, hired a limousine for Valentine's Day, and was able to invest in the numerous causes related to African diaspora studies she had seen detailed on the Internet. Paige was amazed. "He . . . he said nothing to me."

"He wouldn't," Franklin exclaimed. "A man of his background has seen too much oppression from the dominant culture in his country to risk further betrayal by a woman who is only after his money."

"I'm not like that," Paige breathed, alarmed.

"Sure, you're not," Franklin commented quite cynically.

"Look, I don't know what kind of friend you are, but—"

"This is purely business," Franklin shot back in interruption. "Nothing you would understand."

"A big boy's game and my head can only take little girl rules," Paige snarled. *What is it with men?* she mused in annoyance. First Rupert King and now Franklin Coates-Davis. In her mind, she felt completely redundant to the true mechanisms of what was really going on, but as a woman who was not shy to assert her own challenges in life, Paige was not deterred. "Don't underestimate me," she warned, schooling her eyes carefully in bait. "I'm not fooled easily."

Franklin's eyes darkened suddenly as Paige heard the Jeep's engines fire up once again. Someone was pumping the gas signifying they were in a hurry. "I believe you were to redress," he told Paige.

She stared at him in fright, recalling that Rhys had only last night been in that Jeep, but was no longer there now. Paige felt the loss of him, the tangible loss of his kiss and the tremors of being in his arms, as her gaze lowered and she nodded her acceptance of Franklin's instructions before she headed toward the beige tent. Paige knew she could not trust a living soul in this place. Could not trust anyone's word for anything, with the exception of Rhys Langston's, of course. He had kept his word and been at her side at her birthday party. But no one knew where the hell he was. Not even she.

Fourteen

Paige began to feel like the roving, nomadic, sensation-seeker Blanton Blake had once described, who was looking for a brief moment of thrills, as the Jeep Cherokee began to surge through the desert. Not far behind were men on horse-back—Franklin Coates-Davis's herd of henchmen—escorting them along. Seated in the passenger seat, she was all ears, eyes, and expectations waiting for the next riveting drama to enter her life, though deep down, Paige had no stomach for a further emotional ruction. She wanted to go home. She wanted Rhys. She wanted this reincarnation of her worst nightmare to end.

"Where are you taking me?" she demanded of Franklin as he kept his gaze steadfast ahead. He was wearing a black *kef-fiyeh,* which protected his face and showed nothing but his eyes beneath the cloth.

"To the excavation site in Dahshur, of course," he told Paige in a matter-of fact manner. "If your lover has found the correct tomb location, I should be able to match the Egyptian hieroglyphs on the figurine to something there."

"And if you don't?" Paige asked cynically.

"For all our sakes, I hope I do," he answered.

Paige grew alarmed. "My family are going to report me missing," she lied at near-maximum volume, resenting the way she had been camouflaged to fit into her environment. She, too, was wearing a scarf wrapped around her head and lower face. Franklin had folded the *milfeh* and tucked it into the right places so she looked positively Bedouin. He also approved of the clothing he had given her to change into—a simple gray colored cotton *caftan* with a dark throw-over she was told could be removed from around her shoulders when the sun took over the desert. The sandals on her feet were slightly big, but were suitable for the journey ahead. "I suspect people may already be looking for me."

"That is a risk I'm prepared to take," Franklin responded, unmoved. "I'm certain if we find treasure, you will be susceptible to striking a deal."

"Me?" Paige coughed.

"I am not interested in hurting you," Franklin advised, "but it would be better for you if you were to cooperate."

"And what do I tell my folks back home?" Paige reproved. *"It's okay, everybody. I was just searching for some ancient Egyptian bling-bling."*

Franklin laughed at her modern use of vernacular for gold. "You amaze me, Miss Alexander," he drawled, pumping the gas until he felt the smoothness of the wheels against the sand. "I sincerely hope Rhys Langston shares your sense of humor."

"You'd be stealing from him," Paige challenged. "That excavation project is his investment, his work. And the figurine you stole was a gift from him to me. I want it back."

"He should've had enough foresight to check what he had given to you," Franklin protested his behavior. "Such a figurine should've been scrutinized before he handed it over."

"Only you knew the story behind it," Paige debated firmly, "so Sotheby's are at fault, too. They sold it."

"Indeed," Franklin agreed. "And as soon as I am done with it, you are welcome to its return."

"And Rhys?" Paige anticipated.

"We've brokered enough deals in our time for him to understand what is going on here," he breathed shrewdly. "If I know Rhys Langston, he'll seal an agreement."

"I don't see why you just couldn't have asked him," Paige crooned, agitated that matters should have been taken this far.

"I could not do that," Franklin proclaimed strongly, like a true Arabian refusing to banter. "My bargaining position would've been seriously compromised. I know the true meaning to the hieroglyphs on the statuette, while he manages the excavation site. This is a position in which I can reach a pact."

"It's the position of a thief," Paige contradicted.

Franklin winced. "You do something to me that results in the most disappointing solution I may have to make," he remarked sternly.

"And what is that?" Paige asked, fuming.

"You would not wish to know," Franklin told her quietly. "But if you want to stay alive, I suggest you remain silent until this day is over."

Paige gulped.

The journey seemed to take forever. As they crossed the desert, the heat began to rise, and she was soon dismissing the throw-over that Franklin had given her from around her shoulders. The head-cloth wrapped around her head was unbearable. Paige felt less a Bedouin and more a Rastafarian as she began to itch beneath the *milfeh* to her sweaty hairline, where she could also feel her hair stamped to her scalp.

She saw pyramids in the distance during the wake of their journey, and Franklin explained on their way to Dhashur that they were the Bent pyramid—about two kilometers south of the Mastaba Faraoun, the Red pyramid—the pyramid of Sesostris III, and the White pyramid and the Black pyramid—both of Amenemtet III. The last one had an irregular shape that seemed to loom against the vast desert, and it left Paige feeling sickly as she wondered how much longer until they would arrive. She needed water. She needed food. The distress and fatigue were beginning to show on her face.

"There's water in the bag behind you," Franklin offered, noting her weariness and indicating with a simple nod of his head the empty rear seats.

Paige unbuckled her seat belt to reach over, and delved her hand into the bag she could see behind her seat. Her fingers circled a hard, stone object, and she pulled it from its interior to find that she was holding her Egyptian statuette. Paige repositioned herself and stared at the six inch object. The maiden looked as beautiful as the day Rhys had given it to her. It would have been better protected had it been in its box, and she felt annoyed at finding it so haphazardly in the water bag.

"Who would have thought something so small could cause so much trouble?" she proclaimed, upturning the statuette to find the vague markings beneath it.

Franklin looked horrified. "Be careful with that," he gasped. "Put it back, now."

Paige was not accustomed to being ordered about. "This is mine," she railed. "You said there are five more. Why don't you find one of those?"

"That's the only one left in the collection," Franklin cautioned, slowing the engine dramatically. "If anything happens to it, I lose everything."

"Really!" Paige was intrigued. She weighted the statuette in her hand, gauging its weight to be around four pounds. "Do you really believe this can lead you to gold?"

"There are many stories in the Middle East," Franklin insisted, "but if the one my grandfather told me is true, I am certain of it." He stared at her in warning. "Put it down, now."

Paige was reluctant to do so. The Egyptian statuette had been a present given to her by Rhys Langston. Franklin had no right to take it away from her against her will. She was disappointed to know that its true intention was not one of love, but rather to etch in stone the name of an idol god. While that very name was a master clue potentially leading to an ancient tomb where hidden treasure might be found, Paige's aversion to part with what was still essentially her property was resolved in her face.

"I'd like to keep hold of it," she responded candidly, twisting her finely boned fingers around the piece. "It may be the only bargaining tool *I* have."

"Now listen to me," Franklin snarled, moments before his

men began to rush the Jeep on horseback, alerting his attention to their having arrived at the excavation site.

Paige's eyes widened as she looked on ahead, seeing through the windscreen a clearing that was at least twenty feet deeper than their own position. It looked like a crater. She heard Franklin slow the Jeep to a snail's pace before he cut the engine and the scurry of his henchmen outside on horseback gave her the impression that they were about to rally around to plan strategy on how best to proceed.

"What's going on?" Paige asked immediately, looking around in anticipation that she might catch a glimpse of Rhys hiding out.

"We've arrived," Franklin told her, instantly pulling the statuette from between her fingers. Cradling it against his chest, he decidedly stepped from the Jeep and took a few paces forward.

Paige watched as he scanned the excavation site in front of him, seeing the remnants of monuments that had once been located there. It was one mile south of the last pyramid they had journeyed past, and Paige could not see anyone around. No workers. No archaeologists. No one to even indicate that they had arrived at the correct destination. Peering closer toward the windscreen, she would not have guessed that the view in front of her held within its confines a tomb, let alone buried treasure. To her, it all seemed like an empty sandy wasteland where cockroaches, snakes, and ants buried their loot.

Paige stepped from the Jeep, and felt the harsh wind slap against her cheeks as she walked over to Franklin. "This is it?"

He was still scanning the area with his dark, brooding eyes. Paige could see he was in awe of the situation, too. His henchmen on horseback looked equally impatient. The site obviously looked nothing like what they had imagined—this empty oasis of sand, with a few mud-brick constructions and stones mounted about, a clearing of hardened rock, and a heavy wind cursing the place as it blew in all directions. Franklin simply nodded his head, then turned to two of his men, muttering in a bustle of Arabic.

Paige heard the break in his speech the instant a shadowy figure began to emerge from one of the gray limestone shafts on the excavation site. The sway of his walk told her in a heartbeat who he was. As he came closer, his masterful expression began to reveal itself. The rich golden brown of his complexion, his soulful, smoldering mocha-brown eyes, the short black hair smoothed away from his face, and the large pink lips she would always find to be invitingly kissable. Rhys Langston seemed as princely as the day she first met him.

He was wrapped in a dark *keffiyeh,* his arms and legs covered heavily in a *thobe,* and his expectant gaze was unreadable as he stepped over the stones and came toward them. Paige advanced closer. He was alive and well. She could see the fire in his eyes. She could also feel that her desire for him was unchanged. In fact, her deep pining for Rhys had grown even stronger.

"You're chasing a dead end, Franklin," Rhys pounced on his arrival amidst a gush of wind. "Look around you. There's nothing here."

"I will be the one to decide that," Franklin slighted, breaking his lips into a smile. "I see you have received my text message."

Rhys's gaze fell on Paige and held until their eyes locked. He felt the shock bolt of emotion run down his spine before he switched his gaze back to Franklin. "Let the girl go. I have friends who will see she is safely returned home."

"No!" Paige gasped.

Franklin's smile broadened with a sneer. "It seems she has an opinion of her own."

"Only that you're a liar and a thief," Paige objected.

Franklin winced. "This site." He surveyed it arrogantly, ignoring Paige. "Did you find a chamber or a tomb chapel?"

Rhys paused, throwing another glance at Paige as though assessing the situation. "We found the main shaft, discovered during an earlier dig," he told Franklin slowly. "The assemblage of objects in the shaft are relief blocks, small fragments of ornaments, and pottery shards. We think it suggests a period of the early nineteenth dynasty."

"Anything like a burial chamber?" Franklin persisted on a note of disbelief.

Rhys sighed. "Look. This is the third excavation on this site," he informed him adamantly. "I was not involved in the first two. We've only enlarged the grids around the main shaft. The additions we found were jar sealings or sealing stamps on the plaster of the brick walls referring to who my lead archaeologist thought was Atum."

"Ah, Ra," Franklin enthused, his eyes widening as a small burst of wind blew past, throwing small particles of dust into his face. The horses began to appear troubled, but no one seemed deterred as the whitish haze around them began to gather.

"No," Rhys confirmed. "Akhenaten."

"That cannot be true," Franklin fumed. "This statuette . . . I was sure . . ."

"Still the sly old fox," Rhys chortled, taking another pace forward. "You thought I had made a connection with that figurine and this excavation site and was on my way to making a fortune," he accused hotly, surmising the situation. "And of course, you just had to have a piece of the action. Outbidding the house I wanted so you could get access to abduct Paige, knowing full well it would bring me here to bargain with you, and manipulating my financial investments so I couldn't liquidate funds."

"Now wait a minute," Franklin countered.

"No, you wait," Rhys challenged, fired up, noting Franklin's henchmen had inched forward on their horses. "I wasn't closing down my browser software properly every time I was e-mailing you, so a cookie was tracking my net activities and you were storing data on me."

Franklin took a step backward into a cloudburst of dust. "I don't know what you mean."

"Yes, you do," Rhys continued, advancing another step forward. He raised his right hand and a dozen men came up behind him, seemingly out of nowhere, holding rifles. Franklin gave the nod to his men not to make a move. "You knew all about *www.totallyblackdating.com,"* he elaborated, "and that their service did not offer a secure method of access. You, or someone you hired, was watching my network traffic, and extracted personal information which you used to your advantage. That's how you knew Paige's moniker, my nicknames for her. Her name. You've known all along about everything I've been doing."

"He brought down the online dating Web site?" Paige drawled in surprise.

"No," Rhys explained, throwing Paige a glance. "Hackers got into it, but Franklin saw that as an opportunity to download information which he stored." He paused to eye Franklin in combat mode, seeing for the first time how things were done the Middle Eastern way. "I hired a security specialist who was able to analyze and track all attempts to breach my system, They found e-misuse and nailed down your IP address, picked up your electronic fingerprints, and located your damned computer. I've instructed that the info be passed over to the FSA if Paige and I are not safely home within forty-eight hours. All I want to know is why."

"Power," Franklin shot back reluctantly. "How do you think I got you where you are—where I got any of my clients. I *need* to be informed and if I'm not, I find a way. Like this little beauty right here." He held up the statuette for all to see. "It has a name on its base. It is said to be the name of Ra and can lead us to treasures unimaginable. You kept it to yourself. I want to know where the tomb is. I want to find Shamash."

"Shamash," Rhys acknowledged. "That's a Hebrew word. It's the name of a sun god."

"Then it is here!" Franklin declared blindly, pointing at the excavation site.

"You're wasting your time," Rhys told him firmly, as another, much stronger wind lashed out and hit them both.

This time, the horses protested. Immediately unsettled, they began to kick their hooves against the sand. Rhys looked around, and noted the landscape was quickly becoming blotted out by a dense brown fog. The air was smoked with dust, a lot of it, in serried ranks driving past them and leaving a thin film of sand particles on their clothing as it left. The men on his site were beginning to shout, alerting his attention to what was going on. "It's a sandstorm," he chimed in shock.

Paige's eyes widened, not quite sure how deathly this was. "Is that bad?"

"It's not good," Rhys yelled, grabbing her hand. "C'mon."

"Wait a minute," Franklin protested, looking about him, aware he no longer retained control of the situation.

As tiny tornadoes of dust and whirligigs began to pick up the sand and toss it aloft in carousels, and the clouds of brown fog prevailed, the horses began to panic. They kicked up a fuss and began to throw their riders, some of them huddling in bunches expectant of the sand gale, which seemed to be moving ever closer toward them. A dry taste of grit and dust was on Paige's lips as the wind dashed along and the white haze around them thickened until the sun became a great white disk in the sky.

"Where are we going?" she shrieked as she felt Rhys lace his fingers through hers and strongly pull her along in the direction of his men.

"To shelter," he shouted.

"What about Franklin and his men?" she yelled in concern, throwing her head back to find them battling the furor around them, unconcerned that she was making her escape.

"They can take care of themselves."

"But—"

"If I know him, he's probably already making plans to trace the figurine in Israel," Rhys yelled. "C'mon."

Rhys led the way while the brown mass showed light and dark shades of density as the fog bank in the distance began to rise against them. It was such as one might see at sea when a storm was gathering. Paige had never before witnessed the strange spectacle around her, the smoky billows of sand whirling away in gigantic waltzes in irregular gusts that formed the dusty fog.

Rhys knew the desert men called them "sand-augers" because the swirls of sand would sag and sway, hither and thither, writhing and twisting in sinuous grace, exposing their fury to the world. The noise of the horses could be heard weeping in the distance as the gale force of the storm became much harsher, and he used all his might to pull Paige along behind him lest the pull of the wind would cause him to lose her.

The crater of the excavation site was converted to a pit of hell as he stepped down onto the path that led to the main shaft. The air was now full of drifting dust, sand-augers and slender tornadoes sucking up the coarse sand with a burning wind and hurling it so ferociously, it was enough to lacerate their faces.

They jumped headlong into the main shaft, into a space unoccupied by Rhys's hired men, and pressed their backs against the limestone wall as a ferocious whistle of wind, shook the air around them. A tumble of brown sand sagged on the tail of the high wind, and bellowed its own tune as it lashed out with its personal waving streamers of dirt and sand. The dusty squall invaded the entrance of the shaft with particles thrown in by the blast, and Paige coughed as it assaulted her senses.

Besieged by the infestation of desert sand, she closed her eyes, pulled her *milfeh* over her face, and welcomed Rhys pulling her into his arms, where she was able to bury her head into his chest. For what seemed like an eternity, they remained exactly where they were, snuggled, nestled, and entwined in each other's arms as the spiral of wrath outside the main shaft catapulted the great mass of desert sand outside until the torment cascaded. Opening her eyes, and confronted with the harsh sound of the storm, Paige realized that the worse was not over. She looked up, and was met by dark, soulful brown eyes, which seemed to brighten up suddenly at the sight of her.

"It'll soon pass," Rhys said, dipping his head, unsure whether he should plant a reassuring kiss on her lips. "You all right?"

Paige shook her head in the negative. She was scared, confused, and objected to her current malaise. But what galled her the most was that Rhys had not kissed her. Even though her innards desired the simple gesture, her more stubborn side resented his earlier reminder the night before about how she had played him against Rupert King. She felt sure this was why he was hesitant with her now, why he could not offer her a moment of comfort even while they were in the midst of a storm, his mouth a fraction from her own.

"You're still angry with me, aren't you?" she accused, her heart pained with the knowledge that she had hurt him.

Rhys's eyes bore into her. He felt his stomach tumble and his member twitch at how much he still longed to feel Paige beside him, to feel himself deep inside her, bonding their flesh. "I'm not angry," he said quietly. "Just disappointed."

Paige felt a disquiet rise up inside her. "I said I'm sorry." She had not forgotten his abandonment of her, and her mood was beginning to turn as bestial as the sandstorm raging outside. "What more do you want?"

"Nothing," Rhys admitted softly. "Either I'm with you or I'm not. I don't do in between."

"Don't you care what I want?" Paige blurted, tears filling her eyes as she was unable to reconcile the level of her desire with Rhys's rejection. "I . . . I—" *love you.*

"Still giving off mixed signals," Rhys goaded, unmoved by the fragility he saw behind her gaze.

"What?" Paige spat out above the maelstrom of noise drumming her ears. "I'm not asking you to walk back into my life." She waffled for a moment, then shrugged, cynically. "I don't want commitment."

"Liar." Rhys's voice rose.

"Men are optional extras," Paige railed.

Rhys's eyes widened. "What are you afraid of now?" he bellowed as loudly as the sand-augers that continued on their journey past the main shaft. "The feeling that you're giving up something?"

"Maybe," Paige choked.

"You still don't know who you are, do you?" Rhys protested, shaking his head as he tried to conjure up what he had felt the day he had first seen her.

He was on his laptop in the desert, having connected it to his mobile phone. Her picture had materialized as an attachment to her e-mail and, to him, she was like the epitome of a desert princess. It seemed so long ago. Ancient history. As old as the main shaft he was standing in, holding the very image that had conquered his every awakening dream in his arms. Some of the magic resonated still. It danced on her lips, it sparkled in her eyes. He felt the tremor of it pass through their bodies. Who was she to deny it?

"I . . . I . . . ," Paige began.

"This is who you are," Rhys overrode, seconds before his mouth landed on hers.

The pressure of his lips was as ravenous as the raging sandstorm around them. Paige was thrown instantly into an abyss of cascading memories, of renewed feelings of love, of her hopes, dreams, and promise of a future being fulfilled. Yet, still the disillusioned woman, she pulled her mouth free and stepped back.

"Let me go."

Her protest was cut short. As another frightening cloudburst of wind blasted the main shaft and rocked the air around them with a further flurry of sand dust, Rhys's answer was to tug Paige to his chest, masterfully close her tightly into the haven of his arms, and capture her lips into his own. He kissed her profoundly, shamelessly, and robustly. Adrenaline pumped through his veins as the sand-augers whistled their tune down the crevices and niches of the ancient shaft, spurring him on. Converged in a seamless embrace, Paige's resistance momentarily wavered, while the commotion outside continued regardless. As her mind became lost to the power of Rhys's kiss, equal to the force of the whirlwind around them—loud and bellowing like a mad banshee—they kissed on.

A gush echoed. A whirligig tossed a furor of brown fog aloft into the main shaft. Billows of sand left residue along the floor at their feet and on their clothing, but still they could not be separated. Rhys's tongue delved in to taste what he had missed for so long. Paige accepted the sensual onslaught with a response of her own, feverishly licking, sucking, devouring the tongue that leapt about and danced with her own. Their hands roamed in the familiarity of knowing again the limbs, arms, and bony flesh that excited and satisfied. And as the kiss deepened to one of painful ardent need, Paige desperately wanted to experience again the vigor that had driven her into ecstasy.

When Rhys found the disciplined strength to pull back and savor the beauty in his arms, his dark brooding eyes filled with a determination that would have to wait, Paige almost felt vulnerable under his masterly command. She would have given anything for Rhys to have continued, even in light of what she had just told him. But Paige was to receive equal logic to her own when Rhys chose to provide her with an answer to her denial.

"I'm not going to be an awkward encumbrance in your life, resented for taking up valuable product space on the bathroom shelf and leaving my dirty underpants on the floor," he told her in a hoarse tone that spoke loudly of his sense of self-respect and the mark her kiss had left on him. "If emotion-free, commitment-free, post-pill sex is actively what you want, then I'll leave you alone." There. The gloves were off. He was returning her own psychology to its source. Her inner fear of marriage.

"You're really something else," Paige breathed, her heart still pounding from the verve of his kiss as she released herself from his arms. "Well, I know about you, about

Omega Private Equity Funds Ltd. Franklin told me how rich you are."

"What does that have to do with—?"

"It matters," Paige interrupted, "if you're going to try and control me."

"Why in the hell are you so bitter?" Rhys had pondered this before, but did not understand it, though he had suspected from having seen her strength of independence that she would perhaps resent his position over her.

"Because . . . because you had no plans to stay, not really," Paige stormed, ignoring the bout of sand that invaded the main shaft. She coughed and challenged Rhys again. "You went away, as I always knew you would."

"Paige—"

"I know who I am," she interrupted, feeling courageously defenseless, knowing she had acquired some understanding since speaking with her mother. "I'm not going to lie to you. We've been through too much together in such a short time for me to pretend," she told him. "This relationship—meeting you like I did—this whole affair means a lot to me, partly through our bravado, partly through the fact that I wanted to see it through—*ad finem*—but mainly because I've genuinely grown to care for you."

"Paige—"

"Let me finish," she insisted, beginning to see Blanton's point about the spider and the fly and who would be swallowed up first. "If I could really have all of you and with the commitment that we'd still try to live our own lives—not like Mervyn, my brother-in-law who never compromises anything—if you were willing to do all that, then I'd want this relationship. But if you have even the slightest hesitation and don't want to be with me, even though it would be painful, I'm ready to let go, too."

Rhys stared. His eyes blinked away the sand, and then narrowed in reflection of something. When the dawning came, he did not deny himself the truth. "I've fallen in love with you."

Paige felt the sudden thrill of his words shoot through her heart like a cupid's arrow. She could scarcely believe what she had heard, and yet when she met Rhys's gaze in a long, devouring glance that triggered a heavier thumping of her heart, she was suddenly laughing. A more speculative person would have recognized the symptom as that of a woman having found her true love, but Rhys was not a theorist able to dissect the root of Paige's giddiness, even when she reached out to him and grabbed her happiness with both arms.

"We're alike, you and I." She spoke as if an inner struggle had been resolved.

"How do you make that one out?" Rhys wavered, confused.

"We both used the Internet because we wanted to find love until our old age." She chuckled. "We even thought an Egyptian figurine could bless us with that. Instead, it brought us nothing but trouble, when all the time we had found it, but were too blind to see—"

"It was in front of us all along," Rhys finished. He pulled Paige into his arms. "You were trying to tell me before I walked out on you."

She nodded.

Rhys held her close. "How can I ever make it up to you?"

"By believing me when I tell you how much I love you, too," Paige confessed wholeheartedly.

If he had wanted to come to terms with himself, he had done so. If he had wanted peace and love, he had found it. That was how Rhys felt as he took Paige's lips again in another kiss that went on until the sandstorm abated. Only when they both pulled back and heard the lull of silence around them did either realize the worst was over. Rhys's eyes lit up as he looked into the midnight-blue gaze of his desert princess, and suddenly, for no reason at all, he laughed, too.

They rode through the desert on horseback, having found an abandoned black stallion wandering, bedazzled, near the excavation site. Rhys's men, most of them peasant workers, had returned to their homes nearby. Franklin and his men had disappeared. Either they had been beaten by the sandstorm or they had fled the area. Rhys neither cared nor worried. In time, Adabi Mercantile would discover the truth and catch up with Franklin Coates-Davis the moment he closed his account and moved his finances elsewhere.

As for his relationship with Paige, Rhys decided he would take it slow. After all, he planned that they would spend the rest of their lives together. As for Paige, she was just plain lucky.

Epilogue

The site operator of the world's number-one online introduction agency for ethnic minorities posted its forty-sixth announcement on the *www.totallyblackdating.com* message board:

"We are pleased to announce the marriage of two of our online members who met on this Web service sixteen months ago. Omega and Isis are currently honeymooning in the Maldives, and we wish the lucky couple long life and happiness.

"If you are looking for wedded bliss, become a silver, gold, or platinum member now! Simply log on and make a list of your favorite matches with other compatible users. Please DO NOT use this service if you are under eighteen, inviting purely sexual relationships, a married person looking for extramarital affairs, or are adding ads containing pointers to external Web sites.

"Happy hunting and *be safe.*

"Your Web host,

"Cupid."

ABOUT THE AUTHOR

Sonia Icilyn was born in England where she still lives with her daughter in a small village that she describes as "typically British, quiet, and where the old money is." She graduated with a distinction-level Private Secretary's Certificate in Business and Commerce, and also has a Masters Degree in Writing. *Significant Other,* her first romance novel, was published in 1993. Since then, she has added six titles to her name. She has been featured in *Black Elegance*, *Today's Black Woman,* and her work has appeared on the *Ebony* Recommended Books to Read list. Sonia is the founder and organizer of the African Arts and Culture Expo and the British Black Expo in Great Britain. She is also CEO of The Peacock Company. She loves to travel, and realistically depicts her characters from the fine tapestry of the African diaspora. *Roses Are Red* was her first title for Arabesque, followed by *Island Romance*, *Violets Are Blue*—the sequel, *Infatuation,* and *Possession.* She would love to hear from her readers at:

P O Box 438
Sheffield S1 4YX
ENGLAND

or e-mail by visiting her Web site at: *www.soniaicilyn.com.*